BOOK TWO

CURSED CAMPUS

CYNTHIA BRUBAKER

Midnight Tide
PUBLISHING

Cursed Campus
Copyright © 2024 Cynthia Brubaker

Published by Midnight Tide Publishing
www.midnighttidepublishing.com

Cover design by Covers by Jules
www.coversbyjules.crd.co

Interior Formatting by Book Savvy Services

Edited by
R. Walden

Content Warnings

This book contains instances of or references to the following material.

Trigger warnings include but are not limited to loss of loved ones, bullying, physical violence, sexual content and intimate scenes, drug use, smoking, drinking, anxiety, swearing, traumatic experiences/PTSD, racism/discrimination, blood, abductions, death, murder, and fantasy violence.

To William.

Your birth changed my life. You are a ray of sunshine, stronger than any supernatural force depicted in this book. I hope you always keep the magical way in which you view the world, and stay true to yourself.

Love,
Mommy

One

COLE'S DILEMMA

When I woke up this morning, I had felt like I got run over by a fucking freight train. Hell, I was afraid Professor Qadir was going to show up at my dorm and kick my ass for 'Shifting irresponsibly' and breaking curfew. I could get into a whole lot of shit after what happened last night.

But now, I can't remember why I was feeling so freaked out and exhausted.

All I can think about is her.

It may suck that I'm in this position, but what we're doing feels *good*. And if no one ever finds out, what's the harm?

I open my mouth to kiss her harder.

Arya pulls away.

She looks *freaked*.

Fuck! How could I have messed this up so quickly?

"What?" I ask, realizing that she looks confused right now.

I guess that makes two of us.

It's not like I woke up this morning wanting to make out with her. I guess I like her – and I've spent weeks trying to forget about it, pretend it didn't exist – but I never thought I'd actually *go through with* anything.

Didn't she kiss me at the same time that I kissed her? Why did she pull away? Why is she not saying anything?

Fuck. I hate how weird I feel right now.

Am I scared? Worried?

Why is she able to do this to me?

"I... I'm sorry," Arya pants. It sounds like she's having trouble breathing. Wait. Is she more scared than confused? I have no idea.

"Sorry for what?" I ask, more stumped than ever.

"I liked it," I add slowly, just in case *she* didn't. But the way she's talking now is almost like she thinks I didn't want it, the kissing, to happen.

Arya looks pale. "How could you have liked it?" she demands, her brown eyes wide with surprise. "You hate me. You broke my grandfather's Trinket. You almost set my jacket on fire!" she breathes, as if it's all coming back to her now.

I clear my throat. "Uh, yeah. I *did*."

She frowns at me, like I've suddenly started speaking another language. "You *did*?" she repeats, astonished.

I pause. This will be embarrassing as hell, but I have to say it. "I did," I repeat. "I... Uh... Like you."

What the fuck is wrong with me?!

Arya looks shell shocked. Her hands drop from my arms and she backs away from me. As soon as she does, I let go of her waist. I may be confused as shit, but I'm not gonna keep her here if she wants to leave.

I can't say I blame her for feeling weirded out. I've had weeks to *deal with* my feelings (or not, which is my custom), even if I wish they never existed. She's had zero time to process any of this. And judging by her face, I don't think she likes me back.

Again, can't blame her. When you've bullied a girl for a month and a half, it's not like she's your biggest fan.

"I gotta go," she says, not even looking at me now.

"Arya," I try to say. Maybe it's way too late to try and make up for all the shit I've put her through, but I want to at least *try*.

"Thank you for your help last night," she tells me, still looking away.

She's turning around and practically running away from me – no chance for me to explain myself. Once again, I can't really hold it against her.

I crush my back against the brick wall of Feara and yank my lighter out of my hoodie's pocket. I have this weird urge to smash it against the wall. Instead, I put it back in my pocket. I'm trying to control my anger, but I don't think it's working. If I get too angry, the Tedla might burst out again.

I press my hands against my forehead. It aches. I thought the headache was because I haven't had my morning smoke yet – and ghost hunting last night probably didn't help. But I think it's also because I screwed up with Arya.

Looking around, the school grounds are dark and creepy. Still, campus isn't nearly as freaky as it was last night.

Thank God it's deserted and quiet out here, too. I'm relieved that no one saw that humiliating-as-fuck exchange between Arya and I. No one saw me kiss a Nymph.

I feel kind of shitty thinking that way, but I can't help it. I've spent my whole life being annoyed by Nymphs and Enchanters. They only look out for their own kind. They can't be trusted. And now that I'm suddenly *into* one of them, I'm banking on the fact that what few friends I have will shit on me for it. Or, at the very least, call me a hypocrite. Or – what was it Diego called me at the beginning of the school year?

Oh, yeah. A 'judgemental douche.'

Folding my arms across my chest, I suck in a strangled breath. The Fall air is thick and cold. Gomada is usually chilly this time of year, but it's even frostier now. Maybe it's the shit I've been through over the past month and a half. Maybe I'm just losing my damn mind. Everything is piling up. It's not like my life was all hunky-dorey before, but still.

I guess I'll have one less thing to worry about, though, since Arya would rather jump off a cliff than make out with me. That also means I won't have to worry about anyone ever finding out about – God, dare I say it? – *us*.

That should make me feel relieved, right? One thing off my plate? One less nail in my coffin?

But no. It doesn't.

I'm just mad at myself. Maybe if I wasn't such a dick to her for the past month and a half, she wouldn't have run away from me.

I'm so confused. Six weeks ago, I hated her guts and was happy when she treated me like a leper. Now, I'm wishing she didn't.

What the fuck is wrong with me? When did I let my guard down to get hoodwinked by a *Nymph*, of all people? I'd kick my own ass if I could.

I try to think about something cheerier – but not much comes to mind. I'm not really a *cheery* kind of guy. All I can think about now is what happened last night, and even this morning. Fuck.

I'm surprised nothing worse happened last night. I'm surprised Nora survived. Actually–

I'm surprised *I* survived.

I've never Shifted so quickly before. Even with the ghost the first time, it took me longer. But last night, I Shifted in mid-air, mid-jump. I *forced* the Tedla out. I felt him resisting, but I was able to pull rank on him. Sometimes, one of us pulls harder than the other. Last night, it just happened to be me.

I can still remember Nora blindly walking toward the creepy-as-fuck ghost, the weird fog fingers curling around her. It was almost like she was in a trance – just like Lukas Crabtree had been, the poor bastard.

I try to physically shake Lukas' freaked-out screams from my head. If I could scrub that memory out with some Javex, I would. But I can't.

Lukas is dead, or worse.

And Nora could have been next.

Actually, we all could have been next.

Last night could have gone in a totally different direction, and I fucking know that.

The only reason why we weren't ghost toast was because I had the element of surprise on the spooky shithead. The ghost was distracted by trying to nab Nora, and wasn't ready for a fully-Shifted monster entering the game. I took full advantage of that. I jumped it, and dug my teeth right into its right shoulder – or whatever it was I attacked. It was the first thing I could grab.

I wish I couldn't remember the weird-ass scream the ghost made when I did that – yet another job for the bleach bottle. I don't think Nora heard it, because she was still out of it.

Even weirder than that, I could feel my teeth digging into *flesh* when I attacked it. It wasn't like I was biting air.

I thought ghosts were supposed to be untouchable, or whatever. Didn't Ryker and I research that just a little while ago? Ghosts can walk through walls and shit, but they can't physically touch people.

So how come I was able to touch it? How could I make contact with a ghost?

Last I checked, I was still alive and not a dead guy who could interact with ghosts.

How can I kiss a girl but also kick a ghost's ass? I wonder as I pull my lighter out a second time. Maybe a smoke will make me feel better. It's all I've got, honestly.

I jump out of my skin and almost shit my pants when I hear

someone coming up on me from behind. Lighter in hand, I turn around, ready to Shift all over again. I'm tired and sore as fuck, so Shifting may be more of a chore this time. Or worse, the Tedla won't listen and will make me deal with this new threat on my own.

Professor Qadir is standing around the corner to Feara, dressed in a brown suit. I'm not even a hair less screwed than I would have been if the ghost was around the corner. This is just a whole other kind of shitshow.

How the fuck did Qadir show up, just after I thought he'd probably find me here? And how the hell is he so put together, even at six AM? It's like he has no 'off' switch. Not like I'd ever tell him that, though. I've seen Qadir's alter ego – he's not to be fucked with.

"Mister Hudson," Qadir greets me, his tone too serious for this time of day.

I want to say something, anything, but nothing comes out. This might get me deeper into this shit-hole I dug for myself, because I'm a moron. I saw this coming, but I did it anyway. Fuck.

Maybe words will do more harm than good. Talking usually gets me in trouble, anyway. Why make things worse?

"Come with me, Mr. Hudson," the Shifter prof tells me. The way he's speaking tells me I don't have a choice.

I toss my lighter back into the pocket of my hoodie. I'm sure he saw that. It's not like smoking near campus buildings is allowed, even if I actually wasn't smoking yet. Just add that to the dumpster fire that is my life.

So, what am I in shit for this time? My rap sheet is as long as the trek from here to Houssan, the realm where I live. I'm sure Qadir is here to nab me for *something*.

I'm curious what he's going to hit me with now. Getting ready to smoke up next to Feara? Or breaking curfew and kicking a ghost's ass?

Something tells me it's the second thing, based on how freaky Professor Qadir looks.

Thanks to the ghost (or whatever the hell it is) taking Lukas Crabtree the night of the Shifter Campfire, punishments for breaking curfew (not that I pay attention to that crap, as a general rule) are pretty steep.

I'm probably on the on-ramp to getting expelled. Not that it matters, I guess. I've tried to catch up, to measure up to my family's expectations (I wouldn't brag about it), but I had a feeling it wasn't enough.

Whatever. If I get expelled, one less issue for me to deal with, right? I could do with a few less problems. God knows I have my fair share of them, despite trying to coast through life up 'til now. Even if my dad kicks my ass or grounds me for life, it's not like it'd be any worse staying here and probably turning up dead. If that ghost didn't have it out for me before, it sure as hell holds a grudge now. My badass heroics last night are looking a little stupid this morning.

That sounds like me.

Plus, it's not like I don't have a clue as to the proof or evidence they'll have against me. I can't avoid those damned security cameras *all* the time. I'm sure the so-called head of security, Greyson the Brainless, saw the Tedla scampering around campus on at least one of them. Even a blind pig finds an acorn once in a while.

Making things worse, Headmistress Frow and Professor Qadir would know for sure that the big-ass wolf monster was me. No one else would – but they'd see the Tedla and immediately think *Cole Hudson*.

Fucking Tedla and its notoriety.

I ignore the inner growl from the Tedla at my tired and annoyed thoughts.

"Right now, if not sooner, Mr. Hudson," Professor Qadir snaps.

Shit. Have I not started moving yet?

I push myself off the brick wall of my dorm and begin to follow him.

Perfect. This day just can't get any better. Maybe I *should have been* ghost chow last night.

Fuck my life.

That seems to be my motto over the past month and a half. It's always the same shit, just a different day.

Maybe getting expelled will be a good thing.

Two

ARYA'S MEETING

The mist is turning into rain as I continue to walk briskly – or, *run quickly* – back to Meera.

I thought I'd hit rock-bottom, the lowest of the low, when Professor Xhao, my Field Practice teacher, lectured me about my remedial Nymph skills. Then, I thought I sank to a new level of *low* when I got rejected by Ryker at the campfire.

But apparently, the *real* rock-bottom for me was kissing the biggest jerk on the planet (which is way worse than I thought), Cole Hudson.

Ever since I came to Gomada Academy in September, Cole has been making my life a living Hell. He tormented me, broke my Grandfather's Trinket, burned me with his cigarette, and scared me half to death. Now, all of a sudden, he tells me he *likes* me? How is that even possible? Worse than that, how am I supposed to deal with it? And even worse than *that*, why did I kiss him?

Why can't a nice, studious Enchanter like Ryker have a crush on me instead of a dark, twisted Shifter like Cole? Am I just that unlucky?

What will happen now that I blew him off? Is he going to switch back to hating me, and make what happened to me before seem like sunshine and roses?

I want to die.

Maybe I should have gotten chewed up by the ghost last night. I don't think I'm cut out for this life. Even though I love being with Nora and learning about the history and culture of Gomada, part of me can't shake this feeling that Earth, the Over-world, is where I really belong.

As soon as I round the corner to Meera, finally feeling like I'm getting closer and closer to sanctuary, I skid to a halt when I see none other than Headmistress Frow. My stomach crashes through the damp grass, my lungs unable to bring breath into my frozen body.

The Headmistress' Familiar, a red-tailed hawk named Leopold, is circling overhead, waiting for his mistress' prey to arrive.

If I wasn't pale before, I'm white as a ghost now (bad choice of words).

"Miss Willow," Headmistress Frow begins. Her arms are folded and her posture is firm and calculated as she approaches me. "Please accompany me to my office."

I'd be sobbing if I wasn't so scared of what punishment I'll receive for breaking curfew and trying to fight off a ghost last night.

That might be a good thing, though. Tears may be seen as immature and weak right now. That's how Professor Xhao felt when I got weepy during her Field Practice lecture – or take-down.

When will I learn to take the hint? 'Immature and weak' are pretty much *me*, as much as I hate to admit it.

Headmistress Frow's dimly-lit office is even more intimidating at 6:43 in the morning. I can tell by the clock behind me that I've only been awake for less than an hour.

In other words, in less than an hour of being conscious, I'm already in trouble with the administration of Gomada Academy.

I never used to get into trouble. My parents would tease me about 'living a little' – sleeping in, getting detention for once, walking a little slower to get to class. That was how much of a rule-follower I am – or, *was*.

Now, it seems like I'll get frequent flyer miles for travelling to and from the Headmistress' office.

"Please have a seat, Miss Willow," Leona Frow tells me, standing behind her desk, her hands on its wooden surface.

Leona Frow's long black hair with blue lowlights is pulled into a loose clip at the base of her neck. Otherwise, she's wearing a black blazer with dress pants. For some reason, I get the impression that she's stressed out, even though she doesn't let on that she's feeling that way.

There are not one, or two, but *three* chairs in front of me.

Oh, no.

Just as I'm walking over to the chair to the far left, the door to the Headmistress' office opens again. I turn mid-pace as I approach my chosen chair.

I lay eyes on a professor of Arab descent that I've seen before, but have never had in any of my classes. I think he's a Shifter professor. And I know I'm right – not because I'm smart, but because Cole is standing next to him, looking dejected. I've never seen him look like this before. But to me, Cole's only personality is evil wrongdoing with sides of sarcasm and rebellion.

The tension heightens with the addition of another faculty member–but it *explodes* now that Cole and I are in the same space again.

"Sit down, Mr. Hudson," the professor whose name I don't know commands.

Without looking at his professor or even giving him attitude

(I'm not used to seeing that, either), Cole shuffles over to the set of chairs without missing a beat. He sits in the middle chair, beside me, slouching slightly.

The unnamed-to-me professor steps to Headmistress Frow's left and gives Cole a firm look. Cole straightens immediately in response.

The door opens. None other than Professor Xhao appears. A sleep-deprived Nora Leith is in tow.

I stiffen as soon as I see my other bully and teacher. I try not to flash back to the Nymph's Field – but it's impossible to forget how pathetic and insignificant my professor made me feel. I remember it like it was yesterday.

Cole's green eyes dart to me when I tense up at the sight of Professor Xhao. Maybe he noticed my movements in his peripheral vision. He's not the only one who's intimidated by a teacher.

"Here is Miss Leith, Headmistress," Professor Xhao reports, holding her hand out into the office.

Nora quickly moves over to the last empty chair, sitting next to Cole. Even though she says nothing to us, I can see that she is bewildered by Cole's presence. As far as she knows, she and I broke curfew and she almost got abducted.

When Professor Xhao sees the Shifter professor, she nods at him in greeting. "Hello, Professor Qadir," she greets him.

Oh. So that's his name.

Professor Qadir moves his head ever so slightly in response to my least favourite teacher. "Good morning, Professor Xhao," he responds.

"Is there anything else you require, Headmistress?" Professor Xhao asks. She's also dressed nicely in a business suit. I'm not used to her being so kind, so formal. Usually, whenever I see her, she's ready to slice and dice.

"No, thank you, Professor Xhao," Headmistress Frow responds in a tone that sounds *final*, decisive.

Professor Xhao lingers in place for a brief moment, as if she is digesting the response from her superior. I get the impression that she wants to stay and witness this execution. However, judging from Leona Frow's tone, it looks like the Headmistress and Professor Qadir want to keep it private.

Despite being scared out of my mind, I'm thankful that my Field Practice professor has one less thing to hold over my head.

Professor Xhao nods at the Headmistress and leaves, closing the door behind her.

The Headmistress and Shifter professor exchange a quick glance with one another. Professor Qadir leaves the area behind the desk and walks over to the door. Opening it, he leans his upper body out into the hallway. When satisfied, he closes the door and locks it.

This isn't good.

"Well," Headmistress Frow begins, as her Familiar ruffles his feathers while sitting at the perch on top of her desk. He's been quiet and still as a statue this entire time. "It seems the three of you had a bit of excitement last night."

Silence.

I don't know what to say, but part of me thinks that saying anything would be inappropriate. I'm too frightened to look at Nora or Cole, but I imagine they're rigid and soundless on purpose, too.

"If no one is going to regale us, we'll dispense with the pleasantries and begin," Headmistress Frow states, as Professor Qadir leans against the door.

It's almost as if Professor Qadir is acting as another buffer of security. Maybe they're afraid of someone overhearing our conversation?

It's possible, since the five of us know about the ghost.

The email sent from Headmistress Frow prior to the incident from last night, informing students of a 'threat to Gomada Academy' was one thing, but we've discovered the truth: there is a ghost abducting (and likely killing) students from campus.

Nora and I went straight to bed as soon as we got home from her near-abduction last night. We were too exhausted and freaked out to talk. I wish we could have discussed the ghost. I want to be able to tell her everything now – especially since before, I was too nervous to let her or anyone else in on what was happening.

But I don't have any choice in the matter now. Everything will be revealed. I'm concerned Nora will feel betrayed because I kept this from her. I could have saved her the anguish of getting lured out of our dorm room if I'd just let her in on what was going on...

"What did the three of you see last night?" Headmistress Frow asks us in such a way that tells us we need to start talking.

This snaps me out of my dismal reverie. I'm digging my nails into my thighs through my leggings, my breath caught somewhere deep in my throat.

"Someone lured me out of my dorm room," Nora begins shakily. "I wasn't aware of what I was doing. It was almost like I was hypnotized."

It wasn't like Nora and I labelled what we saw last night as a 'ghost,' but I'm still surprised that she wasn't more specific in her descriptions. Maybe she is being vague on purpose. In addition to being a confident and compassionate Nymph with an Earth Affinity, Nora has an intuition that makes her more mature than our Freshmen contemporaries.

Maybe Nora thinks it's best not to reveal too much about last night.

Something flickers across Headmistress Frow's blue eyes, but she says nothing in answer to Nora's statement.

"And you, Mr. Hudson?" Professor Qadir asks. "Security cameras have you fully Shifted and injured, heading back to your dorm."

I stare at Cole, shocked.

He was injured last night?

How come I never saw anything this morning?

When I think hard enough, I suddenly remember Cole limping over to the middle chair in the Headmistress' office. He does have some scrapes on his face. How come I didn't–

Never mind. I know why, and don't want to think about it. Ever.

Instead, I think about the fact that Nora now knows that Cole was the one to save her from the ghost. Sure, I sort of helped with my electrical component (thank God it worked that time), but Cole was the real hero in that scenario.

Cole shifts in place. "I picked up her scent in the Shifter's Field. Heard the screaming. I Shifted to help."

"To *help*, Mr. Hudson?" Headmistress Frow asks. It's like she knows Cole doesn't usually make friends or talk to people outside of his own race, but never makes mention of it.

Cole nods 'yes' instead of answering with words.

"And how did you know that it was Miss Leith who needed help?" Professor Qadir asks. "Your family heritage is impressive – but even that doesn't explain your apparent extra-sensory-perception."

Silence elevates in the room to could-hear-a-pin-drop level.

What does Professor Qadir mean about Cole's family heritage? I guess there is more to Cole than cigarettes and reck-lessness.

Cole hesitates. I'm shocked by this. It makes the hairs on my neck stand on end.

Is he trying to keep me out of trouble by not ratting me out to Professor Qadir?

"Miss Willow, how do you fit into this – besides using your electricity to light up the edge of campus?" Headmistress Frow asks me instead of waiting for Cole to answer.

I grow pale at that. I guess seeing electricity shooting through the air would mean someone with an Air Affinity was involved. They must have seen Nora and I on the security cameras, as well. I knew this would happen, but last night, all I cared about was saving Nora. Nothing else mattered.

"I called him," I finally admit. I feel bad saying that – like I'm implicating Cole. But he was already on camera, too...

I'm so confused.

"I came home before curfew and saw that Nora was gone. it's not like her to break curfew," I stammer in explanation.

Headmistress Frow doesn't miss a beat when she asks, "And you immediately assumed she was under hypnosis, about to be taken?"

I notice that, so far, Headmistress Frow and Professor Qadir haven't mentioned anything about the ghost. They're just asking us what we saw, how we knew to go to the Shifter's Field – in essence, if we were working together.

Are they still trying to cover up the ghost? Or do they even know that it exists?

They're definitely suspicious–but it's hard to gauge the depth of said *suspicions*.

"After the email that was sent out, I... I didn't want anything happening to her," I finally admit. My voice breaks on 'happening,' but no one seems to notice. I guess that's a bit less embarrassing. I really don't want to cry right now.

"What did you see?" Headmistress Frow asks all of us again.

"I can't remember," Nora breathes. "I just remember being cold and unable to think for myself. I guess I recall bright light. I was really scared."

"I never made it into the Shifter's Field," I tremble. "I just saw the bright light and fog. I heard Nora screaming. I wanted to help her."

"Mister Hudson?" Professor Qadir asks expectantly.

Cole clears his throat. "I attacked whatever it was," he admits. "Dug into his shoulder."

"His?" Professor Qadir pinpoints, causing my stomach to jump.

What else did Cole see last night?

Cole shrugs. "I dunno. I think so," he tacks on at the end, when Professor Qadir eyes him.

The two adults share another glance, even with Professor Qadir still at the door.

"Thank you," Headmistress Frow tells us. "Please do not broadcast your adventure to the other students. Miss Leith, I'd like you to stay a little longer. I want to ensure you are healthy. Mister Hudson – please go to the infirmary to get your limp tended to. Miss Willow – you are to go straight home."

To my dorm? Or San Francisco? I panic.

"Mister Hudson is your Mentor, is he not?" Headmistress Frow asks me.

"Indeed," Professor Qadir answers before I can say anything.

"He will escort you. All three of you will need to take extra precautions from now on, because as you are well aware, Gomada Academy is under threat."

"Miss Leith, we expect you to rely on your Mentor for assistance, as well," Professor Qadir mentions.

"Yes, sir," Nora agrees quietly.

My stomach jerks at the reference to Nora's Mentor and the Enchanter who turned me down, Ryker Johnson. Maybe if I wasn't so terrified, I'd be more torn up about that.

"Mister Hudson, please go to the infirmary when you are finished with Miss Willow," Headmistress Frow commands.

Cole says nothing, but gives Headmistress Frow a slight nod of his head.

"The two of you are dismissed," Headmistress Frow tells us, her arms folded.

Professor Qadir unlocks the door and steps aside, opening it for us. Cole and I rise from our seats, more or less at the same time.

I don't want to be any closer to Cole than I already am, so I'm quick to leave the Headmistress' office, filled with fear and shame.

Three

COLE'S AFFLICTION

It's raining harder when we walk out of Gomada Academy. The infirmary is back in here, so once I'm done walking Arya to Meera, I gotta head back to this dump. I'm not sure how my right leg will do heading over here again, but I'm not about to whine about it.

It's quiet but awkward as fuck as Arya and I walk over to Meera. We're about halfway there when she says something.

"How did you get hurt?" she asks.

I shrug, but I'm not sure if she sees it or not, so I answer, "I dunno."

That's kind of a lie. I busted my leg jumping a tall-ass ghost that gave me some pushback when I took a chunk out of it. But I'm not about to tell her that.

The silence continues until we finally get to Meera. I don't know how to fix this weirdness, and I have a feeling I'll only make it worse if I try. Still, I feel like I gotta say something.

"Are you okay?" I ask, just as she's about to walk up to the double doors on her own.

She looks up at me. "Yeah," she answers, but she looks unsure.

Even if she's lying, I can't say I blame her. For weeks, she's probably felt like she can't show me any kind of weakness. Can't expect that to be any different just because I kissed her.

"Are you?" she asks, surprising me again.

I shrug. "I've had worse," is all I respond.

Arya looks like she doesn't know what to do with that.

"Um... Thanks for walking me back," she trails off, sounding nervous.

I clear my throat. "No worries."

I don't think now's the time to talk to her about what happened before the shitshow in Frow's office, so I just shut up and turn around. I walk away, hoping to put this day – the past six weeks – behind me.

"Cole?"

I turn around, shocked that she's still talking to me. I loosen up, even though every muscle in my body feels like it's on fire, trying not to convey my surprise.

"I'm sorry I called you," she tells me. "It's my fault you're in trouble."

I frown at her. "I'm always in trouble," I remind her. "It's not a big deal."

Arya looks unconvinced–like she thinks I'll change my mind and slam her face into the ground for getting me in shit with Qadir and Frow.

"Okay," she says, folding her arms and shifting from one foot to the other.

"Hit me up if you need help," I offer.

Her head jerks up to look at me. She's thrown off by what I said. I was hoping by now, she wouldn't be. But maybe you're not supposed to get used to your enemy helping you out.

"Okay," she repeats warily.

Part of me thinks she won't. She looks freaked. Not as much as before, but still pretty close. Damn.

Shoving my hands in my jeans' pockets, I glance back in the direction we just came. "Later," I tell her, turning on my heel and trying hard not to limp like a loser back to the school.

The infirmary was a waste of time. Nurse Ratchet told me I have a 'mild sprain.' She said something about 'rice,' but I wasn't paying attention. All I really care about is going back to the dorm, having a smoke, and eating back at the Dining Hall. I would've stayed at school for breakfast, but I think that stupid midterm schedule has us eating breakfast at nine AM, so nothing would be ready just yet.

I'm pissed off all over again when I finally get back to Feara and see that teachers and students are walking around. Too many people could rat me out for smoking near the dorm. Not only that, since it's raining more than it was before, I'd have to stick close to a roof or overhang so I wouldn't get soaked. No dice on that front, either. Everyone is huddled around, trying to keep out of the rain.

I hate people.

Since I'm already here and don't think I can manage going back to the Dining Hall to get food, I decide to just go upstairs and see if Diego and I have anything in the mini-fridge we bought at the beginning of the year.

When I unlock and open the door, I find Diego sitting on his bed, stretching. It looks like he's just waking up. I wish that could be me. I'd give anything to not have the morning I just had. Worst part is, it's still going on. It's not even eight thirty yet, and I'm ready to smash my head against the wall.

Diego does a double-take when he sees me.

"The hell are you doing up this early?" he asks.

I frown at him. "You'll never believe what kind of shit went down last night, Jasper," I begin.

He looks like he's not surprised by that. After the crap he,

Ryker and I have been through so far, I guess we're not fazed by much anymore.

"Good God," is all he says. "Well, at least you survived, Hudson."

"Barely," I respond as I close the door, deciding to tell him the whole damned thing.

Diego frowns at me as if he's trying to figure me out after I've told him about last night.

When will people stop doing that?

"How come you always get caught up with that Nymph girl?" he asks.

"*She* called *me*," I remind him quickly, trying to get the heat off of me.

But that doesn't seem to work. Diego raises a dark eyebrow and gives me a suspicious look as he rubs his messy long black hair.

"You gave her your *number*, bro?" he gasps, looking like I just brought about the apocalypse.

I sigh. "I'm her Mentor. I kind of had to."

This 'defending myself' thing isn't working very well. I'm half-expecting Diego to grill me about it when he rolls his eyes. And I really don't want to say anything else about it.

It'd be the end of me if Diego or any other Shifter found out that I kissed a Nymph and liked it.

"Right," Diego agrees. "I guess that makes sense. Can't even sneeze anymore without running into 'em."

I guess he's talking about his own Mentorship Program thing and how Frow's making us Sophomores mentor the Freshmen until the end of term because of *slacking*. That's such a load of bullshit (who cares if she's right?).

Diego's taking his Mentor-Mentee prison sentence better than I am, but I know he finds it annoying, too.

"Pretty much," I agree.

Diego stands, looking stiff. We were sitting for a while. "Well, good on you for helping out – even though I can't believe you helped *Nymphs*," he grins at me, causing me to flip him off.

Well, at least he still thinks I'm a judgemental douche. That helps me, but I know Diego isn't nearly as big of an asshole as I am when it comes to mingling with other races. In fact, he would have jumped in and saved the Nymphs, himself. He's also dating Lucy Chapin, an Enchantress Sophomore who's dangerous as fuck. She has a Darkness Affinity – and we recently figured out that she also has a Light Affinity, just like Ryker.

I keep forgetting to tell Ryker about that – though I'm sure he already knows. That kind of news of 'contradicting Affinities' or whatever it's called travels fast around here. Lucy will have the same target on her back that Ryker, Diego and I have had to suffer with for years.

"Didn't really have a choice," I remind Diego, trying to focus on the conversation. "I don't wanna see anyone else die."

Diego nods, folding his arms. He's wearing a black t-shirt with gray sweatpants. "We gotta meet up with Johnson – tell him what happened," he suggests.

"Yeah. You're right," I agree, knowing we can't get out of this – that *I* can't get out of this. Even if I'm dead on my feet, I know we gotta let Ryker in on what happened last night.

"What did the other Nymph – Nora – have to say about the ghost?" Diego asks, as I open the door to our dorm.

Without talking about it, we both know it's time to leave for breakfast. Right now, I'm so hungry I'd limp to Lesantha for a bagel. I'm still wearing my hoodie from before. Diego's shrugging into his jacket and putting on hiking boots.

"Nothing. She was freaked when I nabbed her from the ghost, and she didn't mention anything at Frow's," I report. "She must have said something to Arya, though."

Girls are predictable – sort of. If Nora's going to tell anyone about the nightmare she went through, it'll be her BFF – not a teacher or a Shifter.

"Hmm," is all Diego says, locking the door and squaring his broad shoulders. We head down the hall, avoiding other Shifters as we go. Most of them look like zombies.

It's midterms, so everyone's on-edge and has their noses poked in books. I don't have a midterm until this afternoon, so I'm just chilling until after breakfast. Then, I'll have to hunker down. I know I need to do better this year – but a fight with a ghost who may not even *be* a ghost took a lot out of me.

The Dining Hall is packed when we head inside. Due to the bad weather and the fact that midterms are happening this week and next week, everyone will be huddled together more often. This is going to be annoying. But that's my life. Everything and everyone annoys me.

Diego and I get in line and finally get the basics: eggs, toast, bacon, sausage. We eventually find an empty table squeezed in the back.

We're not only starving, but we also can't find Ryker anywhere. Not a big surprise. There are dozens of Enchanters eating breakfast now. It's not like it'll be easy to spot the one you're actually looking for, just because you need to talk to him.

We eat in silence. I'm happy about that. It's nice to just hang with Diego. We can do pretty much anything together without worrying about filling the gaps. With other people like Ryker, it's a little bit harder to do that.

Even though things feel normal now – it's midterms, I'm

hanging with Diego, we're eating in quiet, and nothing's in the way – I still can't get that kiss out of my head. I don't know how to get things right with Arya – and I'm not even sure if I should try.

She definitely wants to steer clear of me. Why go to all that effort if she's not interested?

Not only that, it'll make it easier for what happened this morning to fly under the radar – permanently.

Too bad I'm not a talker, and too bad I'm not interested in telling Diego about my problems.

Diego's not a ladies' man, but he definitely has his fair share of girls following him around. This year, it's Lucy. I don't know how long it'll last – but after what happened with Lucy and her messed up cousin, Désirée Chapin, I know she's not who I thought she was. She may be an Enchantress, she may be stuck-up and annoying – but she's Diego's girl, and I know she has his back. That counts for something.

Anyway, Diego could have helped me sort this out. But I'd never tell anyone about my dilemma – not even my best friend.

"You haven't told Lucy about any of this ghost shit, have you?" I find myself asking him. I didn't think he would – but now, I'm not so sure.

Diego frowns across the table at me. "No," he answers. "Don't want to scare her."

Like anything can scare a Chapin bitch.

That thought kind of snuck in there, even if Lucy isn't as fucked up as her cockroach of a cousin, Désirée.

Diego takes a bite of his toast, swallows, and adds, "Unless you think it's safer if I do. It's coming into dorms – or around them, anyway."

Diego has a point. We still don't know if the ghost – or whatever it is – *showed up* in Nora's dorm to lure her somewhere secluded, or if it just hovered outside of Meera.

Either way, we gotta change our strategy. I hate to say it, but it may be better to have a bigger posse than just two or three people at a time.

"Tell her," I proclaim. "Nora and Arya are already in on it. Ryker, too. We may need more help if we're gonna take it down for good."

Headmistress Frow and Greyson are doing jack shit about this. It looks like it's up to us to try and put a stop to this *whatever-it-is*.

At first, Diego appears surprised that I changed my mind. But it doesn't last long. Now, his hazel eyes look determined.

"Alright. That makes more sense. Strength in numbers," he muses.

I nod. "Just need to check with Johnson first," I realize.

Diego frowns at me. "I don't think he'll care if we add on anyone else. This may work to our advantage if the odds are against the ghost."

It's true. Two Enchanters, two Shifters, and two Nymphs against one ghost, or 'whatever-it-is?'

I like those odds.

And when Diego and I Shift?

It'll be a fucking bloodbath.

Maybe we should've added more people on from the start. I guess it's hard to know what to do when you're up against a creepy-ass ghost with weird mind control powers.

"Create a group chat with everyone in it," Diego suggests. "We can meet tonight."

"Whoah," I protest, putting down my coffee cup. "Why the fuck do I have to be in charge?"

Diego smiles at me. "You were the one who put this little group together, Hudson," he reminds me. "Just do it. No one will expect you to take charge – and that'll make them listen to you."

I scoff. "I hate my life," I grumble.

Diego shrugs. "Not much of a change from last year," he responds, waiting for me to growl about that, too.

But he doesn't know how much has changed since Freshman Year. I *wish* I could be that person. But there's nothing I can do about that now.

When breakfast is over, I finally pull out my phone while Diego leaves to call his girl about the ghost. Thanks to Lucy and I more or less settling our shit at the Nymph/Enchanter's Field a while back, I now have her on my social media crap that I never use. The rest, I can hopefully just find and add.

Fuck. I hate my phone and I hate this shit. How did I get in charge of anything?!

When I actually go about making the stupid chat, I realize it's not too hard to find Nora. I just go to Arya's profile and search for Nora. I finally add all five of them into the chat.

> Meet up at Feara tonight. 7 PM.

I'm taking charge. Hopefully this doesn't blow up in my face.

Some of them probably have midterms to finish and more of a life than me, so I'm surprised when Ryker, Nora, and Arya see the message, almost at the same time.

Ryker is the first to answer me, which makes me more annoyed.

> You got it, man. Your place?

> That works.

> Arya and I will be there.

Nora responds after Ryker. The girls are probably reading these messages from their dorm room.

> Don't be late. Don't get followed or blab about it, either.

I add those stipulations just in case one of the girls plans to do any of those things.

Ryker pisses me off when he puts an 'OK emoji' reaction to my message – especially since he knows I wasn't referring to him.

> Relax, Cole. We get it.

Ryker puts a 'laughing emoji' reaction to Nora's message. Lucy and Diego see Nora's chat message. Diego has the same response to it.

Is this the thanks I get for saving Nora? I put my phone away, deciding to go back to my dorm and study a bit more before my stupid midterm. I'm just happy I'll be finished with them by next Monday. I hate tests. They always make me feel like a dumbass.

Just as I'm heading out into the brisk-as-fuck morning air, my phone vibrates in my pocket. I yank it out, thinking it's the group chat.

It's a text from Ryker.

> Crabtree isn't the only victim. Apparently the ghost got a Nymph and a Shifter. People are starting to notice that their friends are missing.

> Looks like it's happening overnight, with no witnesses. No one is saying anything about a spirit, per se.

I almost stumble on the cobblestone pathway as I read his messages.

The ghost has abducted more students than just Crabtree?
There are hundreds of students here at Gomada Academy.

Who knows how many other students have been taken – killed? Worse?

> The fuck did you find this out?

I type my question furiously, narrowly avoiding a moronic Nymph who almost crashes into me as I yank up my hoodie to avoid the rain.

> I'm tutoring a Nymph. She told me her girlfriend is missing. And I heard some Shifters at the library talking about a friend who hasn't been around lately.

Huh. I guess Ryker's an all-around Good Samaritan. Tutoring, reading books in the library, and always smiling. Fucking annoying, if you ask me – but it seems like that makes people open up to him about shit.

> What's the name of the Shifter?

I ask this of Ryker knowing it's pretty doubtful that the missing Shifter would be on my radar. Sure, I keep to my own kind, but it's not like I have a ton of Shifter friends.

Honestly, the people who know me wish they didn't. Even strangers steer clear. They can sense the beast inside me, and want no part of it.

> Patty Mer-something. Can't remember her full name.

Huh. That doesn't ring a bell (big surprise, thanks to Inspector Dumphead), but I file it away for later. Some sleuthing on social media might help me figure out more about this Patty person – and might give me a clue as to whether or not she is truly missing.

I lean against a nearby tree, ignoring the scraping of the hard bark against my soaked hoodie as I wipe rainwater off my phone. I quickly type 'Patty Mer' into the search engine of one of my social media apps.

A few choices come up (just my luck). I zero in on the third one down: Patty Merlotts.

I sort of remember seeing Patty around Feara – mostly because she's a redhead and I have a thing for them. I also recognize her because she and her partner's Field Practice final exam from last year was pretty epic. Otherwise, I never would have remembered *this* hot redhead.

One click on her page (thank God, it's public) tells me she hasn't posted in a couple of days. A bit of scrolling tells me she's too into coffee pictures and silly poses with her friends. From the looks of things, she'd post shit a few times a day. But for the past two? Nada.

This usually wouldn't raise any eyebrows, but if Ryker overheard people at the library saying they haven't seen Patty around, and her socials aren't up to date...

Fuck.

That foggy asshole has struck again – *before* it tried to take Nora.

> Patty Merlotts, idiot. She's definitely missing. Her socials aren't updated.

> Thanks for the intel and lovely compliment.

I roll my eyes at that, noticing a few students walking past my spot under a tree with dripping branches and leaves. I'll probably get pneumonia, but I don't care.

I'm pretty sure these hurrying kids are Nymphs. Thanks to

my keen Tedla senses that can block out the loud-as-fuck rain and howling wind, I can hear them murmuring something about 'what happened last night.'

There are too many shitheads around here. I need a smoke to calm myself down, but there are too many witnesses who'd love to rat me out to the nearest prof.

I guess people are starting to find out about these attacks and so-called 'abductions.' It's going to get around soon that at least three students are MIA. A boarding school for loser teens who love texting and social media basically means Blabbermouth Central. Even people who don't like hanging out with other races will hear about missing students from classes with other entities.

Rumours are going to start.

People are going to panic.

All these crazy kids aren't going to know the real story.

The thing is, *we* know the truth. And it's way worse than kidnapping.

We also know Frow and all the other adults are just sitting around interviewing people and watching security cameras. They don't know what the ghost is capable of – especially since they can't get a good look at it in the first place.

We won't let that motherfucker nab anybody else.

Four

ARYA'S CONFIDANT

"**A**re you sure you're okay – besides the obvious, anyway?" Nora asks as we hustle a little faster to get to Feara.

It's only six forty-five, yet the campus is blanketed in darkness. It's starting to rain again. Thunder rumbles, creating an unnerving backdrop to our clandestine meeting that I can only assume is about the ghost.

Creepy campus, creepy meeting... And spooky subject matter.

Basically, we want to get inside as soon as possible.

Bright lights and being surrounded by Shifters, even if they're strangers, are so inviting to us right now that it's not just the weather that makes us hurry.

"I guess," I answer quietly as we pass some pupils moving in the opposite direction. "I just don't want to be in the same room as Ryker."

Or Cole.

While it's true that I want to repress Ryker's rejection forever, there's another reason why I am absolutely *not okay* with this entire thing. But I can't tell Nora. She hates Cole with the passion of a raging hurricane, and I can't say I blame her.

Plus, I'm still trying to figure out why I'd even kiss Cole in the first place. I'm berating myself for my lapse in judgement – and frankly, I don't need someone else adding to the flames.

Nora rubs my arm. "Arya, you gotta try and move on from that," she advises me. "I'm sure Ryker has already forgotten all about it."

I'm sure that's true. I'm usually entirely forgettable. It wouldn't surprise me at all if my embarrassment and heartache over Ryker turning me down at the campfire thrown by the Shifters was just a blip on his radar; something he forgot the moment it happened. I only wish I could have that skill when it comes to humiliating things.

"Besides, with Cole clearly taking point on this weird meeting, I'm sure you won't have to do much talking with Ryker, as it is," Nora puts forth.

She's trying to make me feel better, but her talking about Cole only makes me feel worse.

Nora nudges me as if she can pick up on that. "Is something else bothering you?"

I frown over at her. "You mean, other than you getting attacked by the ghost and us teaming up to fight it?" I respond.

I say 'ghost' quietly and under my breath since two guys are passing us, approaching Feara. I think they're Shifters, but I'm not sure.

Nora rolls her eyes at my response and likely at my mention of Cole and I *teaming up*. Good God, why did I say that?

Getting back to Nora, she looks tired, like she doesn't want to be out and about on a Friday night. I can definitely understand. After what happened to us last night, we just wanted to have some pizza from the Dining Hall and head back to our dorm for some peace and quiet. Of course, that's out of the question now.

Besides, we're both under the impression that Cole is grouping us together to fight the ghost. What other reason could there be for the chat that involves other students – terrifyingly enough, Lucy Chapin?

Self-care in our dorm is definitely not a discussable option.

"I'd rather just try and forget about what happened – or focus on other things while I still have the chance," Nora confesses to me.

I can understand that, too. After spending all of dinner telling her everything I know about the ghost, Nora's probably done with paranormal meetings. And she wants to repress what happened to her. I shouldn't have brought it up in the first place.

"I'll gladly take any other subject for one hundred, Arya," she continues teasingly.

I give her a small smile through my nerves as we get ever closer to Feara.

Flashes of lightning to our left prompt us to hasten. Even still, my body is alive with the churning wind and electricity in the air. With my Air Affinity, this kind of weather awakens my being and strengthens my control. But I'm too freaked to harness it into anything productive. If anything, I want to escape it now.

I mull over Nora's request for a subject change as rain soaks through my jacket. If I tell Nora what happened to me this morning – before our awful meeting with Headmistress Frow and Professor Qadir, before Nora was awakened by Professor Xhao rapping on her door – there's no going back.

If Cole finds out I told someone we kissed, he may retaliate. I'm still afraid he'll somehow get me back for taking off on him before. If I do one more thing to tick him off–

"You can't tell anyone," I murmur to her, just as Nora opens one of the double doors to Feara.

Thankfully, we made it to the Shifters' dormitory unscathed – soaked and terrified, but alive and uncaptured.

Nora frowns at me. "How many friends do you think I have?" she jokes, holding the door for me. She slides in behind me after I jump inside so she doesn't get any wetter waiting for me to move.

"Really," I press, as we move out of the way for more students to hustle inside. "It's private."

Nora raises her dark eyebrows. "Oh?" she asks. "This sounds scandalous."

"Nora," I protest – or whine.

"Maybe I *don't* want to know," Nora teases as we begin to walk through the lobby.

While we're waiting at the elevator, I shuffle in place, unsure how to explain what happened.

"Geez, you're really upset," Nora observes, placing her hand on my back. "What happened?" she asks, all joking aside.

I give her a pleading look. "It's... I – I kissed him."

Nora gapes. "What? Kissed who?" she breathes when a few people pass us.

These Shifters look like older students – maybe Seniors or Masters. Either way, they scare me. I'm thankful when the elevator doors open: soon, we'll be out of sight and earshot.

"Ryker?" Nora guesses, bewildered. "But I thought..."

We board the elevator. We're alone. Thank God.

When the doors close, I look over at her again after pressing '3' on the number pad. Diego, that boy whose name I never knew until this afternoon, gave us his room number for the meeting.

"No," I murmur, ashamed and exhausted. I really wish it could have been Ryker.

Nora frowns at me. "No offense, Arya, but I don't really want to recite all the names of straight guys I know at Gomada Academy."

Her jaw drops. Her blue eyes flicker with realization.

There's no going back now.

"Cole?" Nora gasps, horrified.

Hugging my chest, I just nod in agreement. I don't know how to tell her about it – how it happened, how I handled it. All I can think about is the fact that it happened – and that *when* it happened, it actually wasn't so terrible. In the moment, it felt *right*. That sticks out to me because I never thought anything involving Cole could be labelled as 'right' or 'good.'

But how can I explain all that to Nora, who's looking at me like she's a witness to a zombie apocalypse?

"Did he force you into it, or something?" Nora demands, ready to switch from surprise to anger as soon as I give the word.

"No," I finally admit. "We – we kissed each other. At the same time."

I murmur those last four words quietly, sheepishly. I'm horrified that I've spoken them aloud. I regret thinking honesty would be the best course of action. Nora and our other friends like Cole about as much as blistering hives.

The elevator doors open. I didn't even hear or feel the *thud* signalling our arrival. The night behind us and the day ahead of us – combined with barely any sleep – must be dulling my senses.

Nora looks stupefied as we step out onto the carpeted third floor. "But I thought you loathed him – and rightfully so," she states after a lengthy pause.

We don't have long to go because Diego and Cole's dorm is Room 301, right across from us.

"I don't know what happened," I begin to protest, but the door swings open and I promptly clamp my mouth shut.

Cole is staring at both of us. My face almost falls off, but Nora saves me by putting on an immediate poker face.

"Look!" she gasps sarcastically, in an overly dramatic way, gesturing to the two of us. "We're not late, and we weren't followed. Oh, and we didn't *blab*, either."

Cole rolls his eyes sourly at Nora's remark. "Get in here," is all he responds, holding the door open and stepping aside.

"How hospitable of you," Nora groans, giving me a 'here we go' look before following Cole.

I follow Nora into the room, wanting this meeting to be over with before it even begins.

When we step into Diego and Cole's shared space, it's pretty obvious they don't concern themselves with things like cleanliness and laundry. Even so, they must have tidied up a little bit for tonight because part of the floor is bare and the beds have been hastily made.

The layout of their dorm is very similar to ours: two desks, a shared closet and dresser, a large window, a closed door off to the side that I'm assuming opens up into a bathroom. The only differences are bigger beds, a mini-fridge, and a slightly larger space.

Maybe Sophomores are allotted a few more perks once they've survived one full year at Gomada Academy. I used to think that was unattainable due to academic reasons. I didn't think it was impossible due to threat of survival.

Ryker is sitting at the desk closest to the window. This is the (marginally) tidier half of the room – likely Diego's side.

When Ryker sees Nora and I, he nods at us enthusiastically. He's looking at us straight-on, as casual as can be. I'm the complete opposite.

I'm suffering from pins and needles and uncontrollable butterflies. We have way more important things to worry about, but I can't help it.

Still, Ryker is Nora's Mentor, and I'll clearly have to work with him, talk to him, more now than before. I'll have to get over this crushed spirit thing – or at least get over it enough to be around him more often.

"Hey, guys!" Ryker greets us. "Nice to see you – even under *these* circumstances," he adds, giving Nora what seems to be a sympathetic look.

Word must have spread between the three boys about what

had happened to Nora last night. Even though I've been relieved over Nora's safe return, a small part of me still wants to know the rest of the story. Maybe those gaps will be filled tonight.

"Hey," Nora greets him stiffly.

I know Nora and Ryker have been hanging out a bit due to Mentor-Mentee stuff, so I'm assuming her discomfort is due to the situation, not him.

Just as I'm opening my mouth to try and greet Ryker in the most normal way possible (which means it won't be normal at all), the door closes behind us. Nora and I walk closer to where Ryker is sitting, so the newcomers can have more space.

Lucy and Diego are now stepping into the room. Diego has his arm around her shoulders in an easygoing way, but it still signifies that they are dating. I suppose it makes sense: why else involve Lucy, an Enchantress related to one of the cruelest students on campus? The only possible reason would be that Diego cares for her and wants to keep her safe.

Great. Now I have to work with Ryker *and* Lucy, someone who's bullied me and knows my family secret. I understand these issues aren't as life-threatening as a ghost haunting the campus, but my allies in this mess aren't exactly the dream team I would have wanted.

One of them knows my biggest weakness.

One of them publicly rejected me, breaking my heart and making me feel pathetic.

And the other one hates my guts – or, at least, he *used to*. Now, I don't know what to believe.

Cole closes and locks the door after peeking up and down the hallway, his posture stiff and uncompromising. He is poised for an ambush.

This all seems so top-secret. They're not taking any chances, I muse as Cole leans against the door and folds his arms. I wonder if he's doing the same thing Professor Qadir did at our shared meeting this morning.

Lucy sits on Diego's bed – making it look carefree and easy. I don't think I'd ever be able to do that if I was dating someone.

Nora leans against Cole's desk, giving Lucy a wary look. I can't say I blame her for that. After telling her about Lucy wanting to make a *truce* of some sort, Nora has been just as unnerved about that as I am.

I step beside Nora just as Cole opens his mouth, likely to start the meeting. I flinch when I think about those same lips pressing to mine.

Thinking about Cole is like a rabbit hole – all-consuming, so easy to fall into. A black abyss of ecstasy and confusion.

"Alright, let's just get started, since everyone's here," Cole grunts, thankfully breaking me out of my reverie.

He looks from one individual to the other. When his eyes drift from Nora to me, I quickly put my head down.

"We all know about the ghost," Cole continues. "We've all seen it or at least heard about it from a reliable source."

Since when does Cole use terms like 'reliable source?' He must be taking this seriously.

That's weird, because the Cole I know doesn't take anything seriously. Except for the ghost. Hmm. Maybe this isn't so weird, after all.

"We brought you here because we need help getting rid of it. The school's not doing their job. More people are getting snatched, maybe even killed. We have to do something about it."

There are more students missing than that boy Cole told me about at the campfire party?

This is awful! That means the problem, the ghost, is escalating.

Lucy frowns up at Cole. "What do you mean, the school's not doing their job?" she asks him.

On second thought, that sounds more like a challenge than an inquiry. But Cole doesn't look fazed by it at all.

"Who else is missing?" Nora gasps.

I clutch her arm in as covert a way as possible. I can feel the terror oozing off of her. I'm sure she's not just shaking from getting caught in the thunderstorm. Her blue eyes are wide with fear.

Cole doesn't miss a beat when he looks down at Lucy, ignoring Nora's question. "Sending out little emails? Scaling back curfew? Do you really think those things are gonna stop the ghost from getting to us?"

Cole turns to Nora abruptly, adding solemnly, "Ryker and I figured it out."

That's all that Cole says in response to Nora's question? Is he serious?

Lucy doesn't look very happy that Cole accepted her challenge – but not in her usual, mean-girl-bully type of way. She looks nervous.

"Nora knows it – no offense," Cole adds, looking over at Nora, who grows pale from the connection. She looks even more frightened than before – which I didn't think was possible.

I don't like that Cole made her feel that way, but she nods at him without hostility or confrontation, turning to face Lucy.

"I was in my dorm room when it manipulated me," she reports. "I wasn't off-campus or breaking curfew. It can get to us anytime, anywhere."

I guess we'll have to find out about the abducted students some other time, because the conversation is beginning to change course.

"Frow knows that Nora, Arya and I went up against it last night, so we can't be seen meeting up," Cole goes on firmly. "We're gonna have to keep doing this in secret."

"Why so many of us?" Lucy asks. "I would have thought it unwise to involve six people."

"Strength in numbers," Cole answers simply. "We've got two Shifters, two Enchanters, and two Nymphs. Those are good odds against anything – even a ghost."

Cole hesitated on that last word, but I don't know why.

"If it *is* a ghost," Ryker cuts in, causing my heart to stop.

What else could it be, if not a spirit of some kind?

It's not like I know much about ghosts, but the fact that this thing seems to float in mid-air and be made of fog are clear signs that it's paranormal.

Just as I'm doubting Ryker (which is hard to do because I still think he's incredibly smart), I'm brought up short when I remember Cole saying he actually bit into the ghost last night. How could I have forgotten about that?

"What?" Lucy breathes.

"Cole took a chunk out of it last night," Ryker relays to everyone, still leaning with his arms propped up against the back of Diego's chair. "Cole and I researched paranormal behaviour that's congruent across all the realms. They can't touch objects or people, and we sure can't touch them."

Cole doesn't look happy that Ryker roped him into some kind of paranormal research investigation, but he nods briefly in agreement.

"So it's not a ghost?" I ask. It's the first thing I say, and I immediately regret saying anything at all, because Cole answers,

"No idea. But I bet it's super pissed off that I figured out it was different."

"Maybe it's a ghost hybrid," Diego muses.

Ryker sighs. "Yes. Let's start speculating on different supernatural creatures while we're at it, Jasper."

Diego rolls his eyes and smirks at Ryker's comment. For two Shifters and an Enchanter, they seem to all get along.

"I've been thinking," Cole segues.

"A dangerous choice," Ryker jokes, but Cole ignores it.

"With Nora's Earth Affinity, she can trap the ghost thing. Arya can electrocute it. Ryker and Lucy can use Dark and Light magic at the same time, to weaken it. And then Diego and I will close in on it, fully Shifted."

How does Cole know about everyone's Affinities? I wonder. Could Ryker have filled him in on Nora's Earth Affinity? What about Lucy? I thought he only associated with Shifters.

No one else seems to be confused by his strategy, so I keep my questions to myself.

Diego stares blankly at Cole while he's talking. It takes me a while to realize Diego is staring because he's surprised.

"That actually sounds like it can work!" he gasps, shocked.

Cole rolls his eyes. "Shut up, Jasper," he orders.

"That does sound plausible," Lucy unnerves me by asserting, her red sweater with black high heeled boots making her look like she belongs on the runway and not in a dormitory.

I'm astounded that Lucy's on board with this, too. What has happened over the past few weeks that I've clearly missed? Does it have anything to do with Lucy's sudden change of heart?

"And I can help you merge your two Affinities together – or at least have them co-exist without the world blowing up," Ryker offers to Lucy. He's smiling at her now, but it looks like it's out of sympathy.

Maybe Ryker better understands what she's going through because he shares the same Affinities. I'm still learning about Enchanters and Gomadian culture, but apparently Enchanters with 'black and white' Affinities – or, opposing Affinities – are rare.

Lucy must have awakened her second Affinity, making her an Enchantress with two opposing elements to control. Being an Enchanter with Light and Dark Affinities, Ryker knows how to tame them. I'm not surprised by him offering to help Lucy. I may be a little envious of it – but not at all surprised. If Ryker wanted to help me by getting Cole off my back, it's not a big leap to see him wanting to assist Lucy in controlling her Affinities.

Lucy beams up at him. "That would be wonderful," she breathes, relieved. Even her shoulders slump slightly, as if she's been tense all day. "Thank you."

"Any questions?" Cole asks, cutting down on the side chatter. "We can meet again next week. And if anyone sees anything, let me know and we can call an emergency meeting, ASAP."

It's still so odd, seeing Cole capable, contemplative, and in charge. Usually, he's just an awful bully. But I know the ghost is serious business, and I hate myself for it, but I happen to agree with Cole. The school isn't doing enough to keep the ghost away from campus.

We need to take charge.

The spirit almost captured Nora last night!

And it's already taking other students.

We can't let anyone else get taken – or worse.

"Well, I need to study for my next midterm," Lucy announces, standing up from Diego's bed and straightening her sweater. "Talk to you all later."

As she walks out, I'm flabbergasted once again that she actually seemed to *mean* what she said earlier – like she actually *will* talk to us later, and she's okay with it.

My head's starting to hurt.

"I should skip out, too," Ryker nods, leaning off of what I'm assuming is the bathroom door. Ryker moved around a bit during the meeting. Maybe it's a nervous habit.

"Later," Cole responds, who actually opened and held the door for Lucy as she walked out of the room.

Ryker nods at Nora and I. "See you guys later," he bades us.

"Bye," Nora and I respond, almost at the same time.

Maybe Nora's right. Maybe Ryker really *has* forgotten about my humiliating display at the Shifter's Campfire. This may make things less gut-wrenching – but it's not like this group gives me sunshine and roses vibes.

If anything, we'll all be lucky to get out of this nightmare alive.

Five

COLE'S A SPECTATOR

It's Thursday. Midterms are over tomorrow, but I've been finished with them since Monday. Thank God that shit is behind me. I actually studied this time, even if it meant I had to take some ribbing from Diego. If I don't get my grades up, I won't have to worry about a ghost coming after me. Professor Qadir will be first in line.

My plan was to sleep and do nothing for the entire week – but of course, that didn't actually happen.

I didn't think that becoming 'leader of the ghost hunting team,' as Diego called me Monday night, meant it would suddenly become a full-time job. But that's exactly what happened.

Suddenly, Lucy's messaging me about practice sessions with Ryker to make sure they 'don't look too suspicious' to Frow and that they 'don't interfere with future meetings'. Diego wants us to figure out a more in-depth strategy than just 'Shifting and closing in on the ghost's ass.'

At least Nora and Arya aren't hassling me about ghost shit and leader crap – but I'm guessing they have more midterms to

45

get through. Last night at dinner, Taylor Hayden mentioned to me that the Nymphs have their Field Practice midterm on Thursday. I bet the Nymphs are shitting themselves about that.

I don't know much about Professor Xhao, the Nymph prof in charge of Field Practice – but I *do* know she's a cold-hearted bitch.

That class can't be fun.

I don't really know why, but I find myself at the Nymph's Field around ten AM, even though my leg is now on fire after all that walking. According to Taylor – the fiery redhead who Shifts into a Fire Bird, of all things badass – the Nymphs' midterm is at ten. I guess I want to see the action for myself. Besides, I want to see if Nora's gonna be strong enough to trap what we think is a 'ghost hybrid,' to quote Diego.

I hope no one notices me. Nymphs are self-absorbed little shits, so hopefully none of them catch on that a Shifter is on their turf.

I never thought I'd be somewhere like this – somewhere so anti-Shifter – but this is all business. I have a job to do. I want to make sure our line of defense against the ghost is, well, *defensive*.

I'd never admit this to anyone, but I guess I'm also here to see Arya. I haven't made a move to go near her since the meeting. Ever since I overheard Arya talking to Nora about the kiss, I haven't really known what to do about the whole thing. I don't know too much about girls – but I *do* know that Arya talking to Nora about the kiss is either very good or very bad. Judging by Nora's tone, it sounded very bad.

I kind of wish my super-hearing wasn't so *super*, because hearing Nora's grossed-out comments could only mean that Arya's upset about it. I mean, I already knew that, but still.

I wish this whole thing could be forgotten about already. But like most shit that happens around here, that seems to be impossible. And at least I feel like less of a moron, because I'm here to make sure the Nymphs coming at the ghost will be able to do some damage. I'm not just here to watch *her*.

Professor Xhao walks out onto the Field, all by herself. She's wearing some purple cloak that makes her look like she's trying to be intimidating and impressive. I've never had a run-in with her before (I don't count the meeting in Frow's office, because Xhao didn't even look at me) – but still, I'm not about to whip out my lighter and a cig right now.

Nymphs begin to fill the Field, hanging out near the sidelines. When more of them are warming up, I walk out onto the sidelines, too, knowing I'll be less noticeable.

It's not like it's a weird thing for other races to watch Field Practice midterms. It's something the Headmistress and profs want. We need to 'foster a community and encourage more tolerance,' to quote that Orientation crap from September.

I lean against the wrought-iron fence and fold my arms. I can sense the fear and anxiety coming from all ends of the Nymph's Field. I don't envy these poor bastards. My Field Practice midterm made me nervous, too – not that I'd ever tell anyone about that. Not even Diego.

A cold feeling hits me. When I glance from the wet grass to the middle of the Nymph's Field, I see Xhao looking at me. Something tells me she's not one of the usual profs who'd cheer me on for watching another race's midterm.

I guess not everyone here – even the profs – agrees with Frow and the other realms about 'togetherness' and all that shit. I can't say that I do, either. In some ways, hanging around with other races is something you just gotta do – like in our case, with the ghost.

This is why it's so hard to like Arya. It goes against everything I've been taught, and everything I've experienced. It's not just that my parents want me to hang around Shifters. It's deeper than that. Nymphs have screwed me over before, and so have

Enchanters. I have real-life experience telling me it's easier to stick with your own kind.

It'd be easier to ignore Arya and just let these damned feelings go by the wayside. But I guess I'm here, so I'm a fucking – masochist? Whatever it is.

Getting back to Xhao, it's creepy that she was able to find me in the middle of all these Nymphs. She could give the ghost serial killer a run for its money.

Whatever.

This uptight bitch doesn't scare me.

I don't cause any shit, but I do look back at her, showing her I'm not gonna back down.

Nymphs these days. Even the profs have attitude problems.

No wonder I feel like I don't belong on this side of campus.

I smell Nora before I see her. She whizzes past me in a blur of green. She's running around the Field now. I guess that's her way of warming up.

If she's into fitness, she'll have stamina and staying power – advantages that can be used in battle against the 'hybrid.'

Even though no one's talking to me or even looking at me, I still feel like I'm standing out – and not in a good way. I'm sure the Nymphs here can sense that I'm different – not one of them.

After a few more minutes, Professor Xhao begins to get every-one's attention. Everyone stops talking, almost at the same time. They even stop moving. They're almost like statues.

Cowards.

But I guess I'd be quiet, too, if I were them. Xhao doesn't look like she's a fan of bullshit.

The rules of the midterm are simple. The Nymphs will be randomly paired (but matched according to skill level) and partici-pate in a mock battle. Even though they won't be trying to wail on each other, I bet Xhao won't stop things if that happens. It's the same with Shifter midterms, and even with Enchanter ones, too, I bet.

Magic is dangerous. If you don't practice, you won't know the consequences of using your Affinities or Shifting powers irresponsibly. Professor Qadir is always talking about that.

Professor Xhao begins calling names. Nymphs walk toward her like trained poodles and pair up. There are dozens of Nymphs here, so I bet this'll take a while.

As Xhao is doing roll call, I glance around at the Nymphs new to Gomada Academy – AKA Freshmen.

You can always tell when new students are enrolled at Gomada Academy, no matter what race they belong to. That look of fear (*Will I fail? Will I measure up? What if I can't do it?*) and self-doubt are like viruses that infect every Freshman within a ten-mile radius. Soon, you've got dozens of Freshmen from all three classes begging to go home. Even transfer students aren't always immune

There are other boarding schools for supernatural races in Chimara (Nymph Land), Houssan (Shifter territory), Valis (the royal people and Enchanters act all high and mighty and live in the main metropolitan areas). But none of them measure up to Gomada Academy. That's why all these pups are shitting themselves.

Come to think of it, only the Overworld (Earth?) doesn't have schools for people like us. We like to make sure humans don't know too much about magic and Shifting – and that's something each of the three races agree on, even if we usually can't stand each other.

Glancing around doesn't change my mind about my first impression of these Nymphs – lots of weak ones, from the looks of things. But there are a few of them that have *some* promise, I guess.

I don't see Arya until Professor Xhao calls her name. When

she comes forward, I can feel the tension between her and Professor Xhao. I remember her tensing up in Frow's office when her teacher showed up with Nora. I'm wondering now if something happened between them, if she's always on-edge around Xhao.

I don't know who Arya's paired up with – but it's not like making Nymph friends is high on my priorities list. I only know Nora because of Ryker, and I only know Arya because I'm her Mentor.

Anyway Arya's partner is some dude in a leather jacket. He looks like a stuck-up douchebag. I'm betting he has a strong Affinity, like Fire or Darkness – something he'd use to overcompensate.

I watch the first couple of mock Nymph battles. They're going faster than I expected. I guess Xhao's been observing them for months and doesn't need much time to see how they've progressed compared to the beginning of the school year. My favourite battle (not that I'd say anything) was a guy and girl with Dark Affinities. When their two blasts of dark magic smashed together, I expected the ground to get swallowed up, sending us all down South – and not in the good, balmy-paradise way.

After a while, though, it all starts to become the same. Girl with Poison Affinity versus a girl with Water Affinity. Guy with Air Affinity versus a girl with Light Affinity. The only other interesting one was a guy who kicked another guy's ass with his Clairvoyance Affinity.

I know nothing about Clairvoyance powers. Mental energy blasts and what seemed to be mind-reading abilities are interesting but intimidating battle strategies. Any kind of ESP ability would be shitty as hell in the wrong situation.

Nora's next, against another Nymph with an Earth Affinity. I pay more attention to this mock battle than the others. Nora's more conscious of her stance and concentration than other first-year Nymphs. You can tell which ones are more experienced than the rest – though, like I said before, most Freshmen Nymphs have marbles for brains.

Nora's opponent somehow gets a hold of rocks out of God knows where to throw at her, but Nora uses vines with the biggest thorns I've ever seen to smack them away. I never would have thought vines would be able to swat big-ass rocks out of the way like pesky flies, but they're super thick and easily controlled. Some of them even grab hold of the bigger rocks to prevent injury.

She'll do well against the ghost if we can get it cornered first, I think. *If the ghost can move through objects, but can still be touched, it may be trickier to catch it in a spot.*

That's why I'm hoping Nora's Earth Affinity combined with Arya's electricity would stop the ghost long enough for the rest of us to go at it. If we can't get it cornered first, we might not be able to stop it. And if it gets pissed off, it can pick us off – one by one.

We have one shot, and one shot only. And I won't hesitate to kick someone off the team if they don't measure up. If one person messes up in battle, the rest of us could end up dead. It's not like these stupid midterms where the worst thing that happens to you is a failing grade and maybe some finger-wagging.

Even though I'm taking this seriously, I'm still shitting my pants about it. I'm not sure if I'm the right choice to be the leader. It's not like I ever take charge in any other part of my life. Just because I saw the ghost first, or whatever, I have to be in charge? Crazy!

But I don't have time to think more on how shitty my end of the deal is because it's Arya's turn, and I want to see how she performs this time around.

And...

I guess I want to see her, too.

Great. More rain on my already-fucked-up parade.

I remember Désirée Chapin, AKA The Original Witch Bitch,

giving Arya a hard time about being a half-Nymph. That probably explains why Arya's so freaked right now. Everyone knows that any race with a 'half' to it won't be nearly as strong as everyone else. Those half-blooded people are made fun of or looked down on in an 'I feel bad for you' way. Even if she's new to Gomada from the Overworld, Arya knows better than to broadcast her secret.

Leather Jacket Douche seems to be psyching himself up. He's bouncing up and down – getting into the zone, I guess. He's taking this way too seriously. Yeah, it's a midterm – but it's not a *war*.

This guy looks like he wants to cause damage. I'd never say anything, but if he hurt Arya more than a few scrapes, I'd send him to the infirmary – or just bury him.

"On my count," Professor Xhao recites, for about the eightieth time. "One, two–"

I'm about to roll my eyes at this. By now, everyone knows they're supposed to attack on 'three.' Xhao must think her students are dumb as doorknobs.

I stop about midway when Arya's eyes happen to land on mine. I'm surprised she could pick me out of the crowd of waiting-slash-finished Nymphs at the sidelines of the Field.

Part of me thinks she could be looking *past me* or *near me* – but there's no way that's what's happening. She's looking at me, and there's this *vibe* I get from her – and it's not good.

"Three."

The guy throws out his arms on either side of his body. Flames crackle out of his palms.

Typical.

Arya's body language screams 'fear.' It's almost tangible. I can't help the lump that forms deep within my throat when her body language stiffens at Fire Douche's literal warm-up.

I want to protect her.

I know it's not my place. I know she has to do this on her own. And I hate myself for making my life more complicated by wanting to save her.

But looking at her now, there's no way out of my feelings.

Damnit!

Dark clouds pop out of nowhere, taking me by surprise. Thunder rocks this side of campus.

This does nothing to Pyro Dick, who's clearly done with his pre-battle show-off shit. He's shooting fire from both palms. It meets in the middle in a freaky orange-and-red blaze, shooting straight for little Arya.

I look across the way at Professor Xhao, who's doing fuck-all about this. I didn't expect her to stop it – but at the same time, part of me thinks this guy's using too much force. Part of Xhao's speech from the beginning was about 'not striking for the kill.'

This guy didn't get the memo.

Arya backs up.

Why is she moving away?

What's her plan, here?

She's gonna get burned alive by this guy!

The air is tense. The heat waves hitting us from the sidelines make breathing hard. The grass is smoking up around the inferno as it rushes for Arya.

Why hasn't she done anything yet?

Why hasn't she at least used her wind, or used her wings to fly away from the flames?

She's going to die!

I look again at Xhao. Nothing. I could be wrong, but it looks like she's almost *waiting* for something to happen – like it's all part of the show.

Now, I *really* think there's bad blood between Xhao and Arya. The Nymphs around me are talking quietly. Some are asking why Arya isn't doing anything. Others are asking why Xhao hasn't intervened.

It makes sense for profs to give rookie Nymphs a healthy dose of tough love. They're wet behind the ears; still learning to control their Affinity. That's one thing.

But this is taking it a little far – even by *my* standards.

When the fire is inches away from Arya, lightning suddenly surrounds her. I think it came from her hands, but the intermittent smoke is making it hard to see.

Lightning is cutting through the wall of fire and thick smoke, coursing around her and over her body.

The fire moves *around* Arya, but I bet she's not feeling very good right now.

I'm no stranger to being around fire – but this is too close for comfort. I'm best friends with Diego, a Phoenix Shifter, but it's not like he's ever tried to roast me. Then again, you don't have to fall off a building to know it's gonna hurt.

With the fire streaming past the battle zone, there's a real danger of it hurting the rest of us. Hell, there's a considerable chance it'll rip through the entire Nymph-slash-Enchanter's Field.

What the fuck is Xhao doing?!

A few Nymphs that I think are Masters jump to the sides of the battlefield and shoot water and mud out from their palms.

The fire explodes.

My ears ring from the hissing steam. My eyes burn from the thick smoke. Ash and sizzling dirt tumble to the singed grass.

Douche Pyro Man doesn't seem to mind any of this, though. I wonder if he'll change from the preppy douchebag grinning at the murmuring, gasping, and hollering of the Nymphs watching the rumble into a crazed arsonist with a superiority complex.

The battle's not over yet.

Arya suddenly whips her hands out. It's an expression of force

– not an act of surrender. Electricity slams toward the guy who's been loving the spotlight like an attention whore.

Pyro Dick looks thrown off track by Arya's counter. He probably figured she would've wimped out by now – and maybe in September, I would've thought the same thing.

Hasty flames shoot from Leather Jacket Douche's palms again. It looks like he used up most of his juice, though: he's tipping slightly from exertion and his fire's at half-power.

This is bad – for him.

Now I'm the one who's grinning.

The electricity and fire blasts collide, each making little progress until the other Affinity pushes it back. It goes back and forth until a third, way more powerful beam of lightning smashes into them.

More ash and a shit-ton of static electricity fill the air. Cracking from more lightning makes most of us cover our ears and shield our eyes from the brightness.

My ultra-sensitive hearing and vision take a beating, too, but I just close my eyes and turn away from the sound as best I can. No Nymph prof is gonna make me flinch.

Huh, I breathe. I didn't realize I was holding my breath until now. *Looks like Xhao is finally stepping in. She has an Air Affinity. Who would've thought?*

I'm surprised that one Affinity can knock out two – even cancelling out its own Affinity in the process – but Xhao is powerful. She may be a cold-hearted bitch, but she's strong.

I've always thought that having an Air Affinity wasn't all that great – unless you could shoot lightning bolts out of your hands. Xhao proves that with her own electrical powers. But then again, Arya growing wings that one time we tracked down the ghost was pretty cool.

I can think this way about Nymphs because no one else will ever hear it.

An Air Affinity would be a pretty good trick to have, after all.

"That is quite enough of that," Professor Xhao announces, her voice sounding exactly like I remember it from last week: nails on a chalkboard.

The lightning from Xhao completely knocked out Arya and Pyro Head's Affinities. The ground around them sizzles. A creepy breeze tosses ashes all around the Field.

It looks – and feels – like the two Nymphs are calming themselves down, which also means turning the dial down on their Affinities.

After Xhao speaks, the Fire Guy and Arya begin to move to opposite ends of the sidelines, knowing their midterm is over. Now that Fire Douche has his back to me, I'm wondering if he has more to prove than I thought.

"Mister Alan Freight and Mr. Blake Carsula, you are next," Xhao finishes, causing me to shake my head free of her weird voice.

Yikes. I'd rather deal with the ear-splitting lightning than listen to *that* noise.

Now that I've seen all I need to, I can skip out and return to Feara. I could do with a smoke, that's for sure. I've had enough Nymph battles to last me a lifetime.

At least I know Nora will do well, even under pressure.

Even Arya has improved.

Still, I don't get why she hesitated like that. Her clothes are singed. It looks like she sustained some burns from the fight. If she'd attacked sooner–

"What are you doing here?"

I'm surprised I didn't sense or smell Arya's approach.

Usually, the vanilla scent is enough to make me notice her – not to mention that typical *burned* smell that follows you around if you're near a fire.

I guess I was distracted.

I look to my left and down at Arya. I know I have to be careful here, so she doesn't think I came around to bully her. I may have been a dick to her, but I need to show her that I've changed – in my feelings for her, anyway. Everything else is still pretty much the same.

"Hey," I tell her. "Taylor mentioned this was happening. Just came to watch."

I'd tell her more about strategies and stuff, but I'm guessing now isn't the time. Not after she almost got burnt to a crisp.

Arya moves her hair away from her shoulder. I can't help but watch. Even with her smelling of smoke, the burns all over her clothes, and the Nymphs all around us who could blow my cover wide open, I still can't look away.

Fuck! I growl. *I **really** like her. This sucks!*

I don't think Arya believes me. Maybe she thinks there's another reason for my presence here. I have to somehow get myself out of this mess before she thinks–

"Did you just come here to–" she begins, at the same time that I blurt out, like an idiot,

"You were pretty good."

Arya stares at me in shock and in disbelief.

"Why did you wait, though?" I ask, really wanting to know the answer. She probably won't tell me, but at least I tried on the off-chance that she does.

Arya is nervous. She folds her arms and steps back from me, turning her head to watch the current battle. It looks like she knows one of the guys who's participating.

"Something bad happened the last time I went up against someone with a Fire Affinity," she confesses, still avoiding eye contact.

I'm stunned she would admit that – to me of all people. I'm also startled that something *bad* happened to her – so bad that she froze up this time.

Before I can ask her what happened, she adds without looking at me, "Professor Xhao told me I could've hurt people and burnt down the entire field. Then she told me I sucked as a Nymph."

I'm guessing Xhao didn't say it exactly like that, but that's what Arya took from the conversation. I'm not surprised that Xhao would have an answer like that.

So this is why Arya stalled. It wasn't just out of fear or nerves. It was out of trauma, or PTSD – or something. I'm not a shrink, but I can pick up what she's putting down.

I don't know how to answer her. I don't know if anything I could come up with would help her. Finally, I just say, "Well, you did okay this time."

Arya gawks at me, still on-edge. "So you really came here just to watch?" she asks – or accuses. It's hard to tell.

I shrug. "Pretty much," I agree.

She's scrutinizing me, looking for a crack in my armour-slash-explanation.

We stare at each other. A weird *pause* happens. I'm sweating.

Finally, it looks like she believes me.

"Well, I have to–" Arya begins quickly.

"Next time, don't wait so long. You were almost a roasted marshmallow, halfling."

Arya flinches as the word 'halfling' is thrown at her by Fire Guy, who's now passing us. I guess the gates to the Nymph-slash-Enchanter's Field are closest to where I'm standing, so it makes sense that he'd come this way. Or, he just came here to be a dick. Maybe it's both.

Looks like Désirée did some damage after that stupid Shifter campfire behind Feara. How many people now know about Arya being half-human? Probably too many, if you ask her.

Arya says nothing back to Fire Guy. I'm wondering if she feels outnumbered because I'm here and a few weeks ago, I might have joined in on the mocking.

But not today.

I turn my head to the right and look down at him. He's smaller than me and clearly only relies on his Affinity – not on common sense or street smarts.

As soon as Fire Nymph makes eye contact with me, I sense cold fear. Like most people here, he can sense I'm a Shifter, and that I Shift into something *bad*.

In times like these, I enjoy making people shit their pants.

"How about *we* give it a go?" I ask him darkly. I was thinking about changing my eyes or voice to match the Tedla's, but keeping this shithead in fear of the unknown is a better tactic.

Sure enough, he crumbles and backs away from us, not even having the guts to answer me before heading for the gates. He's not even a very good bully if he only has one-liners and zero backbone. But it looks like he got to Arya, who seems to be trying not to cry right now.

"Thanks," she tells me quietly – so quietly I wouldn't have heard it without the Tedla's super-hearing that helps me out, even in human form.

I shrug again. "No big deal," I respond.

The thing is, I *hope* it's a big deal. I hope she starts to think of me as someone who can be different from the guy she met. But that may not work out. Too much has happened since September.

"I have to meet Nora," she mumbles after another weird pause.

I nod because I don't really know what to say. And it doesn't really matter anymore because Arya's already walking away from me.

Six

ARYA LOWERS HER GUARD

I shake like a leaf as I stagger through clusters of chatting Nymphs, trying to ignore their eyes on me. I know they're not looking at me with sympathy or compassion. News of my 'halfness' has spread throughout campus thanks to Désirée. I know these Nymphs are taunting my existence and looking for amusement – not concerned in the least that one of their kind was almost killed in a mock battle.

Is that why Professor Xhao waited so long to stop my midterm with that despicable jerk, Samuel Minders? Because I'm a half-Nymph?

I know that's true, based on how the Field Practice professor treated me a few weeks ago once she knew the truth.

If I can't get acceptance from my professors, what makes me think fellow students would be any different?

I force myself to concentrate on my search for Nora, ignoring the whispering and snickers as I move. Still, I can't stop thinking about my midterm – and not just because merely participating in it almost killed me.

I still can't believe Professor Xhao paired me up with Samuel! In addition to being one of the strongest Nymphs in my class, he's also one of the meanest. I never thought I'd meet someone who'd be a match for Cole in the 'bullies' department – but Samuel is just as bad, if not worse. On top of all of that, Samuel's Affinity is Fire. After what had happened with Makayleigh and Nora back in late September, I was dreading going up against someone with that Affinity.

I'm almost certain that Professor Xhao did this on purpose. She was setting me up to fail. Maybe I wouldn't be so paranoid about this had it not been because two weeks earlier, she told the class that she'd pair us up with someone of 'approximate power and strength.' She also told us she'd pair us the day of the midterm – in random couplings, purely based on skill level.

Since I'm not the strongest Nymph in my class, I figured Professor Xhao would pair me up with someone a bit stronger than me, but not by much. So why pair me with the top of my class – *and* he has a Fire Affinity, to boot?

Random pairing, my foot.

I glance down at the scorch marks on my jacket and leggings. My clothing is torn. I can already see throbbing burn marks in between the singed fabric that's sticking uncomfortably to my skin. I'm sure when I go back to my dorm, there will be more burns to discover.

A trip to the infirmary might be better.

He could have killed me!

Even worse than that, Professor Xhao did nothing to stop it!

Had it not been me in trouble, Xhao would have acted sooner. I know it.

At least this time, I didn't use any air blasts or wind. I wasn't the cause of Samuel's fire getting out of control. But Professor Xhao never said anything about that.

Dad warned me this would happen. He told me that people

aren't always as accepting of half-races as they should be. He told me I may encounter racism or discrimination.

I knew it would happen, but I also hoped it wouldn't because I never wanted anyone to find out. But thanks to Désirée and Lucy, there's no way to keep my family secret under wraps.

I'll be a walking target for the next four and a half years at this school.

And it won't only be my contemporaries whispering about me, wanting to see me fail.

Worse still, it's not like that's my only problem.

I let the fog fingers and Nora's screams from the night of her almost-capture take hold.

I let Cole's kiss and supervision of my midterm imprison my mind.

Thankfully I catch sight of Nora and Anja, which snaps me out of the many horrors I can't fully escape.

It just *hurts*. All of this hurts.

Anja and Nora are talking quietly along the wrought-iron fenceline, away from the other students. Nora is my roommate and best friend. She is dating Anja, who is kind yet frank – very much like Nora. I don't want to interrupt whatever they're talking about, so I consider leaving the Nymph's Field and waiting for them. But just as I'm about to turn around to do that, Nora makes eye contact and waves at me.

Approaching them now, I hope that Samuel is gone for good. The way he spoke to me back there, the way he fought against me...

He wasn't pulling his punches. Professor Xhao told us 'not to fight with the intent to kill.' She repeated that cautionary statement over the past couple of weeks – even this morning before the midterms started.

This can't be a figment of my imagination.

*They're all doing this to me because of what I am. We may be of the same race, but in their eyes, I'm still **different** from them.*

I'll never be their equal, even if I get stronger, even if my heart gets harder.

Nora grabs me into a hug as soon as I'm close, making my burden easier to manage.

"I was so worried about you!" she gushes as I return her embrace. "That jackass could have killed you!"

When we put each other at arm's length, I ask, "So you think it was–"

"Totally brutal and an unnecessary use of force? Yes," Anja finishes, stepping to my right and hugging me from the side. I take her arm due to the angle between us.

"I'm alright. I think," I admit shakily when we let go of each other. "I'm just happy it's over with."

But part of me believes all this *isn't* over because Samuel seems to have some kind of chip on his shoulder regarding half-entities.

Nora and Anja believe the same way I do. Samuel used more force *because of* my half-Nymph status. I figure if I try to say that to Professor Xhao, she'll either accuse me of being too sensitive, or she'll just think I'm trying to get a better grade than I deserve.

And it won't matter, anyway, because she shares his hatred of me, too.

It may be best just to suck it up and hope that a pretty girl (if that's who he's into) or a sports event catches Samuel's eye, and he decides to focus his attention elsewhere.

Now that I've survived midterms and half a term of school – literally, survived – other thoughts float to the forefront besides studying and practicing out in the Nymph's Field with Nora.

There's a school-sanctioned Halloween party at the end of the month. I don't know much about it because parties and participating in social events aren't my thing.

Nora and Anja are attending and have been trying to convince me to do the same. The only thing is, I don't want to crash their date. Being a third wheel isn't the nicest thing to do to your two friends who just started dating around the beginning of the school year.

Besides, I don't like Halloween. The scary atmosphere, blood and gore, and weird costumes freak me out. But it's hard not to think about it because the entire campus is buzzing about the event. Flyers are plastered all over the school grounds. Students of all races discuss potential costumes and dates in the hallways between midterm writing. I didn't realize Halloween was necessarily a time to *get* dates in the first place, but then again, it's not like I'm skilled in party-going or dating.

Making matters even worse, attendance is mandatory. Gomada Academy believes in things like 'mingling between the races' and 'the proper socialization of young people.' Headmistress Leona Frow may have said this during orientation, and other professors echo it almost weekly, but that doesn't mean the entire student body is on board with that mantra.

At dinner tonight, Nora and Anja are trying to decide on a couple's costume. I eat my stir-fry in silence, wondering if I should go to this party – and dress up for it, to boot.

I really don't know what to do. Désirée and Samuel are making it pretty obvious I'm not welcome here. And I still don't know if Lucy was a part of the 'half-Nymph' rumour spreading; if she's being genuine in wanting to make peace with Nora and I.

And then there's Cole. I don't even want to go there.

I just don't want to put myself in a situation where any one of them can torture me even further.

If I wanted to go to the party, but also didn't want to ruin Nora and Anja's fun, I could ask someone to go with me. But that would involve talking to a boy and asking him out – and I already know what happened when I tried that with Ryker: disaster.

I don't want to go through that again. Being rejected even once was unbearable. I don't know if I can deal with it again.

Besides, I have way bigger problems than dates, Halloween parties, and bullies.

Dinner ends with Anja and Nora deciding on a costume and then trying to get me to decide on one, too. But since I'm dreading this party, I guess I'm not really in the mood.

But as I get ready for bed tonight, part of me feels like I don't have any other choice. I know Makayleigh is going with her boyfriend, Alan, and I assume Lucy is going with Diego. We know for sure that they are dating now, thanks to a horrific afternoon PDA scene that Nora and I saw.

I guess I can always go alone. Attendance is mandatory, and humiliation seems to be inevitable. Getting nicknames like 'dateless loser half-Nymph' seems to be inevitable, too.

At least if I wear a costume, no one will know it's me. That's one tiny thing in my favour, at least.

I usually call Mom and Dad to say 'goodnight,' and since midterms are over, I have a bit more energy at nine PM than I usually would – especially over the past two weeks. Getting comfy on my bed and putting on my headphones so Nora's reading won't be disturbed, I pick up my phone from my pink duvet and open up my Phone application. Making sure Nora is wearing her own earbuds, I look back at my screen, ready to call home.

My eyes become glued to Cole's name under my 'recent calls' list. That night comes back with a vengeance. Suddenly, I see those foggy claws and hear Nora's shrieking all over again.

Midterms, my mock battle (which wasn't a mock *anything*, thanks to Samuel and Professor Xhao), and that awful night must have caused me to temporarily suppress the kiss – or at least move it to the back burner. I've been so overwhelmed that it's been a continuous cycle from one traumatic event to the other.

Sure, I remembered the kiss when I saw Cole this morning – and I think seeing him triggered some of my electricity to show up earlier than I expected – but it's been buried at the back of my list of worries. Now that midterms are over and the Headmistress knows about Nora's almost-capture, I have more time to worry about this.

How could someone who tortured me for so long have feelings for me now? And what about his obvious detestment for Nymphs and other races?

It just doesn't make sense. My brain hurts when I try to pick apart Cole's confession. I've never had a boy confess feelings for me before – and the first one has to be *him*? He's an obnoxious cockroach!

But on the other hand, there *were* some signs if I'm using hindsight as a compass. Cole started messaging me back on time, even when he doesn't seem like the 'phone' type. He helped me break into Headmistress Frow's desk – and brought me that chocolate bar, seemingly out of the blue. And most importantly, Cole mysteriously stopped making my life a waking nightmare over the past few weeks. I mean, sure, he'd reserve a few choice words for me if he saw me, but he stopped seeking me out, tormenting me, trying to crush my spirits.

So, there *were* clues about Cole's real feelings. I just wrote them off as weird coincidences.

I still don't believe him. But what guy would kiss a girl like that and confess *feelings* for her if he didn't have them? Why would Cole put himself in that embarrassing situation if he didn't have to?

All this makes my eyes linger on Cole's contact information. Suddenly, part of me wants to see how *I* feel about *him*.

I used to think I loathed him. But if I hate him so much, why did *I* kiss him, too? Why did I call him when Nora was in trouble? Was it just because of our ghost-hunting partnership, or was it something more, and I just didn't know it then?

This is the part of the kiss that I've been pushing away. I've been avoiding it because I know the root cause can't be good.

Was I just swept up in the moment of Nora being safe, of Cole rescuing her from the ghost?

Did I kiss him because he kissed me?

I know it can't be the second one. We kissed each other at the same time. It wasn't like he made the first move, and I answered him. This was something we did *together*.

I shiver at that thought and lock my phone, placing it beside me.

Together.

I never thought that word could describe Cole and me. I still don't think it does. But *something* is happening between us, and I don't know what it is. And that horrifies me, which is why I don't want to think about it. That's why I'm spending my time picking apart Cole's motives and words instead of my own.

This can't be good.

"There's no way Parents' Weekend is still happening," Makayleigh interjects as Anja holds her hands up in defeat.

"I'm only telling you what the email said," she defends, tucking her blue highlights behind her ear. "I'm not too sure about it being a good idea, either."

It's Friday morning. The four of us are eating breakfast in the

Dining Hall. You can tell it's the last day of midterms because there's this feeling of *relief* that is almost impossible to ignore.

The four of us are finished with our midterms – but now, the hard part is waiting for our grades to get uploaded to our student portal accounts.

I'm eating banana pancakes – my favourite – but I'm in too much of a sour mood to enjoy them, thanks to Cole Hudson.

I'm still avoiding decoding my feelings for him and figuring out why the kiss happened. Nora hasn't brought up the kiss – probably because she's as grossed out as I am. I'm hoping the Halloween party two weeks from now and Parents' Weekend next week will be enough of a distraction.

"If we're not even allowed to leave campus, why is the administration letting *families* visit?" Nora agrees, nudging me in the ribs as if looking for support.

I choke on my hashbrowns. "It doesn't make sense," I agree hoarsely.

If it's so unsafe to have Parents' Weekend, why do we have to have a Halloween party? I want to ask, but I know I'll be in the minority on that motion.

"Big help," Nora commends me sarcastically.

"I think they're trying to show families that Gomada Academy is a safe place to be," Anja announces, folding her arms on top of the table. "Plus, Headmistress Frow and the rest of the faculty want to discuss what to do about the 'threat to campus safety,'" she adds.

That's right. An entire section of the Parents' Weekend email was dedicated to a large meeting held in the Auditorium about what the realm in general and the school, in particular, are planning to do about the abductions – though the words 'abductions' and 'ghost' are never mentioned. That doesn't make them any less real, though.

"Ha!" Makayleigh huffs. "I'm surprised one of us hasn't

gotten poached yet. More and more students have gone missing. Alan's roommate, Leland, has been AWOL for God knows how long. I'd transfer out of here in a heartbeat, but we all know Gomada Academy is the best place for training."

Nora and I share what I hope is a secret glance. We haven't told the girls about what happened a few days earlier. Judging from the looks of things, Nora hasn't spilled the beans to Anja, either. She told me she wishes she could, but she doesn't want to put Anja in unnecessary danger – both with the ghost and the school administration. It's bad enough that six of us are meeting secretly and dodging faculty as we do it – we don't want to involve anyone else in this mess. It's not like the worst that could happen is suspension or expulsion. The worst that could happen is–

"Maybe he got permission to leave campus, or–" Anja begins, but Makayleigh shakes her head emphatically.

"No. No one has seen him!" she persists, her eyes full of alarm. "He's gone, for sure."

An eerie silence fills the table. Maybe it's up to Nora and I to break it so we can try and keep our ghost-hunting expedition under wraps. How scary, though, that the ghost is picking off more and more people. It's not like it's tried once or twice and decided to call it quits.

How many more students have to go missing before Gomadian authorities take action? Surely the realm has contingency plans for this sort of thing.

Why isn't anyone doing anything?

"I guess the school will address this on Parents' Weekend," I try to theorize.

"Before they get sued, or worse," Nora adds.

"Let's try not to panic. Maybe Leland went home for a while and got special permission," Anja finishes her earlier train of thought by explaining. "I'm sure the school will step in and figure this all out."

Nora and I remain tight-lipped on that. I hate to say it, but I really have doubts about Gomada Academy handling anything ghost-related.

"Maybe," Makalyeligh seems to agree as she looks down at her cappuccino.

As Makayleigh sips her coffee, I wonder if that's how she really feels. The way she's tugging on her white cardigan after putting down her cup tells me she's anxious. Maybe she's afraid Alan is next.

I'm scared of that possibility, too. Who could be next on the chopping block? It will probably be Nora, Cole and I because we all ticked off the ghost. Cole and I have done so repeatedly.

"Well, I still don't want Dad coming," Makayleigh asserts, thankfully ending my train of thought. The other girls must have circled back to Parents' Weekend while I was thinking about the ghost killing us.

From what I remember about Makayleigh's family, her mother died in a horrible car accident because of a drunk driver about a year ago. Ever since, Makayleigh never touched alcohol. She doesn't talk much about her mom. Even though Makayleigh is almost always in a happy, joking mood, sometimes I see a glimmer of sadness in her brown eyes.

Maybe that's why she's so concerned about Leland and Alan. She doesn't want to lose anyone else. After losing my grandpa, I can understand that impulse.

"I don't want my parents coming, either," Anja begins, straightening in her chair, "but they told me they want to 'check everything out.' Something tells me I won't be able to persuade them to stay home next weekend."

"Well, with parents and more school officials around, maybe no one else will go missing," I try to assert – even though I know that's not true.

Ghosts don't care about things like increased security and adult presence. I wish I didn't have this painful *hole* in my stomach, knowing that I can't warn my friends. Keeping the truth from them feels more like lying and betrayal than a form of protection.

"Maybe," Anja nods, getting back to her omelette.

Nora shifts uneasily at her girlfriend's words. I can't imagine how difficult this must be for her – keeping secrets from someone she cares about.

Maybe there's a kind of *nobility* in keeping frightening and painful truths from people we love. At least, that's what I tell myself multiple times daily. But nobility and love don't make me sleep any better at night.

"Well, I'm doing some Halloween costume shopping, so that'll take my mind off the fact that my dad will have to meet Professor Xhao," Makayleigh sighs, poking at her hashbrowns with her fork.

All three of us stare at her.

"You're going *shopping*?" I gasp.

"You know you can't go off-campus, Makayleigh," Anja warns.

"You'll get expelled, for sure," Nora adds firmly.

I'm still surprised Nora and I didn't get expelled after breaking curfew that night – which probably explains Nora's insistence.

Makayleigh laughs long and hard at our warnings and astonishment. "Please!" she scoffs, waving her hand dismissively. "I'm shopping *online,* you Nervous Nellies!"

Nora smacks her forehead, taking in a breath of what I'm guessing is relief. "You could've *started* with that, you know," she critiques.

"Yeah," Anja murmurs, sipping her orange juice. Anja is a healthy eater and loves to exercise, just like Nora.

"Man, you guys are a bunch of sour grapes this morning," Nakayleigh frowns at us after chewing her hashbrowns.

Maybe Makayleigh is pushing away her worries and is trying to be her jovial self again. She's bouncing in her seat, waiting for a reaction to her statement.

Sour grapes? I would've laughed at that if I wasn't in such an unhappy mood.

"Speaking of which," Anja continues, wrinkling her brow at Makayleigh. It's impossible to miss the small smile poking at the corners of her pink lips, though. Anja likes Makayleigh's sense of humour. "Maybe some online shopping is a good idea. They'll deliver it right to our dorm mailboxes."

Gomada and the other magical realms use Mexa, a large online shopping database similar to what we use in the Overworld. I've already downloaded the app to my phone. Unfortunately, it's just as addictive as the other shopping apps I use back home.

I slump a bit in my chair, like a four-year-old. Online shopping puts the final nail in the coffin which is me skipping out on the Halloween party.

"Good call," Nora approves. "You can come over and we can shop together. Is that cool, Arya?" she adds, poking me when I don't answer her.

"Um, yeah. Sure," I agree, trying to sound more enthusiastic about it halfway through my answer.

Nora and Anja frown at me in a confused way.

"What's wrong with you?" Anja asks gently, concerned.

Over the past few weeks, I've grown to trust Anja and Makayleigh – but I still haven't told them about my half-Nymph status or that I kissed Cole. I don't know which of my secrets is the most horrific.

"Yeah," I try to say. "Just worried about my midterm marks."

Anja waves her hand at that. "Please. You studied more than

all of us – even Nora." She winks at Nora, who pouts at her in response. "I'm sure you did great."

All except for Field Practice class.

"Thank you," I smile at Anja instead.

I know my unpleasant mood isn't my friends' fault. I should try to be brighter. I spent so much of the term wanting friends, and now that I have three, I'm not being very *friendly*.

"Why don't you come over, too, Makayleigh?" I suggest, wanting to make good on my vow. "We can all shop for costumes together."

I glance at Nora for confirmation as I'm talking. She grins at me encouragingly.

"Sounds good!" Makayleigh approves, her cheerful mood apparent and vibrant. "Let me just shower first. Now that midterms are over, I can finally focus on other stuff – like *this* rat-pile." Makayleigh tugs on her short black hair, causing the rest of us to scoff or laugh off her comment.

But I know what she means. Now that midterms are finished, other problems or circumstances are coming to light. And no matter how hard I try, I can't escape these *other problems*.

Seven

COLE'S PARENTS' WEEKEND

I'm in a worse mood now that classes have started up again. Time for more torture. But I knew this was coming. Professor Qadir found me on campus last weekend and slapped a paper into my hand: my midterm grades. Sure, they weren't *bad*, but they weren't *great*, either.

I got low-to-high sixties in everything. They're actually an improvement from last year, but based on the look Qadir gave me when he lectured me about being a *slacker* (his words, not mine), I'm guessing he wasn't feeling the same way.

So now I'm at the library, trying to study *again* for my stupid Literature test that's in a week. I don't get how there could be a test so soon after midterms – but whatever. I guess my Lit teacher has a fucked up sense of humour.

But that doesn't change the fact that I have to get my grades up before final exams. If I don't, I'm pretty sure Professor Qadir will feed me to the ghost and not give a shit about it.

Making things worse – and they were already *at* 'worst' – Parents' Weekend is upon us. Today is Friday. Some parents are already on-campus. I've seen them walking around with students who are either freaked out or super-happy.

I'll be neither when Dad shows up. I hate it when he comes to visit. Thank God this thing only happens once a year.

Mom has meetings or something, so she can't come this time. I'm disappointed, especially since there won't be anyone or anything to save me from Dad's torture.

Dad would never pass up an opportunity to tell me I'm a failure. He cleared his schedule for the entire weekend. As the son of the famous Nicholai Germain, Dad definitely wants to check up on the latest Tedla legacy: me.

This will be a shitshow.

I've been so panicked over Dad coming, getting my grades up, and that fucking ghost, that it's been hard to function – even while sober.

The Ghost Busting Team – a stupid nickname Ryker gave us that no one laughed at – had a second meeting. We didn't have much to discuss. Nothing freaky happened since the ghost tried to capture Nora.

The campus has been pretty quiet. No one has mentioned anything about more missing friends or acquaintances.

Basically, the meeting was pointless.

I've spent most of my time in the library like a nerdy loser. Even Diego, who loves reading *way more* than he used to, is giving me a hard time about it. But the only thing worse than Professor Qadir kicking my ass would be Dad coming tomorrow to kick it first. So I gotta prepare as best I can. And if that means holing myself up in the library, then that's what I have to do.

At least I can show Dad my midterm grades but also let him know that I've been hard at work trying to improve things – and I wouldn't be lying for once.

My phone vibrates in my pocket. I'm at the library, bored as fuck but hard at work, all at the same time. Two of my least favourite things.

Now that I know the librarian, Noreen, more than I'd like (that's what happens when you come here a lot), I'm betting she'd smash my phone against the wall if she wasn't so busy at her computer. I take advantage of this opportunity by pulling out my phone and looking at the notification.

I'll be there in an hour.

Great. Dad's coming sooner than I expected. The Parents' Weekend stuff starts tomorrow. I don't know why Dad has to come *tonight*. More time to smash my head against the wall, I guess.

Alright.

I know Dad will want more than that, so I add in another text,

See you then.

I'm sure he'll be coming here with one of his Trinkets. Dad isn't one for travelling. He's even more impatient about things than I am – which means we both fly off the handle instead of talking things out. When we do, Mom leaves the room and lets us duke it out until no one wins. And since she isn't coming this weekend, there won't be any buffer between Dad and I in public or in private.

Great – again.

I'm just about to put my phone away when I see that I have another message that I haven't read yet.

Weird.

No one ever messages me. Usually, it's Diego, sometimes Ryker, or my parents.

> Will you go to the Halloween party with me?

I stare at the message from Arya, wondering if I've had some kind of messed up psychotic break.

Why the hell would she ask me to that party that's bound to be a pile of horse shit? Attendance is mandatory because that's what Gomada Academy does, but I still don't get why Arya would ask *me*. Last I checked, kissing me made her gag.

Is she trying to make Ryker jealous?

Is this some kind of girly game or trick?

Is she scared that Fire Douchebag from her midterm is still out to get her?

Is this some goody-two-shoes way to pass the Mentorship Program?

And then, the embarrassing thought...

This could be my only chance to show her I'm not the asshole she thinks I am.

At the same time, I don't want to be seen at a party with a Nymph.

I like Arya, but I don't want people knowing I'm weak for one of them. It's humiliating – especially since I've spent my entire life avoiding them and mocking anyone who does otherwise.

Maybe I can use this Halloween thing to my advantage and still show Arya I'm not as big of a douche as I made myself out to be at the beginning of the year. Two birds, one rock. Or whatever that saying is.

Someone clears their throat. Creepy Noreen glares at me from across the room. I look back at my phone, knowing I have about five seconds before she kicks me out of the library.

Yeah

This is all I say because I'm still confused as fuck about why she's asking me in the first place. It just doesn't make sense. But whatever.

Maybe she's giving me a second chance. My heart thumps faster at that possibility.

I put my phone away and try to concentrate on my Lit notes, but that's hard to do when all I can think about is Dad coming and going to the party with Arya.

Damn.

I finally close my notebook with my hard-to-read chicken scratch handwriting, knowing I'll never be able to focus now. Besides, if Dad's coming to Gomada Academy sooner than expected, I need to go home and tidy up.

Dad hates messes. Since my life is a mess, that means my dorm room is one, too.

No wonder Dad can't stand me.

I pack up my crap and head back to Feara. Even though I'm distracted and hurrying, I still feel like someone's watching me.

This is happening more often now.

Nora, Arya, and I are pretty sure that Frow and Qadir are watching us. I've seen Frow around more often than usual – and at our last meeting, Nora said the same thing about Qadir.

They're making sure we don't do anything else that's against the rules. I'm sure they know this by now, but I've never once played by the rules. And they won't stop me from getting answers.

I unlock and open the door to my dorm, observing the empty space. It looks like Diego has gone out. More time for me to clean, I guess.

Diego being away from Feara doesn't surprise me. I'm sure he's hanging with Lucy before his parents arrive. I don't know how they'll react to him having an Enchantress as a girlfriend.

They'll probably react the same way Dad would if he knew I was going to a Halloween party with a Nymph.

I make my bed, kicking some dirty laundry under it. As usual, our hamper is loaded with clothes. Adding more to the pile won't be good.

I organize my desk the best I can, closing the window when I see gray clouds and the darkening sky.

It may snow tonight, so Dad will want to spend more time inside.

I've got to tidy up this dump, pronto!

I rush into our bathroom and grab this weird room freshener spray Diego brings with him each year. I walk into the main room and start spraying. Nothing smells bad to me right now, but I'm sure Dad will be able to pick up an odour from a mile away. He once said my bedroom was 'as fragrant as a gym sock'. I don't play sports, but I'm guessing that's bad.

I unpack my books, throwing them into drawers at my desk and grabbing for falling pieces of paper that end up on the carpet. As I'm shoving them into a textbook, there's a knock at the door.

Shit!

Has an hour passed already?!

I look at my phone after yanking it out of my pocket. It's been about forty-five minutes since Dad messaged me. I only packed up at the library five minutes after that. He's ten minutes early. Probably wanted to catch me scrambling around before his arrival. Kind of a smart move, but a really annoying one, too.

I should've expected this.

Fuck.

Walking to the door, I sense I'm moving faster than usual. I take an uneven breath and slide open the lock, opening the door as quickly as possible. But no matter how fast I do all this shit, it won't make him leave any sooner.

There he is.

I guess he looks just like me, but older and with a better sense of style. Dad cares about things like looking *proper* and *dignified.* Those are words he says a lot. At eight PM, he's wearing suit pants with a long black coat. He looks like he just came from work – but I know he's looking good because of our family lineage.

I'm in huge shit.

Dad's green eyes shoot through mine and then behind me. "Cole," he states emotionlessly.

To Dad, this is *just business* – not a father-reuniting-with-his-son thing.

"Hey," I answer, really sure what to do with myself. I finally step aside, inviting him into the room.

Dad walks through the open doorway. He analyzes every inch of the place as he closes the door behind him.

"Just had enough time to make it look somewhat presentable, I see," he observes, causing me to fold my arms in defense.

My stomach sinks and churns when he says that, making me want to toss my cookies. I harden up just before he turns to face me.

I don't want him to see any weakness from me. But I'm sure he can sense it.

"I've been studying," I admit – or protest. I'm not sure which.

Dad frowns down at me. "Oh?" he asks. "When your professor called me on Monday, it seemed you weren't making any effort at all."

Shit! Qadir called Dad!

I'm pissed, but also freaked. This isn't good.

How will I get myself out of this one?

But I know there's no way out. So I just say nothing.

Dad begins to walk around the room. "At least there's no outward evidence of alcohol or drugs this year," he remarks. "But you definitely haven't quit your other habit."

I don't say anything to that, either. I know he's referring to smoking. I even skipped my after-studying smoke to rush back here and tidy up. But as usual, nothing is good enough for Dad.

Dad turns when he gets to my desk. He looks at me while leaning against it. "So," he opens. "I hear there's been some trouble on campus. Do you know anything about it?"

Is he asking that as a general question, or is he thinking I actually have something to do with it?

I shake my head. "No," I add, so he knows I'm serious.

Dad's quiet. He folds his arms and studies me. Everyone always believes the worst in me. I should be used to it by now, but tonight, it's a drain on me.

Finally, it looks like Dad believes me – or, believes me *enough* – because he leans off my desk and stares at me differently this time.

"I'm pleased you're spending time at the library – though I find that difficult to fathom," he adds, just when I think I've done the impossible and impressed him.

I'm not dumb enough to say 'thank you' or to even blink. I just stay quiet.

"Your mother sends her regards," he continues. "She wanted to send along a care package, but it looks like you're managing just fine."

I guess he saw the mini-fridge and the garbage can full of wrappers from pizza pockets. Still, getting some of Mom's home-made muffins would've been nice. Dad doesn't like it when she 'babies me' – which, in Dad's world, is showing me any kind of affection.

"Where's Diego?" Dad asks, surprising me.

"Out," is all I answer.

"Hm." Dad approaches me. "Well, I've skipped dinner. Is the Dining Hall still serving pizza on Fridays?"

Dad used to go here – and so did my grandfather. Basically, Germains have always gone here; even more reason for Dad to kick my ass for not doing well on my midterms. I did even worse last year – I'm surprised I made it out alive in June.

"Yeah," I agree. "But it's almost over," I add.

Dad rolls his eyes. "Let's go, then," he huffs as if it's my fault that he came at the end of dinner hour.

When Dad and I get here, the Dining Hall isn't very full (except for other stragglers). Students and parents move out of the way for us as we approach the small line to the kitchen. Dad must have gone to school with some of these parents. They must know who he's descended from – which means they know about me, too.

Tedlas don't always pick each generation of whatever family they're drawn to, for some reason or other. It's the same with the Phoenix, Fire Bird, and other creatures. We've learned about this in Shifter Studies.

Case in point: Dad never got the Tedla gene. He got some kind of in-between monster that I haven't seen in my seventeen years of life. But I don't think that matters.

No one asks questions. They just know to be afraid.

Pizza day is usually one of the only things I look forward to in the week – and I almost forgot about it because of studying and Parents' Weekend. Now that I'm with Dad, I doubt I'll enjoy it. Dad doesn't believe in *enjoying things*.

As if my life can't get any worse, I suddenly sense and smell Arya somewhere in the Dining Hall. It's weird, though: her scent's a little *off*.

Suddenly, a kid jumps in front of us.

Dad hates kids – probably why he didn't talk much to me until I was twelve – so he looks down at this girl like she's some kind of cockroach.

"You're a Shifter," she asserts.

It takes me a minute to realize she's talking to me, and a minute longer to realize why Arya's scent was weird before.

I was smelling Arya (who isn't in the vicinity) and what must be her little sister.

Well, the kid's definitely more of a chatterbox than her sister.

Dad's green eyes narrow in condescension. "Do you realize you're interrupting a conversation, little girl?" he asks, even though we've been like depressed mimes the entire time.

I'm expecting the little girl to freak out. Instead, she frowns up at him. "You weren't saying anything," she points out.

I quietly bite back a laugh. Dad must sense it because he leers at me.

Arya skids to a stop behind the little girl and takes her shoulders. "Oh, my God. I'm so sorry," she protests to Dad.

Dad fixes his stare at her. "I can now understand the unruly behaviour. Half-Nymph or not, you and your relatives should keep yourselves in check."

I'm shocked Dad would say that, even if he's usually a douche. Being mean to a kid is kind of taking it up a notch.

I'm also surprised that Dad can discern *halfness* from Arya and her sister. Maybe because he's more experienced as a Shifter, he can distinguish those things.

I really have no idea. That hasn't been covered in class yet. Or maybe it has, and I just wasn't listening.

Arya looks like Dad just took a sledgehammer to her head. Her sister looks surprised, and then *mad*.

"That's a really rude thing to say," the little girl snaps. "You should set a better example for your son."

Arya slaps her hand over her little sister's mouth, who's clearly on a roll with her rant. She quickly drags that hilarious kid away from us. Even with the distance, we can still hear the end of their conversation.

"Macey, you can't talk to people like that!" Arya hisses.

"But he was being a total miscreant," the little girl who must be Macey insists. "This is why you get bullied, Arya. You never stand up for yourself."

Dad rolls his eyes as we head into the now-tiny line. "It's clear the school's admission standards have dropped since I attended," he comments.

I don't say anything, but I'm having a party inside my head.

That whole thing with Macey was fucking hilarious! I've never seen anyone stand up to Dad – especially a kid who should've wimped out on sight.

That made my day so much better.

It looks like Dad is mulling something over as we eat pizza. It's not the food pissing him off, that's for sure. Dad usually eats super-healthy, but I know he has a soft spot for pizza. As a kid, we had 'pizza night' every other Friday. Maybe that's why I look forward to pizza day here at Gomada Academy – besides the obvious, anyway.

What's he thinking about? I wonder – or worry because with Dad, there's always something to worry about. There's probably some random thing I was supposed to do by now that I didn't, and he'll nail me for it. That's just how my life works.

I jump a mile when someone slaps me on the shoulder from behind. I guess I'm too distracted to sense the people around me. That's a great vulnerability. I'm sure a lecture will follow.

But when I turn around, Ryker Johnson is behind me, with someone I'm guessing is his dad.

"Hey, Hudson," Ryker greets me. "Dad, you remember Cole and Mr. Germain, don't you?" he adds, looking at his dad, a little taller than Ryker, with facial hair and a business suit.

Why are these dads all dressed up like this?

"Of course," Ryker's dad nods as Dad and I stand up around the same time. "Nice to see you both again."

"A pleasure, Andres," Dad says, shaking hands with Ryker's dad.

"Give my regards to your wife," Andres tells Dad, giving me a nod with a small smile before he and Ryker head out of the Dining Hall. Or, I think that's where they're going because they're not walking to the kitchen for pizza.

"A peculiar family," Dad mentions, sitting down again.

I'm kind of pissed off that Dad would say that. Sure, I'm not the biggest fan of Enchanters, either - but out of the lot of them, Ryker's not half-bad, even if it sometimes makes me nauseous to admit it. And his dad didn't have a bad thing to say about mine. At least not in front of us.

But when Dad continues, I almost spit my chewed-up pizza all over the table.

"His brother was a piece of work. Must be why Andres comes here every year. Trying to repair the damage."

I don't know if Dad's talking to me or himself, but what he's saying definitely interests me.

I guess Dad, Ryker's dad, Frow, and Ryker's uncle were all in the same grade – or, they went to school around the same time. Either way, they all knew one another. What did it matter if some were Sophomores and some were Seniors?

The point is, Dad may have intel about this Izaak Johnson guy.

Ryker tried to ask his dad about his uncle Izaak a few weeks ago. It was a dead-end. His dad didn't open up. This made us even more suspicious.

Whatever happened around here with Izaak was bad enough that Frow has stuff about him locked away in her office.

I want to find out more.

I'll have to do this carefully or Dad's antenna will go up.

"What kind of damage?" I ask, adding casually as I sip my soda, "Ryker seems pretty chill."

Dad doesn't say anything for a long time. "There's a reason

why Enchanters are dangerous people. And you better not be wasting your time with them, son," he adds sternly.

"I'm not," I respond.

Dad returns to his pizza like we didn't just have a conversation. I guess that wouldn't be a *conversation*, though.

Asking Dad about Ryker's family was pointless. I already knew Izaak was dangerous. He got expelled from Gomada Academy for experimenting with dark magic (AKA black magic, according to Ryker). I was hoping Dad was going to elaborate. Sometimes, I get the vibe that Dad still thinks I'm twelve and can't handle real-life shit.

If he only knew what I've been putting up with so far.

I'm not going to get any answers from Dad right now.

I just need to wait. Maybe asking him about it later, when he's not expecting it, will work better than asking him now.

I've never been good at waiting – and neither has Dad.

This will go well.

The good thing about Dad – and there aren't that many *good things* to choose from – is that he doesn't insist on staying with his kid on campus, like some other parents do. He booked a hotel in Upper Gomada – probably the same one he and Mom stayed at last year. Last Parents' Weekend was a little easier because Mom was there.

So when Dad leaves at nine o'clock, I slump onto my bed and hold my temples. My entire body aches, like I'm getting sick. I know that's not the case. Being with Dad is just painful and tiring – literally.

Even though I want to go to bed at nine PM like an old guy, I know there's something I have to do first. It'll be hard, but I know I can't escape it.

I lean over to my bedside table and pick up my phone. Of course, I don't have any messages. I didn't see Diego and his parents tonight. Maybe they went off-campus. When families come, the school *throws away* the rules it usually has when it's just students on-campus.

"Sorry about my dad."

That's all I can think of to say to Arya. I'm not good with words – and I'm even worse with apologies.

I just hope it's enough.

She doesn't answer. She hasn't read the message when I check just before collapsing onto my bed again, tired out of my mind. She's probably thinking, 'like father, like son' – or whatever that saying is.

If things don't *work out* with her, it will definitely save me a lot of grief. I won't have to deal with liking a Nymph. I'd have one less problem.

I should be relieved that she's not talking to me now.

Except I'm *not* relieved.

And that's pissing me off.

I don't like caring about this stuff. It makes me feel weak. But I can't avoid the fact that I like her.

I guess that means I'm stuck feeling this way.

Fucking great.

Eight

ARYA AND MACEY

"You can't just talk to people like that, Macey," I repeat to my little sister in reprimand as we rush out of the Dining Hall. Actually, it's more than that: I'm dragging her out.

Part of me knows there's no point in lecturing her. She never listens to me, anyway. Macey may be a seven-year-old, but she's hard-headed and stubborn beyond her years. She's more like a teenager than a kid. I worry that her impulsivity – like challenging Cole and his dad – is going to get her into trouble one day.

"You're overreacting," Macey protests, like I'm the child and she's the older sibling.

I probably look as aggravated as I feel despite my efforts to keep a poker face.

I didn't know words like *miscreant* and *overreacting* when I was seven. And if I did, I definitely didn't use them in conversation – especially against grown-ups. I didn't get into trouble – not in school, with my teachers, or with my parents.

Macey doesn't necessarily *get into trouble* – but during parent-teacher meetings, her teachers often tell Mom and Dad that Macey contradicts the lessons and argues her opinions.

It's not that I don't want my little sister to have her own mind. It's just that Macey thinks she's always right – and won't hesitate to tell you just that, even if she gets in hot water for it.

When I say nothing, Macey pulls her arm free and looks up at me. "Why, are you just *okay* with people being mean to you because of something outside of your control?" she accuses condescendingly.

"Obviously not," I respond instantly, knowing too late that I got baited by my little sister for the trillionth time since her birth. But I guess since Cole's dad fell for it, too, I shouldn't feel too badly about it. "I just think there's a time and a place for that. And you don't do it with Shifters."

I clamp my mouth shut, suddenly filled with regret.

I shouldn't be teaching my baby sister these sorts of things. Just because these have been *my* experiences doesn't mean the same will be true for Macey. Plus, Mom and Dad never taught us to hate or discriminate against other races. They just always told us to be careful. I believe those are two totally different things – especially when they even told us to be careful around Nymphs. You never know who may be out to get you when you're different.

I want to tell Macey about that – but I think she's too young. I don't want her to be introduced to how evil the world can be just yet. Of course, thanks to Mr. Hudson, she got a good taste of that just three minutes ago.

Before I can correct myself, Macey beats me to the punch by folding her arms over her new Winter jacket, showing me I've missed my chance. I can tell her blue and white sports jacket is new, because Macey doesn't like to get new clothes, and only does so when our parents tell her it's necessary.

"Isn't that kind of discriminatory?" she criticizes.

"Yes," I sigh. "I was just about to say that."

Macey gives me a smug expression that annoys me even more – even though she *is* right this time – so I hastily explain,

"I guess I just meant that I've let my guard down around Shifters, and it hasn't always worked out."

Kissing Cole, for one thing.

Then, asking Cole to the Halloween party after stewing over it for a week.

I don't want to dwell on that. Kissing Cole was a mistake. Anything to do with Cole would be a mistake. But for some reason, it doesn't always seem that way when I'm around him and only him. How can that be?

Macey frowns up at me. "O-kay," she dismisses.

Clearly, she doesn't want to hear any more of my *sage advice*. I can't say that I blame her. Besides, I don't really want to give out much more of it, anyway.

When we get outside, it's snowing. Macey loves snow – maybe because San Francisco never gets any, maybe because she's always dreamed of snowboarding or other Winter sports I know nothing about. Either way, she's instantly fascinated by the tumbling white flakes.

I'm bothered by the weather. I'll be colder now than I was yesterday. To top it all off, the hot air in our dorm isn't working very well.

"Are you excited to see the rest of campus tomorrow?" I ask her, trying to cheer myself up and change the subject away from Shifters and discrimination. "Today's only the beginning."

Macey shrugs. "I guess. But I won't be coming here for another nine years, so there's no point in getting *too* excited."

Like me, Macey is half-human, which means her Air Affinity won't be as strong as someone like Professor Xhao, who is a full-blooded Nymph.

My body jerks at the thought of Professor Xhao looking

down on Macey in nine years when Macey tries to summon her own Air Affinity.

"Well, we have some time before we meet up with Mom and Dad," I remind her. "Do you want me to show you around? Take you to the campus store, get you some hot chocolate?"

Macey seems to stew over my proposition, which interests me. Normally, my inquiries don't initiate that much thought from her.

"Well," Macey begins, twirling her long brown hair, which she almost always has in a ponytail. "I wouldn't mind seeing the Gymnasium. I hear you're allowed to play sports in there this weekend."

I would have preferred getting hot chocolate with my little sister, or even having her chuck a snowball at my head (not that we have enough snow for that yet) than taking her to the Gymnasium, but I know she deserves to be shown a good time, so I try to put on my best smile for her.

"Okay," I agree, which causes shock to pulse through Macey's body as a flinch. "Let's go to the Gymnasium."

"Seriously?" Macey gushes as we veer right to return to the school. "You're really going to play sports with me?"

I pause. I don't know how Macey will take this. She hates hearing mushy stuff like this.

"I've missed hanging out with you," I confess. "So if you want to play sports, we'll play sports."

"Are you sure you're okay?" Macey asks me, for maybe the eighth time.

I lean the back of my head against my propped-up pillows,

reapplying the makeshift cold compress Nora brought me courtesy of Anja's mini-fridge. The ice cubes in the plastic bag crinkle against my pink face cloth. I try to focus on that instead of the pain I'm currently experiencing. The throbbing heat hasn't subsided even though it's been about an hour since the 'incident.'

"I'm fine," I mumble.

"I've never heard of someone getting hit in the head by a basketball before," Nora remarks, unable to hold back a smile when she passes us.

I frown at my roommate as she tries to conceal her grin.

"My sister's always doing stuff like this," Macey proclaims matter-of-factly.

"It wasn't my fault," I hear myself whine.

And it's true. Dad, Mom, Macey and I were playing basketball. Macey threw the ball, but I couldn't get it. The basketball went over my head, bounced off a wall, and when I turned to grab it, it got *me* instead.

"Maybe I should take you to the infirmary," Mom suggests, removing the concoction Nora made for me. "You're already getting a bump."

"I don't want to go to the infirmary," I try to protest, but Mom gives me one of those *motherly looks* that can only mean, 'you're going if I say so.'

I slump against the pillows in defeat.

I turn to the right when my phone vibrates, knowing it's on my bedside table. I retrieve my hand when the pain intensifies.

Maybe looking at screens isn't a good idea.

I still have a headache when I wake up on Saturday morning. At least it's not as bad as it was on Friday night. That is a relief because I had nightmares about going to the hospital and the infirmary. In the last one, my skull exploded.

It's cloudy and windy this morning. Cascading snow freezes the grass, making it crackle under our boots.

In other words, it's perfect weather for practicing my Wind Affinity. It may be cold, but it's pristine training weather.

Dad wants to show Macey the Nymph's Field, also telling me privately that he wants to see how much progress I've made. Of course, the way Dad said it was positive and encouraging – as if he's assuming I've already made an improvement. The way Professor Xhao says it, it's as if she doubts you've made any headway in the first place.

Macey and I are walking to the Nymph's Field after stopping for some hot chocolate along the way. Mom and Dad are catching up with some alumni friends before joining us for our morning practice.

Macey is referring to our time at the Field as 'the big event.' She thinks it'll be fun and exciting. All I can think about is not messing up and hoping that Désirée and her cousin aren't practicing in the Enchanter's Field. Since the two races share the same practice space, it's entirely possible that we could meet.

Ever since Désirée blabbed about my 'halfness' status to 'all who would listen,' I've wondered what else she has in store for me. Bullies always try to outdo themselves.

No mean girls in sight so far, I observe as we close in on the immense, snowy training area.

Even if Lucy seems less evil than her cousin, Nora and I are still unsure of her true intentions. For now, we want to keep our distance. Between ghost abductions and near-misses, we have enough to worry about without factoring in teen girl sabotage.

I know Mom and Dad have questions and even suspicions about my life at Gomada Academy. They've been watching me closely ever since their arrival. I know my parents as well as the other families had a morning meeting with the Headmistress about the goings-on at school.

I really want to know what was discussed during the meeting.

If I bring it up, though, my parents might start asking questions that I won't be able to answer.

Mom and Dad already know I got detention for breaking curfew. I don't want to add ghost hunting to my list of extracurricular activities.

Macey's presence here means our parents won't ask me anything too unsettling. If we ever get a moment alone, though–

I keep searching for the Chapin cousins. Other Enchanters are scrimmaging with their families, but there's no sign of Désirée or even Lucy. The rising of relief in my chest is impossible to suppress.

"Do you have a boyfriend yet?" Macey asks, breaking me out of my imprisoning thoughts.

Macey casually sips her hot chocolate, thinking she hasn't just posed an earth-shaking inquiry. Moreover, I find it odd and even *humourous* that she added a 'yet' to her question – as if she's expecting that I'm skilled enough to find a boyfriend, let alone someone who likes me back.

Neither of which have happened yet.

I'm about to dismiss her line of questioning quickly – I feel like she needs an interrogation lamp and a detective's outfit for this conversation – when a horrifying thought stops me.

Cole.

I drink my own hot chocolate, hoping the burn on my tongue will distract me from the waking nightmare of a theory I just conjured.

It doesn't.

Never in my wildest dreams would I have thought that *Cole* could be the answer to such a thing. It definitely doesn't make sense.

But we kissed. And I asked him to the Halloween party, and he said 'yes.' I keep thinking the kiss doesn't mean anything, that it was a mistake of epic proportions, but...

Cole might have been *(have been?)* a bully, a tyrant, and a judgemental jackass – but lately, he hasn't been that way. I really don't know what to think. I ended up giving into that 'not knowing what to think' feeling and asking him to the party. I'm sure I'll regret it.

"Well?" Macey asks as we finally near the outskirts of the Nymph's Field.

Snow is crunching under our feet. My fingers are numb, even though we took the tried-and-true shortcut to the Nymph's Field normally used for Field Practice class. Ten minutes of walking and hot chocolate do nothing to protect against this frosty weather.

Macey, on the other hand, is practically skipping to the Nymph's Field in glee.

I'm not sure how much time has passed since Macey asked me about having a boyfriend *yet*. Probably ten seconds. But Macey's winter joy quickly morphs into impatience. She demands immediate gratification.

"No," I respond flatly, causing Macey to roll her brown eyes at me.

At first, I think she already knew the answer to her question and is responding accordingly – but when Macey speaks again, as we're nearing the fenceline to the Field, she says,

"You sure took your sweet time answering – which means you're probably lying."

"That's a nice thing to say to your big sister," I retort evenly.

I once again scan the Nymph's Field for anyone who could further persecute me – like Samuel Minders. But the students I see aren't anyone I recognize. Maybe they're Seniors or Master Nymphs.

"Maybe, but you're still lying," Macey scoffs.

I'm even more annoyed than before!

When someone calls us from behind, we stop arguing and turn around.

Dad is approaching us. He's wearing a dark gray trenchcoat with the collars pulled up. His graying brown hair has a light dusting of snow on it from the gentle flakes hitting the ground.

"Let's get going!" he calls to us.

Even though he's prompting us to practice, Dad is so casual and easygoing that we know he's not being too serious. Dad cares about doing your best and working hard – but at the same time, he understands struggles and hurdles.

My parents never pressured me to do well in school or life. Yes, they *want* Macey and I to succeed – but there aren't any ultimatums or punishments if we sometimes fail. And for that, I really appreciate my parents – in a different way than when I was younger.

"I want to go first!" Macey, ever the perfectionist and eager beaver, asserts quickly as we find a secluded section to use.

Dad rolls his eyes affectionately and gently tugs on Macey's ponytail. He's now in front of both of us. "Your sister will go first when your mother catches up with us. I'm sure she's learned a lot in the past couple of months."

Dad may be talking to Macey, but he's looking at me with admiration in his brown eyes.

This makes me feel bad – not because I think he's putting pressure on me, but because I don't want to disappoint him. He seems proud of me. I don't want to let him down.

Before I can open my mouth to warn him that I may not be as 'improved' as he thinks, Dad rubs my arm and says,

"Just show me what you've been working on. I know I'll be proud, no matter what."

I give him a thankful smile as he lets go of me. With supportive parents like these, and them being here in Gomada, things feel less *doom and gloom* than they did before. Ghosts, bullies, and tough teachers seem like blurry details of the past that no longer matter.

I just worry about tomorrow afternoon when Mom, Dad, and Macey leave. Everything will come back to the surface.

Macey and I are returning to Meera against the intensifying snow. Training went excellently: I could fly and show Mom and Dad better control of my electrical component – a huge contrast from summertime when I couldn't summon any electricity at all. Even Macey, who's also having trouble with electricity, was impressed.

It takes a lot to impress Macey, but I don't let my family's approval go to my head. I know I still have a long way to go, but at least I showed them *something*.

Mom and Dad are at a second parents' assembly in the Auditorium. It wasn't mentioned in the email, which has my antenna up.

Maybe the families of enrolled and captured students had more questions – or the authorities are getting involved. Either way, I'm betting on the fact that there will be no mention of ghosts or 'ghost hybrids,' to quote Diego from our first-ever group meeting.

"Is that an Enchantress?" Macey interrupts my inner thoughts by asking. She points up ahead, where a large tree dusted with snow hovers over a few different students.

Even though one of them has her back to me, I can tell from the flowing black tresses and the practically tangible feeling of evil emanating from her that it's Désirée Chapin. The black cat Familiar draped over her shoulder is also a dead giveaway.

Macey is much better at sensing and recognizing different races than me. But it's good that she can do this now because if she gets her own Désirée Chapin when she comes to Gomada

Academy (God forbid), at least Macey will be better able to protect herself.

"Yes," is all I can think of to say.

I don't want to tell Macey that Désirée is a horrible villainess who doesn't just make *my* life worse but the lives of everyone around her, as well.

It takes me a moment to realize only one other student is with Désirée – not a few like I originally thought. When Désirée shifts slightly in place, telling me she's trying to look haughty and *in control* even from this distance, I see that the person she's talking to is Cole.

Macey, who has a memory like an elephant, immediately recognizes Cole.

"Isn't that the boy whose dad was so mean to us last night?" she asks as my headache returns with a vengeance.

Seeing my two bullies in the same place is enough to make my head explode – which might actually happen.

"Yes," I repeat.

Numbing exhaustion seeps up my chest, spreading to my limbs. I'm sure I feel overwhelmed and sapped of energy because my two nemeses are within throwing distance.

We don't have to be close to Désirée and Cole to know they are having an altercation. Désirée's tone is condescending and malicious. Even her black cat is hissing at Cole like he's a mouse she wants to smother.

Macey and I are out of earshot, so I'm only left with my imagination to envision what she's saying to him.

Macey and I get closer – mostly because we have to pass them to get to Meera, but also because I want to hear what Désirée is saying. Even if Cole can more than handle himself, there's a deranged part of me that's actually *worried* about him.

I don't know why this is happening. Cole can Shift into a wolf-man on two legs, with ferocious oval green eyes. He even gave that ghost a run for its money. It's not like Cole can't handle mean girl nonsense from Désirée Chapin.

But at the same time, I see Cole's hunched shoulders. Despite the glare he's giving her, I know Désirée is getting to him – and not in the way I'm used to. Usually, Désirée gets a rise out of Cole, but it doesn't do anything to scratch the surface.

So what's different about today?

Maybe it's not my business. Maybe I should stay out of it. Still, I don't want to see Désirée picking on him. Or anyone else.

Just because Désirée is a powerful Enchantress with two opposing elements at her disposal (a rarity that makes her of interest to teachers and peers) doesn't mean she can treat people like garbage!

What I want to do is a major violation of school rules, but I just can't help myself.

I feel more than ready now that I've been working hard to perfect my electrical powers. After practicing with Dad, Mom and Macey, I'm charged-up enough to focus, and focus well.

Looking down at my left palm, I visualize electricity sparking from my skin. In seconds, crackling sounds of electricity erupt from my hand.

"Arya, what're you–" Macey asks in a startled voice. She's to my left, so she sees exactly what I'm doing.

Ignoring her for now, I use my opposite hand to flick the electricity away from us. I visualize the electricity travelling from my body to the ground, surrounding Désirée.

I'm not trying to hurt her. I just want to stop her from being a horrible person to innocent people.

I take Macey's hand and resume our pace from before. Macey protests, staring up at me in shock.

"Arya, why did you–" she starts but is interrupted by screaming.

Macey and I steal a peek over our shoulders. Désirée's madly jumping around a circle of electricity, her cat balancing on her shoulder. Cole is himself again: he's throwing his head back, laughing hysterically at Désirée's misfortune.

I used to think Cole's laugh, his voice, and his proximity were as painful as nails on a chalkboard. But today, they don't seem so bad.

"Why did you do that?" Macey finishes her question as we walk away from the commotion.

Other students are around campus now, so it's not as if Désirée will see us and connect the dots. Besides, we're already a good distance away.

"She's a bully, Mace," I explain quietly. "She's been picking on my friends and I since the first day of school. I didn't want her doing the same thing to anyone else."

Macey looks surprisingly satisfied with my statement. "Well, fighting fire with fire isn't any better," she muses – which is surprisingly accurate when you think of Désirée's Fire Affinity. "But I guess you've grown a bit of a backbone, so that's good."

"Gee, thanks," I grumble sarcastically as we pass a few Nymphs on the way to Meera.

We're closer to the warmth of the dormitory – and further away from Désirée's cruelty.

We may not be near her now – and I didn't use enough power for it to have a life of its own and close in on her, so it probably dissipated when we left – but I don't want to take any chances with Désirée. Not with my little sister here. I'd protect Macey if I had to, but part of me fears it wouldn't be nearly enough against a full-blooded Enchantress.

Nine

COLE'S DATE

Diego slaps his knee as I take another drag of my cigarette. It's late Saturday night. We're behind Feara, leaning against the wall. A specific corner back here is free of surveillance cameras when you factor in nighttime and shadows. We use this area to smoke up. Snow and damp air won't stop us. And I guess the chance of being kidnapped by a ghost isn't doing that, either.

"That's fucking hilarious, Hudson!" Diego chortles.

I'm glad Diego finds Désirée's pain as entertaining as I do. Tonight is actually okay. It's like old times: Diego and I smoking up in the dark, breaking the rules, harping on anyone and everyone.

The brick wall is cold but comforting against my back. The night air feels good. Nostalgia (or whatever that's called) creeps through my veins. It's easy to forget about the ghost, my dad being here, and Arya when I'm with Diego like this.

Tonight, Diego's choosing to smoke pot. I smoke it now and then, but I usually opt for my own addiction.

To Diego, smoking is a partying thing. To me, it's life.

"Who did that, anyway?" Diego adds after blowing smoke into the crisp air.

Party time's over.

The answer to his question is easy.

Without even looking, I could tell that the electricity came from Arya. I picked up her scent and her sister's.

I don't know why she did that. Sure, it pisses me off knowing I needed help at all, but at the same time, I sort of appreciate it. Usually, Désirée's shit doesn't get to me – but with Dad around and Qadir calling home to tell my parents how much of a fucking failure I am, I just didn't have much of a backbone.

That cold-hearted Fire-Water Bitch is going to get a nice surprise from me once Dad leaves and I'm feeling a bit more, well, *me*.

I'd text Arya to thank her, but she still hasn't answered my message from Friday (not that I blame her). I'm not in the mood to humiliate myself even more by trying again.

"I dunno. Probably some Nymph who's been pissed off by her enough times," I dismiss.

We all know Désirée sticks to her own. She doesn't hang out with many Enchanters or Enchantresses unless they're worth her time – but she won't screw with them the way she does with Nymphs. She hates Shifters, sure, but there's something about Nymphs that makes her turn up the mean girl shit. My theory is that Enchanters look down on Nymphs because they can only wield one Affinity, and Enchanters-slash-Enchantresses can work with two.

Diego snorts in agreement. "I'm glad Luce is steering clear of her now," he tells me. "Désirée is a snake. Imagine what she'll do when she has more power."

Even though I haven't mentioned this to Diego yet, I'm glad Lucy is staying away from Désirée, too.

I wouldn't have believed in this 'rift' if I hadn't seen their catfight a few weeks ago. Since then, Lucy's usually been by herself. It's weird because Lucy and Désirée were always *followed*, if you know what I mean.

I roll my eyes. "Someone, somewhere, will cut her down before that. She's way too annoying."

Someone like me, I hope.

But Diego is right. When people of any race go through the ranks at Gomada Academy, they get stronger and stronger. And with Désirée's Fire and Water Affinities, she'll be even more unstoppable when she's a Master Enchantress. She'd be able to put out her own fires – literally. Her and nobody else. That makes me want to puke.

Diego shrugs as he takes another drag. "Maybe. Maybe not. Bitches like that know how to survive," he reminds me.

That reminds me of Lukas Crabtree. He was a dick, but he wasn't able to stand up to the ghost. I guess he finally met his match.

Even if he *was* an idiot, I feel bad for him. I even *miss him* sometimes. Not like I'd ever say that to anyone, but–

My phone vibrates in my pocket. I pull it out, wondering what fresh Hell Dad's gonna unleash on me now. He left for the night a few hours ago, telling me he'll be back 'bright and early Sunday morning.'

So much for giving me any kind of a *break* until then.

I'm surprised when I see that the text isn't from Dad.

It's from Arya.

My heart picks up speed. I'm fucking thrown off guard, and totally nervous. I never thought I'd hear from her again, after what happened in the Dining Hall. And it's pretty late for her to be up now.

It's okay. Not your fault.

That's all she writes.

Not my fault.

Well, I guess there's a first time for everything. But I know she's right about what happened. I guess I could have stood up for Arya and her sister – but going up against Dad, especially about Nymphs, is a no-go.

> Thanks for your help before.

I send the text before I chicken out.

Diego's close by. I don't want to spend too much time messaging her in case he sees what's on my screen.

> How did you know it was me?

If I didn't before, I do now.

But thanks to the Tedla's ultra-keen senses, I already knew that.

> Shifter senses.

"Who're you talking to, Hudson?" Diego suddenly teases, slamming his head over my shoulder to try and find out for himself.

His reflexes are fast, thanks to the Phoenix. But since mine are also on fire (accidental pun), I can shove my phone back into the pocket of my jeans before he sees too much.

"Nobody," I dismiss.

Diego laughs. "You always get so squirrely about your phone when Daddy is here," he teases, causing me to glower up at him.

"Can it, Jasper," I order. "We can't all have dads like yours."

Diego nudges my ribs with his right elbow. "Boo-hoo, Hudson," he laughs.

We stare out at the darkness in front of us. Far ahead, we see treetops and a weird half-moon. It's creepy when the points of the trees make the moon look even stranger than usual.

"D'you think we'll see it again?" Diego asks as we look at the black nothingness.

I sense that Diego is scared, like me.

By now, we all know what the ghost is capable of. We know it's been taking other students – but weirdly enough, there are no rumours of a psycho ghost haunting the campus. People are just vanishing without a trace, and nobody knows who or what is to blame.

This motherfucker is crafty. Clearly, it knows to do its *haunting* when there are no witnesses. Even with the stricter rules around curfew and going out in groups, the ghost is nabbing people one by one. I guess that's what happens when you can hypnotize people.

With our luck, it'll come for all of us before we can finalize a plan of attack.

"No clue. Probably," I admit, deciding not to cut corners with Diego.

We've been best friends since we were ten. There's no use trying to hide stuff from him. He'll find out, anyway.

He'll probably find out that I've been texting Arya, too. Unlike me, Diego is smart. Stalling him is the best I can do when it comes to liking Arya.

"No news is good news, anyway. No one else seems to think a ghost is behind all this disappearance shit," Diego breathes, leaning back against Feara and closing his eyes.

Further proof that stalling him is all I got going for me.

Diego must be high. It takes a lot for Diego to feel the effects of anything.

I don't get how the school can keep the ghost under wraps like this. They must know that there's a spirit behind these kidnappings. Frow and Greyson the Dumbass were already speculating about weirdness in September. They must've connected the dots by now.

And since the missing kids aren't coming back to campus, clearly Frow and the rest of them are thinking one thing and one thing only.

The MIA students are dead.

So how are they keeping everything so quiet? Wouldn't the parents of those kids want answers?

Gomada puts a shit ton of money into this school. Are the families being bought off? Sworn to secrecy? Who the fuck knows?

With more people noticing their friends disappearing out of the blue, it's gonna get harder and harder to keep families and the press at bay like this. No matter how many friends Frow has at the top, or whatever, numbers don't lie.

"Yeah," I try to agree. "I don't think Frow will be able to keep things quiet forever."

Diego nods in affirmation.

We smoke in silence for a while.

I love this. It's not just being with Diego. It's about being myself, not having to hide anything.

"I still can't believe that little bugger is dead," Diego murmurs, breaking the now eerie-quiet. He's probably referring to Lukas.

I take another drag of my cigarette. "I know." More emotion leaks out of me than it would have with anyone else.

Diego glances at me, his hazel eyes catching on to my feelings. I'm surprised, though I guess I shouldn't be, that Diego also feels bad for Crabtree. Diego's a much nicer guy than I am.

"Well, we can help him out by being ready next time the weird-ass ghost shows up," Diego asserts, looking straight ahead, pensive.

He's determined. I feel the same way. Now that we have a team of people *in on* everything, it'll be that much easier to take down this POS.

We have to do this for Lukas and the other so-called 'missing students.'

Enough of that bullshit.

We know the truth. They're dead. And Gomada Academy isn't doing anything about it. It's up to us now.

"Agreed," I respond, looking out at the mysterious darkness with him.

It's Sunday. Halloween is tomorrow, but the party is tonight.

I don't care about partying when it's a school-wide thing. Parties put on by the school are lame – but they're mandatory, so I have to put up with them.

Diego is putting a lot of effort into his *get-up*. He used to think school events were lame, too. I guess Lucy likes them, so now he does, too.

He's dressing up as a vampire. I can only imagine what Lucy will be. Ugh.

Just as Diego finishes his fake blood, he looks over at me. "Aren't you gonna get ready soon, there, chump?" he teases me.

He knows how much I hate parties – and any party that requires more effort to get ready beforehand is even worse.

My heart is pounding through my ears, making me dizzy. I don't think I've ever felt this way before. Even though I don't want to go to this party, the thought of seeing Arya–

"No rush," I shrug, trying to sound calm as can be.

What a big-ass lie!

I'm shitting myself on the inside.

I wish Diego would leave so that I could get ready by myself. It's annoying, sure, but it has to be done. The key to getting through this night is making sure no one recognizes me – including Diego. If I want to have the night I'm hoping I'll have, Arya is the only person who can know who I am.

Of course, Diego doesn't know I'm bringing anyone to this stupid party. We also didn't talk about costumes or any of that garbage. That stuff doesn't matter to us. But we know the school administration cares about that crap, and the girls we're taking care, too. So we suck it up.

Diego rolls his eyes at me. "Typical of you, Hudson," he continues to mock me like he's in his freaking happy place or something.

I fix my eyes on him from my desk. I'm trying to focus on my History homework that's due tomorrow. I'm almost done, which makes it even harder to concentrate. But I know as soon as Diego leaves, I'm getting ready, and I won't be able to focus on school-work until tomorrow morning.

Diego finally leaves to pick up Lucy when he's satisfied that he's rattled my cage. I spend twenty minutes of torture on my History homework. I get up from my desk as soon as I'm finished. I yank out the parcel from its hiding spot under my bed.

I never order stuff online. She's already changing me – and I don't like it. If things work out how I want them to (depending on the time of day, anyway), it'll only worsen.

My costume choice was simple. I needed something with a mask to hide my identity. I also needed something that wasn't plastic and suffocating.

TLDR: I chose to be a Grim Reaper.

The costume I bought online came with a black balaclava thing, a hooded cape, and a scythe. I don't think I'll use the plastic weapon, but I'll need everything else.

I step out into the cold and deserted hallway after shoving the hood of my costume well over my head. The heat's been iffy in the dorms for a while now.

Leaving for the party later than everyone else means a deserted departure. That's what I wanted.

The party started at seven, and it's seven-thirty when I close in on Gomada Academy. Lots of other students cluster around the perimeter of the school. Their costumes are stupid – but mine is too, so I don't say anything.

I also see professors and other faculty members spread out around the school grounds. I guess everyone's on double duty tonight because of the ghost-and-party combo.

Surprisingly enough, nobody looks freaked about being out here. But I guess when only a handful of us know what's *really* out there, it's easier to downplay everything.

As I walk to the Reception Hall, I'm hit with a gripping and unavoidable feeling. I guess it's worry. I don't have many of those so I couldn't figure out the nagginess at first.

Maybe I'm arriving to this thing too late.

What if Arya thinks I've skipped out on her? Or that my agreeing to go to this party with her was all a big joke?

After everything I've done to her, it won't be hard for her to suspect that.

The Reception Hall is different. The tables and chairs are gone. It's dark and creepy – which is saying something, because the school did this. But I guess with Xhao and Qadir as inspiration, it kind of makes sense.

Flickering lights and the booming of a stereo from somewhere in the room make it hard for me to concentrate.

A dull ache spreads across my temples. I'll be glad when I can head out of here.

I try to focus. If Arya's here, I'll be able to smell her – even in a crowd as big as this one. The Tedla's senses enhance my own despite the overwhelming noise around me. I'm starting to pick out scents after a few seconds of lingering at the wall closest to the exit.

After a while of tracking, I come up short.

Finding Arya might be harder than I thought.

Fuck!

I could have texted her, but I didn't want to be *that guy*. Since we didn't make any other arrangements, meeting here was kind of a given.

My nerves are taking a big-ass beating. It gets worse with each passing second.

Damnit!

I'm such a dick!

Arya will *definitely* think I'm messing with her head. I'm already late. She's never gonna trust me again (like she does, to begin with) if I don't get my ass in gear.

Wandering the fringes of the party, I still don't smell her anywhere. Searching for Nora's scent doesn't help, either.

This is hopeless! I snarl. *Why did I even bother thinking that I could make things up to her? This whole thing is fucking–*

There it is.

I smell Arya.

She's around here somewhere. Maybe I haven't screwed up yet, after all. But that's a big 'maybe.'

I weave around groups of talking Nymphs and Enchanters, all with something to prove. The guys are acting tough, while the girls are giggling and talking nervously.

Morons.

I'm finally closing in on Arya's scent. She's no less than twenty feet ahead of me. I'll probably bump into her soon enough.

Just as I'm avoiding crashing into an Enchantress who looks like she's a Désirée-in-training, the lights flash above me at just the right time, illuminating partygoers ahead of me. I see an Enchantress prof, a few Nymphs, and *her*.

Arya is hovering close to the wall. Her long brown hair is braided at the side. She's wearing a light blue dress (not a pink one, which seems to be her thing) with a small crown, arms folded. Even though I can sense that she's pissed, she still looks hot.

I bet this isn't her scene either, which accounts for her being alone and close to a wall.

We have that in common. A similarity like that makes me happy, which could only mean one thing.

I'm in deep shit.

Anyway, I pegged her for doing something girly, like dressing up as a princess – but that doesn't mean she doesn't look good doing it.

I approach her, worrying more and more about what to say with each step I take. It's hard to focus on ghosts, midterms, and my shitshow of a Parents' Weekend right now. All I can think about is her.

She turns just as I'm walking up to her. I can see her clearly in the dark, but I'm guessing she doesn't know shit about who I am, thanks to my reaper costume.

"Hey," I finally announce – which is stupid, but it was the only thing I could think of to say. I guess it's better than nothing.

"Cole?" she guesses. It sounds like she's frowning.

"Yeah," I assure her.

"I thought you stood me up," she admits after a brief pause.

Fuck. Just like I thought.

"No," I respond. "Just came late."

I realize I need to add more to that – especially since I'm actually trying to make a good impression – so I add, "I'm sorry."

It looks like that *does something* to her because her voice sounds different when she answers,

"It's okay."

Maybe because I apologized for once (or, maybe twice, if you count last week), she believed me? I hope so.

This shit is freaky. I may have to talk more, do more, to get my point across.

Fuck!

Why am I doing this again?

"What's your costume?" she asks over the bass boom.

The lights flicker as she asks. She sees me and jumps.

I laugh, but for the first time, it's not a mocking laugh. She still hits my chest, though, frowning up at me as the lights shut off.

"Figures as much," she grumbles. "It's not like your inner self is much of a–"

"I like your costume," I tell her while I still have the guts. Even if it's a lame-ass thing to say, it's true. And I guess if I want this *thing* to go anywhere, she has to know I really do like her.

Arya looks brought up short by what I said. "Um..." she trails off, sounding nervous, all of a sudden. "Thanks," she murmurs.

"Do you want food?" I stammer as the bass changes pace. Another song must be playing.

Arya looks around. "Yeah," she agrees.

I'm just about to tell her we can go looking for the buffet table when someone jumps behind her and screams weirdly. It's some guy in a ghoul's costume. Clearly, he's just out to be a dick and isn't a real treat, but Arya yelps in response.

It's not her fault. It's not like we don't have real-life nightmares stalking us to make us paranoid. Either way, Arya grabs me and holds on for dear life. Maybe she actually thinks the ghost is behind us. I have no clue.

Ghoul Guy chortles at her reaction – but he's not smiling for long. I push Arya closer and slam my other hand into the dude's chest, shoving him away from us.

"It was just some asshole," I begin to say, but quickly change my tune in case I sound mean. "You good?" I ask.

Arya looks up at me. It's hard to tell if she's still ticked at me for being late, if she's thinking I was making fun of her for being scared, so she's mad all over again, or if she's just plain *nervous* because we're on a date and it's *not* 'business as usual.'

"Yeah. I'm fine," she answers quickly.

When I slowly put my other arm around her, her dark brown eyes widen as she stares at me. Darkness or not, I can tell she's surprised,

I'm smiling at her. Thank God she can't tell because of the mask.

We stare at each other for a while longer. It's still like Arya doesn't know what to think about me – like she's waiting for me to say 'just kidding' and knock her into the punch table.

My chest jumps in this weird and uncomfortable way when she places her head against it and holds onto me tighter than before.

I'd push them away if it was anyone else – but I don't move a muscle now.

"Is this what you're like when you're not..." she trails off, likely nervous to say the wrong thing.

"A dick?" I attempt to finish.

Arya takes in a breath against me. This makes me realize that I've stopped breathing. I'm dizzy, and my head hurts. But I don't feel half-bad if I'm honest with myself.

Arya nods in agreement, which causes me to inhale slowly.

I clear my throat. "Uh..."

Truth is, I'm usually a dick to everyone. I may be nicer to a few select people, but even that doesn't spare them if I'm ever in a bad mood. So what do I say now?

"Yeah. I guess," I finally try to admit. I don't want to go too far, so I just hold her waist and don't move an inch.

"Let's go get food," I finally suggest again after a weird pause. Maybe it's weirder for me than it is for her. I really have no idea.

Arya steps out of my grip, so I let go. "Yeah. Sounds good," she agrees as we make our way to the buffet table.

It's probably dick-ish of me to think this way, but...

I'm glad I'm wearing a costume with a mask. I'm thankful Diego's not around. I'm relieved that the Shifters who pass us don't give us a second glance.

I don't know what to do about these two feelings I have that want to rip me in two.

I like Arya. I really like her. There's no way to deny it anymore.

But she's a Nymph.

That embarrasses me. It would get a rise out of every Shifter within spitting distance. Diego would never stop lecturing me about being a hypocrite. Even bitches like Désirée would try to make my life Hell for it.

Between Dad and Qadir riding my ass and me trying to fly under the radar at school thanks to the Tedla, I really can't afford to be seen with Arya.

I swallow the big-ass lump in my throat and try to just enjoy this crazy rollercoaster ride I decided to jump on, all of my own free will.

Ten

ARYA'S CONFESSION

I'm thankful when Cole asks if I want to get some fresh air. This party is too much for me to handle – practical jokes and the booming bass, combined with the fact that Cole and I are actually on a date, are too overwhelming to take on all at once.

The lack of snow falling from the sky does nothing to eliminate the chill from the air as we walk around the side of the school. We end up sliding around the corner, heading toward the back wall of the enormous castle-like structure. We now have some degree of shelter from the harsh wind and the air thick with the change in season.

Cole pulls his mask off in a flourish, subsequently fixing his hood. Maybe it was hard for him to breathe in the Reception Hall, too.

Maybe we have more in common than I thought.

Cole leans against the dark wall to my left, staring at the wooded area beyond the Academy. The Gomada Pond follows it, and to the extreme other side of that is the Gomada River, but

I've never been on that side of Upper Gomada before. I just know all this from maps and what we've discussed in class.

The brisk temperature and my rattled nerves make it difficult to know what to say. I hug my chest, trying to wrack my brain for a conversational topic. Worse still, Cole isn't a talkative guy. I guess if he's making fun of you, he has more to say, so maybe I should be thankful that he's quiet.

I'm also tongue-tied because I don't have much experience talking to boys in any capacity, let alone a date with an ex-enemy.

I still can't believe I'm doing this.

"Do you like Halloween – dressing up, partying?" I tack on the rest after he looks down at me in a quizzical way.

"No," he responds. "It's lame."

"Then how come you came to the party?" I can't help but ask.

Cole shifts in place, his green eyes looking *nervous*. I'm not used to seeing him in this light.

"Because I had to," he reminds me.

"Oh, right," I murmur, embarrassed that I asked such an obvious question.

"And because you asked," he abruptly finishes.

My stomach juts upward in a painfully anxious way. I bite my lower lip as he stares down at me. I never would have thought that something I said would have had an influence on Cole Hudson.

He frowns suddenly, freaking me out until he speaks.

"Are you cold?" he asks.

The wind has stopped, but that doesn't change the frigid temperature or the fact that I can hardly form a coherent thought or suck in a normal breath.

I nod in agreement, abashed for jumping back to the beginning of term, when all Cole would have for me were discriminatory, crude comments or downright malicious behaviour.

It's clear he's trying to show me that he's changed over the past several weeks. The least I could do was see this through, and meet him halfway.

It's been hard to stop thinking about him, and it got harder once I asked him to the Halloween party. At least if he shows me he's still a jerk, I can forget about these weird, uncomfortable feelings. And if he shows me otherwise–

I'm still too nervous to speak, for some odd reason. Or, maybe it isn't so odd. When Cole stares down at me, his eyes are so *green* that it's hard for me to concentrate.

I'm startled when Cole places an arm around my back, leaning his head down to look at me. His dark wavy hair and vibrant eyes make his grim reaper costume look not quite as scary as before. In fact, they cancel it out entirely.

I step closer to him, ignoring my heart pounding in my ears.

Is this all a big mistake? Will I regret getting close to him?

When I'm staring into his eyes, it's hard to remember that we used to be at odds. I didn't think that could be my reality.

For weeks, Cole has been aloof, quiet, and even *kind* – stark opposites to what he was like when we met. All this prompts me to think his *confession* was true. I'm also starting to wonder if my uncomfortable, overpowering feelings will be easy to shake.

Could it be possible that I like him, too? It would make sense. I've been fighting, denying, and dreading my inner thoughts ever since I kissed him. And now–

Cole bends his head down, his face closer to mine. For a second, I think he's just doing it so he can see me better in the dark.

But that can't be, because his face is inches from mine. No one gets that close to someone unless–

His soft lips press against mine, abolishing my train of thought and throwing me off course.

*Oh, my God! He's **kissing** me!*

Just like before, a fire wells up inside of me as soon as our lips touch. Even though it may look wrong on the outside, it definitely *feels* right.

All I can think about is giving in to these uncomfortable sentiments swirling around in my chest like tangled-up spaghetti. I'm having trouble breathing.

I kiss him back, wondering if our second kiss – *my* second kiss – leaves something to be desired. It's not like I have practice in the ways of romance.

But Cole doesn't seem to think so. He leans in closer, both arms around me now. My hands are suddenly on the inside of his elbows.

I brought him closer to me without realizing it!

I thought I'd smell cigarette smoke on his breath, but all I smell is the pizza we ate and a hint of something else – mint?

When we kiss again, Cole opens his mouth wider. He brings me closer. I hesitantly take a hand off his arm and weave it through his dark hair, which is mostly hiding under his hood.

Cole flinches. At first, I think he has disdain for what I did – but when he exhales shakily and kisses me again, I realize that's not at all what happened.

I startle when a snapping sound in the wooded area beyond us breaks this used-to-be perfect moment. I'm surprised I was able to hear it. Maybe it's because it's a clearer evening, with less wind to hinder nighttime noise?

I guess I'm more attuned to these kinds of things now that I've seen a ghost. My Air Affinity helps, too, but being on the lookout for paranormal threats has had an enormous impact on my heightened sense.

Cole follows my gaze to the other side of the Gomada Thicket.

"Did you hear that?" I ask, wondering if he'll think I'm crazy, or a crybaby, or–

"Yeah. I did," he affirms, scrutinizing the unknown, that transformed from our quiet backdrop into a harrowing hiding spot for creatures of the night.

There's no fog. No creepy, damp feeling that crops up whenever the ghost shows itself.

So what could be out there? Just an animal? Could we be that lucky?

Doubtful.

Cole yanks down his hood. "Holy shit," he breathes, just as a barely-visible silhouette steps out from the shadowy shrubs.

I can't discern anything about the figure from this distance. I look up at Cole to gauge his reaction.

"I can't believe it," he proclaims, focused on the stumbling shadow mostly hidden by Fall trees dusted with snow.

"What?" I inquire breathlessly when he doesn't elaborate.

Though Cole makes eye contact with me, it's obvious his mind is on what's ahead of us. "It's one of the missing students – a Shifter," he announces. He lets go of me, turning his attention back to the silhouette, who is actually one of his contemporaries.

All I see now is a person flickering in and out of the shelter of the treeline – not a monster or a mysterious entity.

Could this student have escaped the ghost? We didn't think any of the abductees survived because we surely would have heard about their return to campus.

"But I thought they were all – Cole!" I protest as he races for the other side of the fenceline.

I rush to catch up. Cole turns mid-pace and takes my wrists. "No way in Hell," is all he says, letting go of me and continuing to sprint for the Shifter.

I don't really want to stand here and wait for him – but at the same time, I'm suddenly really scared.

Despite my fear, I don't want Cole to go out there alone. What if the ghost is nearby?

I stare at Cole's soon-to-be-reunion in disbelief. I can't get over this. We didn't think the ghost was in the business of keeping people alive. But now, one of the spirit's victims has *escaped*?

My phone vibrates from inside my dress's small pocket. I pull it out, wondering if my incoming notification could be important. If everyone's at the party, I doubt they'll be sending messages. Unless–

I saw Crabtree. He just kicked my ass!

I reread Diego's message to the group chat, dumbfounded.
Lukas Crabtree is alive.
What's more, Lukas just hurt Diego?
I don't think Diego and Cole are very close with Lukas, but the news still stupefies me.

Did he poison you? Go to the infirmary.

Already there. Watch your backs.

Diego's response to Ryker sends a shiver down my spine.
I guess Lukas has a Poison Affinity. I never knew much about him. It feels weird finding things out about him now because we thought he was dead for so long...
A holler makes me almost drop my phone. Only seconds have passed since I took my eyes off Cole and the Shifter – and now, they're on top of him!
Shoving my phone into my pocket, I study my options as Cole rolls around with this student who shouldn't have anything against a fellow Shifter.
If I run to catch up to them, I'll never make it in time.
If I fly, I don't think it'll make much of a difference. I may be unable to yank Cole away from this person if they're stronger than me.

That leaves me with one last alternative.

Thunder rumbles in the dark clouds above the two wrestling Shifters. If I'm lucky and able to concentrate well enough, I can aim my electricity at Cole's attacker.

Too late. Electricity is pouring down from the clouds, which have spread to cover me.

I grit my teeth, my braid flying around me with the increased wind and electrical current in the air.

There's no time to chicken out. This could be life or death. It's not like Professor Xhao is around to stop things if she sees fit. This isn't a mock battle.

It's the real thing.

I have to try and get a handle on my electrical component, my wind control. If I don't steady my nerves–

I'm using my hands to try and tame this massive amount of power I've summoned. My heart is thumping in my ears. I'm terrified of losing control.

That can't happen!

If I lose control, Cole could die. I shudder uncontrollably at the thought.

This is a lot of electricity – but not as much as there was during my midterm. Maybe I *can* handle this. Maybe.

I need to try to manipulate this summoned energy now if I want to have a prayer of helping Cole!

Forked and jagged electricity surrounds the two Shifters and throws Cole from the tangled fray.

Lightning surrounds Cole. He struggles to his feet, backing away from the bright static. Even though his back is to me, I can tell that he's confused and maybe even *scared* of what's happening around him.

I try to ignore the hiss and crackling of my Affinity as I use every ounce of courage and focus I have to try to save him.

With the brightness of the electricity, I can now see that the

Shifter who was attacking Cole is female. She's retreating from the erratic sparks. That's what I hoped would happen. Instead of hurting the attacker, I thought protecting Cole would be the safest, wisest, thing to do.

The Shifter keeps backing away until she seamlessly disappears into the black trees.

It's a very *unnatural* thing to do. You would think that the unpredictability of the thicket would cause people to watch where they were going – but not this girl. Her actions are just so... Robotic.

Other than churning lightning surrounding Cole, there is nothing but quiet.

The coast is clear.

Now, how am I supposed to–

The lightning gathers away from Cole and swarms toward the dark horizon, getting absorbed by the ominous clouds.

My temples ache. I'm nauseous. I waver slightly when Cole calls my name.

Something cold and stiff meets my senses, and I'm almost consumed by blackness. Somehow, my eyes detect a flicker of movement in front of me.

"Arya?"

I strain my eyes to stay open, but I've used up so much energy that it's almost impossible to stay alert.

I finally make out a blurry version of Cole, staring down at me. Is he crouching? It's hard to tell.

Wait.

Did I pass out – *again*?

Cole sucks in a breath and mutters something I can't make out as I shift slightly in place.

"What the fuck were you thinking?" he demands, putting his hands under my shoulders and slowly hoisting me up into a sitting position.

His comment isn't cruel. He sounds – *worried*?

"You could have gotten yourself killed," he continues firmly.

"Is she gone?" I ask, finding it hard to talk. Each word seems to take longer to get out than the one before.

Cole frowns at me, but again, he looks worried. "Yeah, but who cares?" he counters. "You almost gave yourself a concussion."

Before I can even open my mouth to answer him, Cole swings me into his arms. My head lolls against his chest in response.

"Are you–" I begin to fret.

"I'm fine. No big deal," he dismisses, his feet crunching on hard grass as he walks around the side of the school. I don't know where we're going, but I'm too weak to ask.

I shouldn't be surprised that Meera is pretty much a ghost town (bad choice of words) as Cole makes his way down the deserted fourth-floor hallway. As soon as he gets to Room 407, I rummage inside my pocket, weakly handing over my room key. All I brought with me tonight were my phone and my key – and I'm glad about that.

After unlocking the door, Cole walks purposefully into my shared dorm room and places me on my bed. I'm surprised he knows which one is mine – which side of the room is mine, and not Nora's. Maybe Cole pays closer attention than I thought.

Cole closes the door, locks it – again surprising me with his attention to detail – and looks around the room like he's waiting for someone to jump out at us. When neither of us sees anything (though I'm too disoriented to look as thoroughly), Cole leans against the door, folding his arms.

"So, that was one of the missing students," he tells me – or, recaps. I'm not really sure.

"How come she attacked you?" I ask, barely able to get that out as I prop myself against my hastily put-together throw pillows.

Thankfully, my side of the dorm doesn't look too bad. If I'd known Cole was going to be coming back here–

Embarrassed, I shut that thought out of my mind as Cole's green eyes go to the window near Nora's side of the dorm.

"No clue," he admits. "I knew of her, I guess. She's a Junior. But we never had any beef. Don't get why she'd come at me."

"Diego messaged the group a little while ago. He said he was attacked, too," I suddenly recall. "By Lukas," I add, when Cole stares at me, open-mouthed.

He yanks his phone out of his pocket and stares at the messages I read what seems like hours earlier.

"Fuck," Cole breathes. "Lukas may be a dick, but I don't get why he'd go after Diego – 'specially if Diego was just trying to help."

Diego definitely seems like the more level-headed one out of the two of them. It would make sense that he'd be trying to help Lukas, not hurt him. So why would Lukas attack him – especially weeks after getting abducted, when Diego did nothing to deserve that?

Cole looks over at me, surprising me. "You good?" he asks.

I hesitate. "Um... Yeah," I deliberate, as he crosses over to my side of the dorm.

My heart beats a little faster as he approaches my bed, folds his arms and looks down at me sternly. "That was a crazy-ass thing you did back there."

Before I can comment or even think about how freaky it would be if Cole got mad at me, he rolls his green eyes slightly, a small smile on his face.

I guess I'll have to get used to Cole's *other* emotions – besides hate, judgement, mockery, and unpleasantness. He's not mad at all.

"But it was kind of badass, too," he adds, smirking down at me.

I give him a small smile – mostly because I'm exhausted, but also because it's hard to even move my face when Cole is looking at me like this.

Cole glances toward the window and the door again before telling me, "Stay here. Don't open the door for anyone."

"Where are you going?" I ask.

He clears his throat. "To check on Diego. Lukas has Poison and Earth Affinities. Could've done some real damage to Diego if he wanted to."

Lukas has both Poison *and* Earth Affinities? Enchanters and Enchantresses always have two Affinities, but I wonder how lethal an Earth and Poison Affinity combo could be, especially in the hands of an angry Enchanter.

"Wait," I blurt out – definitely by accident – as Cole is turning on his heel and walking away from me.

He turns to look down at me. "What?" he asks.

I pause.

I can't really get myself out of this now that I've started to say it in the first place.

Here goes nothing.

"I – I had a good time tonight. Until this," I admit.

Cole looks stunned for a minute, but then he smiles at me. "Yeah?" he asks.

I nod, still dumbfounded at how I could be saying these things about Cole Hudson and not being in some alternate dimension.

Cole folds his arms. "I did, too," he tells me.

Wringing my hands together, I finally finish my train of thought by adding, "And, um… I like you, too."

Cole raises both eyebrows, the smile completely gone from his face. Before I can panic about that, he walks over to the bed again and bends his head down, his mouth pressing against my proba-bly-messed-up braid.

"God help me," he says, smirking at me before turning on his heel and heading for the door.

Eleven

COLE'S ATTACKER

A thousand different questions slam me as I rush for the infirmary, ignoring the tumbling snow and the hovering clouds that threaten to dump even more white shit on me.

Each time I try to fend off one question, another one takes its place. It's annoying. But I guess I'm panicking, so everything's coming out all at once.

Why would Lukas attack Diego?

Why did Patty jump me? I've never done anything to her. Hell, I barely even know her.

The way she looked tonight – it reminds me of how Ryker described Lukas the night the ghost nabbed him.

One word. One word that I used to scoff at because these things are lame, useless, and oozing. But it seems to be the only thing that makes sense

Zombies.

Sure, there are some differences between Patty and those dopes. For one thing, Patty wasn't scabby and dirty. She wasn't making those fucked up groans, either. But still, she wasn't *herself*. Something was missing – like she was on autopilot or something. No lights on upstairs.

I don't have time for any more craziness. I'm at the door to the infirmary. Time to take action.

A nurse is in front of me, closing and locking the door.

Fuck.

This isn't good. I've taken enough trips down here to know that when they lock up tight for the night, with people in there, whoever's in there is pretty laid up.

Shit.

"Can I help you?" the nurse asks tiredly, like she's in a hurry and I'm holding her up.

Of course she can help me! Why else would I be here if I didn't need something?

I guess being a dick won't get me very far. I try to take a deep breath (weirdly enough, Diego's always telling me to do that).

"Yeah," I answer simply. "I'm here to see Diego Jasper. He got into a fight tonight."

I'm not sure if that's how he spun it, but it has to be. It's doubtful that Diego would spill his guts about a thought-to-be-dead Sophomore Enchanter to a nurse. We all agreed to keep this crap quiet.

The nurse seems to think about that. "Visiting hours are long past over," she tells me, in a sort-of firm voice.

Great. I'm never getting in.

"I just need to know if he's okay," I finally beg, surprised that I went from zero to a hundred in five seconds.

But it's true. Diego is my best friend. I don't know what I'd do without him. Sure, Diego could take Lukas in a fist-fight, but if Lukas threw the first 'Affinity punch' and Diego didn't have time to Shift–

"Your friend is fine," she tells me before I can panic further.

"We extracted the poison. He's recuperating from the ordeal. Please come visit tomorrow."

The nurse stashes the keys into her pocket, gives me a *look*, and walks away from me.

Figures. Adults around here don't trust me. I can't fault them for that – but still, it's annoying. I bet she would've let Lucy in, or Arya.

I stare at the door, wishing I could use my super-strength to smash it open. I mean, I *could* do that, but it wouldn't win me any brownie points with Frow or Qadir. They're still watching Arya, Nora and I after what happened that crazy Thursday night.

I can't rock the boat now. And if anyone's going to do that, it'll be me. I don't want to prove everyone right.

I turn away from the infirmary. I'll be back tomorrow. However, my resolve to do that doesn't make me feel much better *now*.

That makes me remember.

I pull out my phone and message Lucy.

> Diego's okay. They got the poison out. He's resting. I'm going to see him tomorrow.

I don't know where Lucy was when Diego was attacked, but she definitely knows about it. She was in the group chat with all of us – she saw those messages, just like Arya and I did.

Turning the corner in the hallway, I again think about adults who don't trust me.

Dad is a huge example. When I asked him again about Izaak Johnson, Ryker's uncle, he gave me that same firm-and-irritated look that everyone else gives me.

"I didn't peg you for being a gossip, son. That doesn't concern you," he'd answered gruffly.

I grit my teeth and push open the door, heading into the

night. I can still hear Dad's voice, his condescension, like I don't know shit.

I hate that he doesn't trust me; that he thinks I'm just asking these questions to stir up trouble. I'd never tell him *why* I wanted to know about Izaak Johnson – but at the same time, Dad doesn't think I'm even smart enough to ask something for an important reason.

People dressed in costumes are everywhere. Curfew got extended until ten tonight, like it used to be, so I guess that's why people are still hanging around campus without looking like they've seen a ghost (funny – not).

I don't even know where I'm going as I pass by a group of chatting Shifters, sipping out of those stupid plastic cups. They're definitely drunk. One of them probably brought a little something extra to the party.

Maybe I'd be up for having more fun tonight if all this shit hadn't happened first.

Then again, I imagine getting drunk isn't Arya's thing – so maybe I wouldn't have *indulged* (that's what Diego calls it), even if the zombie--attack from Patty and Lukas hadn't taken place.

I glance around me for what feels like the first time.

Okay. I'm near Feara.

Turned off of going home, I make an about-face to go check on Arya. I slide to a stop when something bright and freaky catches my eye.

Trails of fog seep into my peripheral vision. I'm suddenly cold and damp, similar to what would happen if I got caught in a rainstorm.

A tall, pale figure is ahead of me. Its hole-shaped eyes bore into mine. A chill clings to my bones.

That's the ghost!

What the fuck is it doing here?

Is it here for me?

Of course it'd use a Halloween party to show up like this. Coward.

I want to move – go anywhere, do something – but I suddenly *can't*. I feel like my feet are a part of the hard, wintry ground. I can't even move my eyes away from the 'ghost hybrid.'

Is this how it got Lukas, Patty, and the others?

My thoughts about zombies – what the ghost has done to others and will likely do to me – make me even more freaked. But there's nothing I can do to save myself. I can't move. I can't even Shift.

The holes of the ghost's eyes are getting bigger.

Wait. That's not it.

It's getting closer.

Oh, God.

Now that I don't have the element of surprise, or the Tedla to use as power, I can't do jack shit against the ghost now. It's pretty damn obvious that the ghost knows that, too.

If I can't move, maybe I can force the Tedla out – scare the ghost or at least make it think I'm a worthy opponent. It knows I can take it on because of last time.

But I'm not an idiot. I know I don't have a chance in Hell against it without lead-time and speed. Right now, I don't have any of those things.

Whatever. I need to try to fight against this weirdness and Shift. There's no other way!

Nothing seems to happen when I try to dig into my usual urges for Shifting – anger, annoyance, frustration, and even fear.

Fuck. I'm ghost chow now. And I can't do anything to stop it.

The ghost is closing in on me. I'm shitting myself. Everyone is walking past me, thinking I'm drunk or high (which *does* happen sometimes, to be fair). No one thinks I'm being attacked by the 'threat to Gomada Academy,' to quote Frow.

Where's all the tough talk now? I can't help but fume, as the ghost closes in on me. *Where's the vigilance, protection, and safety the school promised? It's all bullshit!*

Well, I'd rather be dead than a mindless zombie robot in whatever game this ghost is playing – and it's pretty obvious it has an end-game, because people aren't turning up dead, like we thought earlier.

I'll fight back in any way I can. But I won't become one of them.

One of them.

A damp blast of fear travels down my spine at that thought. I may act like a tough guy, but when faced with my death – or something worse than that – well...

The earth trembles under my feet. I'm surrounded by bright light and darkness. These two forces are like thick trails of smoke, making it hard to see.

It's really weird. One side is bright, warm, and almost *welcoming*. The other stuff, on my right, is dark, creepy, and really hard to handle: like if I stared at it too much, I'd be sucked into Hell.

The ghost actually falters as the two different but sort-of-working-together forces close in around me. I can barely see through them.

The ghost vanishes.

I turn around, ready to shit myself, for real.

The white-and-black smoke evaporates. Sitting down, looking at me like I'm an idiot, is a white fox.

Whitney.

Which means–

"Lucky for you, I was heading in the same direction."

Lucy steps out of the shadows that seemed to have crept in when I was being attacked. It's darker now than it was before. Whitney moves aside so her mistress can be in front.

Some passersby are staring at Lucy like she's nuts – like she made a big deal out of some dude in a costume or party trick.

But there's another reason for those looks, and I know it well.

She makes them nervous. They know how powerful she is, and don't want to cause any problems. Diego and I know those lingering stares, that's for sure.

People fear power.

I'm not in the mood to play tough or to brush off her help. I just suck in a breath and try to steady myself.

My entire body is on pins and needles. It hurts to move, but at least I'm actually *able* to move now.

"Yeah," I agree shakily. "Thanks, Lucy."

Lucy gives me a side smile. She looks surprised but also happy about what I said. She's still a Chapin. At least she's not nearly as bad as her cousin, who I'm assuming is around here somewhere, screwing with someone else.

But on the other hand, maybe Lucy's relieved that people are finally starting to trust her.

I know how that feels. Usually, I don't care, but it *does* suck when people believe the worst in you.

I hate to say it, but I'm actually starting to feel sorry for her.

Kissing a Nymph? Feeling sorry for an Enchantress? What the hell is happening to me?

I never would've thought those two things could happen to me – not in September. Even now, I'm having trouble believing it.

"Are you okay, Cole?" Lucy distracts me by asking. Whitney jumps onto her and loops over her shoulder, like always.

Even though I think they're useless, Familiars *are* pretty smart. If Whitney's relaxing and content, there isn't any more danger. At least, not tonight.

I'm not sure how to answer the Enchantress' question. After a while, I shrug. "Yeah. I'm good."

Just scared shitless.

"How did you know I needed help, anyway?" I ask as we begin to walk.

I'm not really sure where we're going. All I can think about is the fact that I'm actually able to move again.

"You never knew what the ghost looked like," I add.

Lucy and Diego were given descriptions of the ghost from those of us who've seen it. Lucy had no idea what she was up against, and she still managed to get me out of trouble.

She'll do well when we battle the ghost six-on-one – that is, if we all survive 'til then.

"I sensed something dark about the ghost coming toward you," Lucy admits, weirded-out about what she's saying. Whitney nibbles on Lucy's collar, acting like the craziest thing ever didn't just happen.

"Dark? You mean, *evil*?" I ask. I don't want to add 'straight out of Hell,' but I'm hoping Lucy gets my point.

Now that Lucy is discovering more about her Light and Darkness Affinity Combo, I'm sure she knows what I'm getting at. Besides, she's been training a lot with Ryker. I'm sure he's let her in on the secrets of the trade or whatever. That's probably why Lucy looks uncomfortable right now.

"Not exactly," she surprises me by admitting as we close in on Meera, of all places. "It was something dark, yes, but not inherently evil."

"But it's a ghost," I remind her. "Sort of," I add, thinking about Diego's 'hybrid' comment.

Lucy is quiet for a while. I notice she looks deep in concentration as we walk. Her blue eyes look like she's in an alternate dimension.

"I don't think so," Lucy disagrees.

Shock radiates through my body at her statement. Even though we were kind of wondering about this, ourselves – especially me, because I bit a chunk out of the thing as the Tedla – it's still crazy to hear someone say it the way Lucy did.

This isn't just a theory she's spewing out. It sounds like she has concrete proof to back up her assertion. And that makes me nervous.

"A ghost would mean that it died, and would therefore give off a celestial or hellish aura," Lucy continues as we stop in front of the entrance to Meera. "All I could sense were dark intentions. But I do think the creature is very much alive."

"Is it human?" I ask.

Lucy looks stumped by this. I notice now that she's not wearing a costume, but she's all dressed up. Figures. Rich girls like the Chapins don't always do Halloween. Can't say I blame her, if I'm honest. I feel stupid in this reaper costume – especially since *I'm* the one who almost became deader than dead tonight.

"I'm not sure," she confesses. "If I had more time, maybe I could've gotten a better read on it. It's definitely an enigma."

I don't want to split hairs or use fancy words to talk about that thing – but I know I need to tell her this ASAP.

"I wasn't able to move or Shift," I explain, eyeing the dormitory as discreetly as possible.

I still don't really know why I'm here at all. Maybe to see Arya? It's been such a weird night that I can't remember what I was doing before shit hit the fan.

Is that because of the ghost, or… ?

"Ryker said he was immobilized a few weeks ago, as well," Lucy recalls.

I remember that Arya and I *weren't* 'immobilized' that Thursday night when it saw us – but Nora was.

Maybe the ghost can only freeze people if it sees them? This makes me think that the element of surprise may be the only strategy worth using against the ghost.

Lucy must notice me looking at Meera (shit), because she gestures to the building, a frown on her face.

"I didn't think you frequented Meera," she tells me, confused.

Damn.

Lucy can't know that I come here more than I thought I would. She can't even know that I was maybe planning to come here at all.

I shrug. "I don't know where I'm going. Just happy to be able to move again."

Lucy nods in understanding but that hint of curiosity is still in her eyes. Maybe Diego digs that, but I find it annoying. It's like Lucy can figure you out at any second. It's freaky.

"Thanks again."

My thanks is genuine. If it wasn't for Lucy–

Lucy waves her hand dismissively. "No need to thank me, Cole," she responds calmly. "I'm just happy I could help."

After a short pause, Lucy says, "Please keep me posted if you hear anything more about Diego. I'm going to visit him tomorrow, too."

Lucy looks worried while Whitney nibbles on her short hair. Eventually, Lucy folds her arms. She's probably trying to make herself look tough.

"Will do," I assure her. "He'll be fine," I add, causing Lucy to give me a very small smile before turning around and walking away – maybe to Gleera.

We're all done with Halloween. We have enough nightmares to last us a lifetime without this party shit.

Twelve

ARYA KEEPS QUIET

It's Tuesday, November first. I'm so glad October is behind me. I don't even care that it's snowing again.

The Halloween party was horrifying. I was so traumatized that I hid in my dorm room the night of the thirty-first. After what happened to Cole, Diego and I, I didn't want to risk any 'repeats' by venturing out on Halloween night. I'm sure the school wouldn't have allowed any 'extra-curricular events' on Halloween, anyway.

In fact, everyone involved in the 'ghost hunting expedition' stayed in last night – even someone as tough as Lucy. I didn't peg her for having weaknesses.

It makes sense that Diego stayed in – he had no choice, what with being locked up in the infirmary for all of Monday. Thankfully, his condition improved. As far as I know, he was discharged last night.

I scan my surroundings now that I'm outdoors. I want to make sure I'm not being followed – by professors or paranormal prowlers. The ghost might have used the Halloween party as a backdrop for its *haunting*, but that doesn't make us any safer on November first, in broad daylight.

I'll have to keep looking over my shoulder because we're going to have another group meeting tonight.

I doubt these meetings will do any good. The ghost (or whatever it is) is clearly trying to pick us off, one by one. If we all gather in the same place, it'll just make its job even easier.

Can it sense us?

Is it watching us right now?

I jump a mile when something moves in my peripheral vision. I'm just about to lose it when I recognize Lucy.

I definitely didn't expect to see Lucy at my side this morning – or ever. I was thinking it was likely Nora, who wanted to catch up with Anja before morning classes. Or maybe even Cole (as hard as *that* is to believe). But definitely not Lucy.

"Good morning," Lucy greets me. She's wearing a black trenchcoat with high black boots. A large black bookbag is slung effortlessly over her shoulder. She smells of lavender.

The Enchantress looks very *put together*, especially for a cold, snowy Tuesday morning. I still don't understand why she wants to get close to Nora and I. Girls like Lucy never want to hang out with girls like me – and I don't get why Gomada would be any different.

In some ways, the Overworld is the same as the other realms I've learned about here at school.

"Hey," I respond, just so she doesn't think I'm trying to be rude. I may not trust her – but I don't want to tick her off, either.

It looks like Lucy is uneasy, too, because we walk in awkward and unsettling silence. It's only when we get close to Gomada Academy that Lucy clears her throat and queries,

"Did you attend the Halloween party?"

Since Lucy and I don't spend much time together (other than

the mandated meetings by Cole), I guess it makes sense that she's asking me that question.

Is she just making conversation, or is she trying to talk about what happened? Either way, anxiety floods my stomach in the form of tight knots.

I hesitate to regale Lucy with the events of the party that are personal to me and those I care about.

I refuse to tell her about Anja and Nora's magical date. I also refrain from mentioning that Cole was my date to the party. I'm still having trouble believing that, myself.

I'm not ready to tell anyone about my shared moment with Cole pre-ghost-attack. I don't know if I'll even tell Nora. Based on her reaction when I told her about the kiss...

"Yeah," I affirm, not sure what to do with my hands as we get closer to the school. I end up tugging nervously on my pink bookbag.

A bright flicker cuts through the falling snow up ahead. It looked like a spark. Fire makes me nervous.

Nearing the school, we pass a shadowy alcove. I'm surprised to see Cole, lighting a cigarette. Smoking this close to school is a big risk. It's so gross that he chooses to smoke at all.

My disdain for his behaviour evaporates from my mind when he lifts his head, making eye contact with me.

Should I smile at him or wave? Shouldn't I try to talk to him if we went on a date together (even if it ended in paranormal attacks)?

My chest twists into even more knots than before when he abruptly puts his head down, getting back to his habit.

An impossible-to-ignore sinking feeling takes precedence over my stomach issues.

Lucy clicks her tongue, eyeing Cole, too. "He's not only risking his health, but his place in the Academy by engaging in such riff-raff behaviour," she observes.

I swallow unevenly, but an embarrassed lump stays lodged in my throat.

Was it my imagination, or did Cole ignore me just now? I know Cole doesn't like associating outside of his own race. He only does it when he has no other choice.

It has to be me.

Did I do something to make him lose interest in me (big surprise)? Or is it something much bigger than that?

"It's a disgusting habit," I agree, hoping that Lucy will buy my poker face.

"Did you go to the party?" I change the subject by inquiring.

Lucy nods, pulling her phone out of her pocket. It looks like a calendar alarm is going off. From the outside looking in, Lucy is very organized. We have more in common than I thought.

"Yes, I did. Excuse me, but I have to pick up a book from the library before class. I'll talk to you later," she announces, putting her phone inside her bookbag.

"Bye," I murmur as she breezes ahead of me, probably in a hurry to run her errand before first period.

The cold weather overtakes me for a moment as I stand still, listening to the wind. I turn quickly.

Someone is watching me.

It wouldn't surprise me if the Headmistress or even Greyson, the Head of Security, is behind this.

I should be used to this feeling by now. Between ghosts and faculty members, someone or *something* is always keeping tabs on me.

Students of all races and ages rush past me. Class must be starting soon. Nothing seems to be out of the ordinary. It's almost like a regular day. Giving into that sentiment is dangerous, though.

In any case, I force myself toward the school. I must keep my grades up and do my best to improve my Air Affinity.

The normalcy of life beckons, even when you're tangled up in a web of horror stories.

Nora and Anja are at the library, so I walk alone to Feara. This draws attention away from the six of us. Even though some Nymphs and Enchanters frequent Feara (not everyone steers clear of other races), I still feel conspicuous as I open one of the doors.

It's no better when I'm in the lobby of the dormitory. Every nerve in my body is burning, pushing me to go home.

I know I'm unwelcome here, but I have no other choice. Now that the ghost can manipulate both mind and body, we need to work faster. In some ways, it was a little easier when we thought the ghost was just killing people. Using students as puppets for some sick and twisted end is much worse.

I board the elevator, recognizing no one along the way. I press 'three,' fidgeting against the back wall.

I'll be seeing Cole for the first time since this morning, making me unable to control my nerves. The way he ignored me earlier further proves that Nora and my other friends would be unwilling to accept that there is (or *was*) anything between us.

The elevator drops to a halt, the doors sliding open. I disembark quickly, hesitantly approaching Room 301.

It sucks that I'm already here. If the room was further down the hall, I could've had more time to prepare myself.

The hallway is empty as I look at my phone for the time. It's almost seven o'clock. I'm early.

Can't go home now, I think as I knock quietly on the door.

Shuffling occurs from the inside. The door unlocks and opens. I can hardly breathe.

Cole looks down at me, paralyzing me with uncertainty. I have no idea what he's thinking, or how he views me now. It's hard to keep track.

Cole's green eyes dart to either end of the hallway. After that, he jerks his head into the room, pushing the door open. I step inside, wondering if he's being secretive because of the meeting or because of *me*.

Professor Xhao's criticism takes over my thoughts. It's hard to concentrate. Everything she told me – how I'm *remedial*, how I'm as skilled as a child – rattles around in my skull, causing me to think twice about getting involved with anyone.

Cole closes and leans against the door. His black hair is wet. Maybe he just got out of the shower. That explains the misty air.

"Hey," he says, folding his arms.

I don't know how to act. "Hi," I eventually muster out. My throat is like sandpaper.

"What's up with you?" Cole frowns.

Cole seems to have a knack for noticing details. He must notice that I'm freaked out of my mind right now.

Will it do me any good to be honest?

"Did you see Lucy and I this morning?" I blurt out.

Cole is bewildered but doesn't hesitate to answer. "Yeah. Why?"

This changes nothing. I knew he had. It just would've been easier if, by some miracle, he hadn't.

"You acted like you didn't," I admit, hugging my chest so I don't look as shaky as I feel.

Cole's frown disappears. He puts his head down. He's deep in thought.

This can't be good.

He leans off the door and approaches me. It doesn't take long. "I just think it's better if no one knows," he confesses.

It takes me a painful minute to register his statement.

*I just think it's better if no one knows **about us**.*

"Why?" I ask even though alarm bells are going off in my mind.

I'm sure I won't want to know the answer to this question – but here I am, asking it anyway.

Cole looks *caught* again. He clears his throat. "It's easier," is all he says. "I like flying under the radar," he adds.

I can't say I disagree with the whole 'flying under the radar' thing – but what about the rest? How is it *easier* to hide a relationship – if that's what this is? Yes, it'll invoke scrutiny from everyone else – but it makes me wonder...

Is he embarrassed of me?

Is it because I'm a Nymph?

Cole's discriminatory comments from the beginning of the term begin to poke at me like angry wasps.

I'm startled when Cole steps closer to me – closer than is socially acceptable for acquaintances.

"Arya?" he asks.

My heart skids to a painful stop when he takes my hand.

I swallow back an enormous lump in my throat. "You still like me?" I ask, dumbfounded.

Cole rolls his eyes, but I notice a fond smile as he does. "Maybe," he says, feigning dismissiveness.

I look down. Cole's large, rougher hand is holding onto my smaller one. I can sort of understand why he wants to keep *whatever it is* we have a secret – maybe for now, anyway. But what about later? How is this a permanent solution?

My head is spinning.

"And you?" he asks, shocking me.

His face and stance are casual, but his green eyes are *concerned*. He's wondering if I'm re-evaluating everything.

My eyes dart away from him. Being in Cole's orbit is like standing beside a fire. It's warm and inviting, but it's lethal and hard to breathe if it's left unchecked.

I'm playing with an inferno. I know I'll get scalded, but I can't help myself.

"Yeah," I confess quietly.

I gauge him for a reaction, promptly caught off guard when

he leans toward me.

Oh, my God! We're going to kiss again!

Memories from our past *moments* swirl around inside my head. It's hard to focus.

His lips press to mine. Any hope of concrete thought is now helpless mist.

I place my hand on the inside of his elbow. Cole takes hold of my windblown hair. Sparks flicker from my neck down to my spine. It feels so good but so frightening, like the fire is spreading out of control. It's hard to fight back the shiver that knocks into me.

The door begins to unlock, extinguishing the blaze between us. Cole pulls away from me and lets go of my hair. I release his blue hoodie. Even if I didn't want the fire to become ash, I have no choice. Cole is already at his dresser, acting like nothing happened.

Did he use his Shifter speed to get away from me?

Diego and Lucy enter the dorm. Diego nods at me and gives Cole some weird boy-like greeting. Lucy and I make brief eye contact before I turn to regard Cole. His eyes may casually drift from Diego's to mine, but I see a flicker of something *different* in them. I turn from him, not knowing what to think anymore.

My feelings for him make no logical sense. He was cruel to me for so long. But I can't fight it anymore. I want to be close to him, despite our past, despite everything that threatens to undo us.

At the same time, Cole wants to keep everything so secretive. I can't shake the feeling that he's embarrassed, that there's more to his reasoning than just 'flying under the radar.'

Is this the price I pay if I want to be with him? Maybe it would be good to keep things quiet for a time – with ghosts, uncertainty, and leering school administrators around every corner of this school.

If that's all true, why do I feel so disheartened?

Thirteen

COLE THE AVENGER

It's late Wednesday night – right around curfew. I'm heading back home after spending way more time than I should've at the library. I almost flunked a History pop quiz today, so I decided to catch up on my damned readings.

I've already been attacked by a 'ghost hybrid' and its crazy-ass minions – the last thing I need is Professor Qadir ripping me a new one for 'slacking on my academics.'

Then again, what's the point of worrying about school shit when I can get killed or zombified at any second?

The ghost is getting ballsier: it's ripping through campus whenever it wants, even with people around. We all need to be on our guard. No time for other stuff.

The only problem is, I *am* thinking about other stuff. I'm thinking about Parents' Weekend and how my dad clammed up about Ryker's uncle (which is sort of on-topic, but still). I'm thinking about school and how I'll ever 'pass *well*,' to quote Professor Qadir. I'm thinking about my family and knowing that I'm not pleasing them. Normally, I wouldn't care, but thanks to

Dad, I guess it's starting to eat me up inside. And as much as it sucks, I'm also thinking about her.

I'm worried that Arya isn't a fan of the whole 'let's keep things a secret' situation.

It's easier for both of us if we keep quiet.

It's not just because she's a Nymph. I don't like people knowing my business. It comes with being a Germain. It's why I used Mom's maiden name to apply to school. That's why I never Shift on campus, even if it gets weird comments from everyone. It's why Diego and I don't hang out with many people.

Our private lives are, well, *private*.

Okay. So even though I have all these good-sounding reasons to keep things classified, it doesn't take away from the fact that it still bothers me that I have a thing for a Nymph. In the beginning, I went along with it because I wasn't gonna do anything about it. No one would ever know. But now that she likes me back...

It's complicated. I don't want to lose her. But I also don't want everyone on my ass about it.

I've always been pretty vocal about not trusting other races. I tolerate Lucy because of Diego. I get along (-ish) with Ryker and Nora because of the ghost. It's not like I'd have much to do with them otherwise. Sneaking around to have ghost-hunting meetings in my dorm means no one knows I associate with them. And that's good.

If anyone found out about me dating a Nymph, I'll not only be shit on for being a hypocrite, but I'll also draw attention to myself. I can't let people talk *more* about me, discovering more about me. It'll only lead to bigger shit – like people finding out about the Tedla.

I'd rather skip those floggings.

Still, maybe I need to explain myself to Arya. I'm sure she'd understand the family angle, but I think she's worried about the *Nymph* angle. I'm worried because I know she's right.

No matter which way you slice it, I'm still being a dick.

I just don't want to hurt her feelings in the process. I may be a jackass, but I really do care about her. This would just be so much easier if she wasn't–

My thoughts are interrupted when I spot Lucy and Ryker hovering close to a shadowy corner of Feara. From what I can remember, Diego told me he and Lucy were studying today in Feara's tiny common room. Maybe that's why Lucy's in this neck of the woods.

But why is Ryker here? What are they doing in the dark?

That's sketch.

I'm just about to go about my business when Ryker bends down and kisses Lucy in a way that's way too fucking tender. It's hard to tell if she's kissing him back, because it's over almost as soon as it started.

Rage burns in my chest. Anger pulses through every vein in my body. I want to kill Ryker and then kill him again.

What the fuck is he doing? That's his friend's girl! Why is he–

"Just think about it, okay?" Ryker asks.

They are standing way too close. I didn't notice that before, but the kiss made me see things from a whole new warped angle.

Lucy stares at him, but I can't tell what she's thinking. She has a damn good poker face.

What the fuck is happening?

I should've listened to my gut instinct this entire time.

Enchanters and Enchantresses aren't worth shit! They shouldn't be trusted! I knew Lucy was going to screw with Diego! She messed with my mind and made me think she was halfway decent!

Fuck! The two of them are worthless!

This is why we need to stick to our own. Shifters have a code of ethics or whatever shit Taylor calls it (but she hangs out with other races, so I tune her out after a while). We wouldn't do this to each other.

Ryker is walking in my direction. I use my Shifter speed to dart around the other side of Feara. I peer out from around the cold brick.

Lucy is retreating from the dormitory, several paces behind Ryker. It's clear they're not leaving *together*, or anything like that. At least that means I won't have to watch any more of this bullshit.

My whole body is shaking. I can feel the Tedla wanting to come out.

Whenever I get frustrated, angry, or irritated, my emotions fuel my Shifting powers – whether I want them to or not. Sometimes, I need to let out my anger in other ways if I refuse the urge to Shift. I may have to do that now, so no one – especially Ryker – gets their head ripped clean off their shoulders.

Gripping the brick with my right hand, my knees buckle, forcing me to grit my teeth.

Get yourself together! I shout at myself.

I'm so pissed at both of them – especially Ryker. Diego was good to him, and this is how the Enchanter repays him? Asshole.

As much as I hate Ryker, I know I can't Shift. If I do, he'll die.

Every bone in my body is tensing up, preparing to be broken and reset to be a part of the Tedla's skeletal system. Everything in me is screaming *do it*.

I shut my eyes. Will I be able to get over this urge?

When it comes to people I care about most, like Diego, it's tough *not* to Shift, especially if it's because I'm trying to protect or avenge them.

I may not be able to resist the Tedla. My eyes are churning into an oval shape. My vision is a thousand times better, even if it was pretty good before. I look down at my right hand. My knuckles are white against the dark brick.

I'm going to lose this fight. The Tedla will chase Ryker down and kill him. I'll wake up covered in blood. It wouldn't be the first time. I've lost control more than once. But no one's ever died because of it. No one human, anyway.

I need to make this stop!

I can beat up Ryker in human form tomorrow morning.

If I get caught Shifting and attacking a student, I'll be expelled, for sure!

A loud *snapping* sound hits the air. I slump into the brick.

Fuck! I'm in transition!

Shifters everywhere will pick up on this. Any Shifter who has an alter ego with heightened senses will hear me Shift, even if they're in human form. Even worse, I'm screwed – and so is Ryker – if I Shift and find him.

I try to remember where the security cameras are. I try to think about how I can't afford to get caught.

More snapping sounds. My clothes are ripping apart. My vision is getting blurred from all the pain. I clench my teeth together and drop to the ground, fighting with all my might to at least slow down the transition.

Snow-crusted grass prickles against my body as I roll around like an idiot, trying to buy time – as much as possible.

Maybe if I can hold off the Tedla for more than a few minutes, I can get control – or Ryker can get back to Gleera. If he gets back to Gleera and I Shift, I *might* be able to avoid killing him. The Tedla knows that a dorm full of Enchanters and Enchantresses could spell trouble (I didn't mean for that to be a pun) – it may not overpower my mind enough to crash through windows and hunt Ryker.

God help me! Nothing I'm doing is working! My spine is aligning into position. My bones are snapping and resetting.

I can't stop the transition. I can only slow it down. And even *that* is failing, because I'm almost fully Shifted now.

For the first time ever, I feel helpless and angry that I can't do anything about the Tedla inside of me. I hate Ryker, but I don't want to kill him.

For the first time ever, I'm mad that I'm a Shifter.

Now on all fours, I race for the Shifter's Field. I can *feel* the Tedla's pull to turn around and crash into Gleera. I'm trying to let my mind overpower the Tedla's. Usually, we work together. I guess I was too mad before to stop it – and now, it wants blood.

Man, I suck tonight!

The Shifter's Field is dark and deserted (thank God) as I begin to race around it, trying to get my body under control. I've probably been spotted by the three security cameras I just passed. Maybe all Clueless Grey will see is a blur, but still.

I can't take any more chances. I'm already trying not to kill Ryker. I also have to make sure I don't get expelled from this school – or worse.

The adrenaline is taking over. I want to go home and sleep – but there's no way I can calm down.

The only other option is to take out my anger on something else – but what? Where's that fucked up ghost when I need it?!

A low growl from the far left corner of the Shifter's Field catches my attention.

I thought I was alone. Why didn't the Tedla pick up on that? I'm too out of control – and now, I'm gonna pay for it.

My thoughts are beginning to race around in my head like that broken pinball machine I used to play at the arcade as a kid.

If the ghost is here, I'll be able to kick its ass! Problem solved!

*If I'm too pissed off and the ghost **is** here, it may kill me before I can do any real damage.*

Wait.

Ghosts don't growl. What the fuck is out there?

Now on two legs, I tense into a crouching position as I was

taught by Dad and even by Professor Qadir. I open up my fore-arms and fix my stance.

As I wait for the monster to show itself, I realize something.

That growl wasn't really a *growl* – not the way most Shifters give off warning calls. This one was different. It's almost like there was a weird twinge of laughter to it, which is why I got ready to strike so quickly. It was so messed up that I didn't want to take any chances, even with the new threat being on the other side of the Shifter's Field.

Dark bushes rattle, concealing my new attacker.

Man, I can't catch a break these days! I've got shitheads of all types coming after me. What the hell?

Even though the human part of me is scared as fuck, the Tedla isn't – not like it was with the ghost.

It's ready. It wants to fight. That must mean it considers whatever's out there to be its equal.

Now, I'm almost positive there's another Shifter in the Field with me.

Is the ghost controlling a Shifter? The scent is familiar, but not so much that I can pick out the creature behind the foliage. Either way, this entity could be zombified, like Patty and Lukas.

Great. Another threat to the school, to my friends, to me. Things just keep getting better and better!

A huge-ass *figure* rises from the bushes. Pure terror hits me like a sack of bricks, overwhelming the Tedla's confidence.

This creature is way bigger than I thought – over seven feet. Even bigger than the Tedla. What's more, it's not walking on two feet. It's on all fours, and it's stomping – no, *clomping*.

The moonlight illuminates the thing just as it's approaching the centre of the Field – too close for comfort, even with the distance between us.

I'm frozen to the grass. I know what this creature is – and I might know its alter ego.

It's a Cuda.

I'm in deep shit.

I drop my arms, fixing my stance as fast as possible into a submissive one. The Tedla doesn't like it, but I know I have to do it. I recognize the Shifter's scent. I'd know it anywhere.

We learned about Cudas in Shifter Studies. They're a cross between a hyena and a horse. Their hooves can stomp through metal. Their teeth can rip through ships. They're unpredictable, just like Tedlas.

I can't say that the Tedla's scared – but I sure as fuck am!

The Cuda's not getting into an offensive or defensive position. It's not pawing at the grass, ready to charge me. It's not growling-laughing anymore, either. Its red eyes are just *staring* at me.

Normally a Cuda is supposed to be aggressive and out of control. This one is strangely calm. And I know why.

This isn't some random Shifter from school. This isn't some mindless zombie student that's being controlled by the 'ghost hybrid.' This Shifter has done an awesome job of distracting me from wanting to rip Ryker apart. Instead of feeling violent and mad, I'm cut down to size. I'm ready to Shift back. Hell, I'm ready to turn tail and run home – as long as no one will be able to find out about it

It's Professor Qadir.

His alter ego is wickedly badass. I'm impressed by it, but I'm also shitting myself. Plus, now is not the time to be impressed.

His red eyes are studying me. Silence overpowers both of us – but it's not like he needs to say anything. I'm wondering how he knew I was going to do something reckless and crazy. Maybe he saw me on the cameras? Maybe he was patrolling the grounds and heard me Shifting behind Feara?

Either way, I need to get my shit together before he kicks my ass – and something tells me that Shifter Qadir is actually *worse* than Professor Qadir.

Qadir must believe that I've calmed down and won't cause any shit, because he slowly backs away from me. I guess the fact that he's a prof also means that *he's* not going to attack *me*. Maybe his plan was to restrain me if he couldn't get me to calm down.

The way my prof is moving, though – it's not what Shifters do when they're threatened, when they've been outmatched, or whatever. His red eyes stare at me the entire time.

He's waiting for me to change my mind.

That makes sense. Qadir knows how wild the Tedla can be. As a Cuda, he has to fight those same impulses.

It's only when he slips back into the shadows, never turning his back on me, that I suck in a normal breath for the first time.

I guess 'lecturing' as the Cuda just means scaring the shit out of me. It's still pretty damned effective, though.

Sweaty and exhausted, I decide to gather up what's left of my energy and head home.

I knock on the door, rocking on my heels every few seconds. I'm nauseous. I'm also nervous and confused as fuck.

I *hate* being left in the dark. I have a few theories about what I'm doing here, though.

Headmistress Frow wanted to see me in her office 'as soon as classes were finished for the day.' The email she sent me at seven AM not only woke me up, but made me crap myself.

She's probably going to give me detention for breaking curfew last night and almost losing my shit on another student. Maybe she'll expel me. Or worse.

Basically, this can't be anything good.

The door swings open.

I'm face-to-face with Professor Qadir.

Oh, shit!

It's like nothing happened last night. He's still dressed in one of his fancy brown suits. His black tie is straight. His short dark hair looks combed. He's normal, straight-laced, which makes him even scarier.

"Ah. There you are, Mr. Hudson," he says as if I've taken forever to get here. I guess class *did* end ten minutes ago...

"Sorry I'm late," I mumble, just in case he Shifts in the next ten seconds and offs me.

He opens the door wider and steps to the side. "I'm just satisfied that you've come," he states as if it's a miracle that I actually listened, for once.

He's probably right about that, too. I don't listen much – not even when it counts. But I guess when it comes to Qadir, I *do* pay more attention. He's a fucking menace as a Shifter. I respect him for it.

I walk into the neat-looking office that always smells of sage. The antique window offers a bit more light in the dimly-lit space. Snow is falling from the already-darkening sky. Winter *did* come early this year – and so did whatever punishment I figured I'd eventually get for being, well, *myself*.

Headmistress Frow is at her desk. Her creepy hawk Familiar is perched on the bar thing to her right. Its beady little eyes glare at me. Maybe it senses what I am.

Who knows what these weird animals pick up on, anyway?

All I know is that this bird freaks the shit out of me.

"Mister Hudson," Frow says. "Please, have a seat."

As Professor Qadir closes the door, I sit down at the only chair across from the Headmistress' desk.

At least no one else is joining us this time. That may make this a little bit easier. Maybe.

I see Professor Qadir leaning against the door in my peripheral vision. Maybe he's making sure no one spies on us. Great. That can only mean one thing,

"I'm assuming you know why we've called this meeting with you, Mr. Hudson," Frow begins.

So, the email came from Headmistress Frow, but she and Qadir planned the meeting? I suspected that, but still.

"Yeah," I finally admit.

There's no way out of this. I might as well just give in now.

"I Shifted irresponsibly," I proclaim, knowing that's what Qadir would say.

If I take *some* responsibility for this, maybe they'll go easy on me (yeah, right).

The Headmistress looks at me like I've just kicked her hawk across the room. I can feel Qadir's stare.

They must think I'm not being serious. I'm trying to be – in a way. I'll say whatever it takes so I'm not kicked out of here. Deep down, though, I *do* know what I did – what I was planning to do – was bad. Even if Qadir and Frow don't know I was trying to stop myself from ripping Ryker apart, they still figure I was up to no good out there. After all, it's *me*.

Neither of them say anything for a while. Finally, Frow looks over at Qadir.

"Professor Qadir has a solution to this troubling situation," she tells me, but is still looking at the Shifter.

It's weird, but I think I see worry in her blue eyes.

I don't get it. Ever since Frow became Headmistress, she's acted like she knows all the answers. Now, she looks like she doesn't.

Before I can worry about whatever punishment I'm in for,

Professor Qadir leans off the door and approaches the Headmistress' desk. He leans against the front of it.

"Mister Hudson, you've demonstrated that your alter ego is capable and proficient under fire. However, you're still as reckless and irresponsible as last year."

I slump in my chair. Here I was, thinking I was doing a bit better, and then–

Professor Qadir reaches into the pocket of his brown suit. He pulls out something small that jingles with his touch. He looks uncomfortable as he walks up to me. As soon as I look at what he's holding, I understand why.

Damn!

This will be way worse than suspension, expulsion, detention, or anything else they could do to me to get me to behave. This fucking sucks!

"I'm sure you are well aware of Curios, Mr. Hudson," Qadir continues, holding the necklace out to me. It's a gold chain with a dangling ball made of the same metal.

I bet there's dry Marjoram in there – the herb that stops Shifters from transitioning. It's a gross-as-fuck herb that makes you sick when it's in close range. The lecture about Curios was the one time I actually listened in Shifter Studies class. The dry form of the herb is the worst.

There's more to Marjoram than that, though. If you've already Shifted and the herb is used on you, you'll go down like a sack of bricks. You can't fight or defend yourself. Veteran Shifters like Professor Qadir can usually hold off the herb's effects – at least for a while. Or they need to get a ton of it on them for it to work. But the stuff makes a difference for someone like me, who's only been a Shifter for less than ten years.

"You have much promise – but you're dangerous," Professor Qadir asserts, making me feel even worse. "However, I don't want to see you leave the Academy. Your grades are improving. You're even fraternizing with students from other races. I personally think you can improve, with assistance."

My teeth smash together. So, I'm improving – but it's not enough? And what the hell is he talking about, *fraternizing with students from other races*? Is he talking about Arya? Ryker? Lucy?

Do Frow and Qadir know that we've all been meeting in secret to stop the ghost? But wouldn't the rest of us be in attendance if that was the case?

Fuck. If Qadir is seeing this, then I'm sure others are, too.

I can't do this. This can't be me.

On the bright side, though, at least Frow and Qadir don't seem to know about the ghost-hunting meetings.

Qadir holds out the Curio to me, the little gold ball moving from side to side in his palm. I'm getting sick just looking at it.

"I hope you understand the gravity of the situation, Mr. Hudson," my teacher tells me. "The Headmistress wanted you expelled. I wanted to give you a second chance. This was our compromise."

Shit. So, I was a goner until Professor Qadir suggested this?

I didn't want to be expelled, but I didn't want *this*. Not being able to protect myself by Shifting is a pretty lousy punishment – especially with a ghost waltzing around here!

But I can't protest or whine to Frow and Qadir. I can't let on that I know too much about the ghost. Can't risk further scrutiny on the others.

"I know you Shifted with dangerous intentions," Qadir says firmly. "With all that's taking place on- and off-campus, we can ill afford that."

I reach out my hand. I have no choice. As soon as my fingers touch the gold necklace, nausea creeps into my stomach. I put the Curio around my neck.

I feel fucking helpless right now.

"I'm glad you've agreed to our terms, Mr. Hudson," the Headmistress says, startling me.

The Curio made me forget about her and the red-tailed hawk that's still eyeing me. With the uncontrollable nausea and despair surrounding my current predicament, I can't focus on much else.

"I do hope you take this alternative form of disciplinary action seriously. This is your last chance before expulsion is our only option," the Headmistress finishes, still as a statue at her desk.

Yikes. I guess I'm not too far from the noose, after all.

"I curated this Curio, Mr. Hudson," Frow surprises me by explaining, rubbing her red fingernails as she speaks. "I've spelled it specifically so only Professor Qadir or myself can remove it."

Well, damn!

Enchanters and Enchantresses always make Curios – *that's* nothing new (and another reason why I don't trust them). Sometimes, Curios are spelled even more by making specific people the only ones who can remove them without experiencing extreme pain. It's a way to 'keep Shifters obedient,' Qadir said last year.

I think it's a way to keep us locked up and screwed over.

I clear my throat. I try to speak, but I'm too sick to talk. I just nod my head in agreement.

Now that I'm forced to wear the Curio or face getting expelled, I can do nothing to protect my friends when the ghost comes back. That *strategy* we were planning won't go so well now that I can't Shift.

If I didn't let my anger get so out of control, I wouldn't be in this shit right now.

Fourteen

ARYA'S TURMOIL

I'm in the Dining Hall by myself on Thursday night. Nora and Anja's LGBTQ+ club meeting changed to tonight, so they had a quick dinner after class before attending. Makayleigh and Alan are busy, too.

I don't know where Cole is – it's been hard to get a hold of him today. That's probably why I'm sitting here, feeling like I'm going to get an anvil dropped on my head any time now.

At the same time, after going through midterms, Parents' Weekend, and a chaotic Halloween party, it's nice to have some quiet time. I'm way more introverted than my friends. Some alone time might help me recharge, even though I dislike being by myself in public.

I'm in a room filled with people. The ghost probably won't come here. Then again, it crashed a Halloween party – what's to stop it from invading the Dining Hall? I try not to think about that as I take a sip of my bottled water.

I try to look on the bright side, something Mom has been encouraging me to do since I was a child.

It's pasta night. That improves my mood a little bit. Midterms are over. I've already gotten some marks back. I'm doing really well in History and Nymph Studies. Professor Xhao hasn't been lacing into me since midterms finished. Maybe things are starting to look up for me – at least, as far as school is concerned.

The good mood that I'm trying to create doesn't last very long when a sudden shadow looms over me. Then, I smell that sickening candy scent that could only mean one thing.

"Can't find any friends to eat with you, halfling?" Désirée taunts, turning my blood cold.

Désirée's brown hair is in a ponytail. She's dressed head to toe in an expensive ensemble: a white dress with a black trenchcoat, showing off her curves. Her black cat Familiar is at her heels, as usual. Even though the cat is about as wild as a mountain lion, I'd rather deal with it than its mistress.

Maybe Désirée is going on a date, which makes me wonder why she's wasting her time with me. But knowing Désirée, she probably can't resist an opportunity to make one of her victims suffer. I should be used to this by now.

Instead of giving her a retort (not that I'm skilled in that department), I resume eating. Maybe if I ignore her, she'll disappear. But with my kind of luck, that probably won't happen.

"What's the matter, Arya? Too dim-witted to come up with a comeback?"

I grit my teeth in anger – maybe because she's right – but I still don't react.

"Fine. I know of a surefire way to get your attention."

She's just baiting me. She won't do anything in a public place. Professors are everywhere.

A strange odour wafts through my nostrils. I jump a mile when I see a ring of fire starting to pool around my tray.

Visions of training at the Nymph's Field, and what happened to me because of Samuel Minders (burns, a ruined outfit, nightmares) causes awful splotches to cloud my vision.

Without thinking, I grab my bottle of water and dump it all over my tray and the fire. Thankfully, I just sat down to eat, otherwise, the fire may not have been put out so quickly.

I look up at Désirée in shock. Why would she do something so dangerous in the Dining Hall? Someone could have been killed!

There's no point asking her. She's already laughing and walking away from my table. She probably didn't want to stick around in case a professor or security spotted her.

Thanks to the ghost, there's a lot more *presence* here – but extra security doesn't seem to stop typical teenage bullies like Désirée Chapin and Samuel Minders.

My heart is beating in my throat. I can't think. I feel like I'm going to throw up. I push my chair out and run for the nearest bathroom, vomiting as soon as I get to the toilet closest to the entrance.

I'm sitting on my bed, trying to calm myself down. All I can see in my mind's eye is the red-orange flames circling my dinner that I never got to enjoy.

I just can't deal with fire.

When did it start? When Makayleigh and I accidentally combined our Affinities during Field Practice class? Or when Samuel almost killed me during my Field Practice midterm?

Part of me thinks it also concerns Professor Xhao and her apparent dislike for me. If Samuel was going to injure severely and maybe even *kill* one of her favourite students, would she have stepped in sooner? What if it was a full-blooded Nymph who was in trouble?

A dark, quiet part of me is angry about this. How could a professor get away with blatant discrimination?

Nora's words ring through my ears as if she said them just an hour ago instead of a few weeks.

For a school that's supposed to be so inclusive and tolerant, Professor Xhao is being a complete bitch.

This is so hypocritical. We need to talk to the Headmistress.

I remember promising Nora that I would think about approaching Headmistress Frow regarding my issue with Professor Xhao. But I worry about Professor Xhao finding out – or that Headmistress Frow may side with her colleague instead of a half-breed.

Maybe saying nothing is the best course of action – even if it feels like the coward's way out.

A knock on the door startles me. No one really comes to visit our dorm other than Anja and Makayleigh. And Nora never forgets her keys. I untangle myself from my pink throw and hesitantly approach the door.

It can't be the ghost. Ghosts don't knock.

So why am I still scared?

I unlock and open the door. If I'm going to get attacked, I'll grow a backbone for once and fight back. Maybe the solution to my bully problems is to just suck it up and fight fire with fire (bad choice of words).

But it's not Désirée at the door, or even Samuel (I doubt he knows where I live, but it wouldn't be hard to figure out).

Cole frowns at me. Maybe I look as surprised as I feel.

I guess I'm also thrown that Cole is here to see me but won't pick up where Désirée left off. Sometimes, it's hard to separate what *used to be* from *what is happening*.

"Hey," he greets me.

My knuckles are white against the door. "Hi," I respond as I let go of it.

Cole's green eyes look me over – but not in the normal way a boyfriend would. "You okay?" he checks. "You look freaked."

He's concerned about me? That fills me with relief. Maybe Cole cares about me more than I thought. Maybe he's *not* embarrassed of me.

"Désirée set my tray on fire in the Dining Hall," I admit quietly.

Cole rolls his eyes, unimpressed by my statement. "She's a real pain in the ass," he comments, shifting from one foot to the other.

When Cole moves, I notice he's holding something: pizza pockets on a napkin.

Why would he be walking around with food – especially food they don't serve at the Dining Hall?

"I kind of heard about it," Cole tells me, holding out the napkin to me.

Did he bring me dinner?

When Cole's eyes glance down at the food and then at me, I slowly reach out and take it from him.

I guess it shouldn't surprise me that people are talking about what happened in the Dining Hall. Of course, students would see that and not a professor or security guard. 'Désirée picking on the halfling' has a frightening ring to it.

"Um, thank you," I murmur, still shocked by his gesture that doesn't seem to be very *Cole-like*. The Cole I was used to was a bully and a narcissist.

But maybe I was wrong. I keep seeing evidence of that the more time I spend with him. There's definitely more to him than I would've thought in September.

Cole gives me a small smile. "Yeah. No worries," he dismisses, but it looks like my words did something to him. He looks awkward.

"Do you want to come in?" I ask. "We can watch a movie or something," I tack on in case he thinks I'm referring to something else.

Cole doesn't seem to, though. He shrugs and leans his hand against the doorframe. "Can't. Need to talk to Diego."

I feel like there's more to what he's telling me, but he doesn't elaborate. Maybe if I knew him better, I'd be able to pick up on what it is.

Did something happen to Diego – other than what happened the night of the Halloween party?

Cole glances up at me, interrupting my thoughts. That overpowering fire wells inside me when his green eyes stare into mine. A strange sensation pulses between my legs, making me flinch.

"Another time, okay?" he seems to check.

Thank God he didn't notice any of that.

Being alone with the cute and mysterious Cole Hudson makes my stomach twist and my throat as dry as the desert. But it also makes me... Excited?

Just thinking about it makes that pulsing sensation return, so I put it out of my mind as quickly as possible.

"Yeah. Sure," I agree.

Maybe when that 'move night' comes around, I'll be less of a chicken than I am now.

Cole nods at me. "By the way... You have powers, too," he tells me, stepping away from the doorway. "You can electrocute her – or at least blow her away."

It doesn't sound like he's joking. Wasn't that sort of along the lines of what I was thinking earlier?

However, there are two problems with that...

"I don't think any kind of air attack would work," I frown. And I don't want to–"

"Get into trouble," Cole finishes for me.

Instead of berating me for that as he would have in the Fall, he gives me a small smile.

"I get it," he adds gently.

"Are you okay?" I finally ask, still unable to shake the feeling that there's something he's not telling me.

Cole looks surprised by my question. "Yeah. Just a long day," he responds.

Maybe I'm imagining things? It just seems like something is *different* about him.

"Okay," I assert, not wanting to pry. "Thanks again for the food. It was really nice of you."

Again, Cole shrugs dismissively. "It's no big deal," he replies, leaving my doorway without another word.

Shooting up in bed, I force my still-dazed eyes to look across the dark dorm room. Even though nothing seems out of place, I *feel* like something is in the room with Nora and I.

I've been having nightmares about the ghost (and now, its zombie-like minions) for the past few weeks. But nothing compares to reality: what the ghost is capable of, and all we don't know about it.

The scariest part is that the ghost can control students to do its bidding. At our meeting, Cole told us that Patty Merlotts, a fellow Shifter and friend of Taylor's, never would have attacked him under normal circumstances.

The ghost is clearly *doing something* to those thought-to-be-dead students. But what is it? And why? Is the spirit closing in on us, wanting to add us to its collection?

I glance at Nora's bed. She's resting peacefully. If Nora doesn't sense anything, maybe my mind is just playing tricks on me. It wouldn't be the first time.

The thing is, ghosts don't care about things like locks, doors, walls, or gates. They're going to get in, whether you want them to or not. And that's the second-most terrifying thing about all this.

What really scares me is the chance that any one of us could be next. It's not like the ghost needs to try very hard to make that happen.

I pick up my phone in an effort to distract myself. It's Friday, around three AM. I really wish it could have been earlier than this – like before midnight, for example – so I could call Mom. But at the same time, I know I probably can't do that. My parents are still on-edge about the safety of Gomada Academy. If I call home, they may take that as one more tick in the 'going back home' column.

As much as I don't want to be *next*, or anything like that, I also don't want to leave school. I don't want to abandon my friends. I may only be a half-Nymph, but I want to do everything I can to protect them and the school.

I think of Cole and the possibility of calling him. After everything that's happened between us, I'm pretty sure we're *together*. My inexperience with boys means I have no idea what I'm doing.

I wish I could discuss this with Nora, but she isn't Cole's biggest fan. She was already shocked that I kissed him. I don't want to make things worse by explaining the rest of the story to her. But, knowing Nora, she'll eventually circle back to the issue and ask me about him, all over again. Nora doesn't forget anything.

Stop thinking about boys! I chastise myself. *There's a ghost manipulating people, and you're thinking about a* **boy**?

At the same time, Cole isn't just *any* boy. He's the most infuriating, obnoxious, and difficult person I know. He's also the most surprising, complex, and caring guy I've ever met.

Even though Cole's not one for hand-holding or PDA, his gestures – the chocolate bar, dinner, swooping in to protect me and my friends – all point to him being a kind person underneath all of his relentless snark.

My feelings for him still surprise me – especially the *heat* that captures me when he's close by. But I'm also worried about what will happen if I push too hard. All of this could go away. He could go back to being the boy who broke my grandfather's pocket watch.

I'm thrown off track by something moving in my peripheral vision. One quick glance at the window shows me that it's nothing but a tree branch with some snow hanging off it. Maybe the white was what startled me?

I squeeze my temples with my index fingers. I'm getting a headache. I'm exhausted, but too afraid to go back to bed.

I jump a mile when someone taps me on the shoulder. Now that I'm going to class, I need to be on the lookout for more enemies.

I whirl around on my heel, almost spilling my just-purchased coffee all over myself. Coffee isn't my favourite beverage, but I know it's a necessary sacrifice whenever I can't sleep.

A peel of laughter from Makayleigh does nothing to alleviate my surprise. "Man, you look like a zombie! No offense," she adds when my face must have dropped further.

The ghost and its zombie-like minions...

"Sorry," I breathe. "I didn't sleep well last night."

Makayleigh adjusts her purple coffee thermos and gives me a playful frown. "Don't apologize to *me*, silly," she teases. "You *may* have to apologize to Professor Xhao if you nod off this afternoon, though."

"That'll work," I grimace, alert faster than a jack-in-the-box. Makayleigh laughs at my response.

"Did you get your midterm marks back yet?" I ask as we walk past the small café inside the school.

"Yeah," Makayleigh grumbles. "Nymph Studies went well, but there's definitely room for improvement in Field Practice."

I rub her arm in consolation. At the same time, I'm relieved that someone else is struggling, just like me. Then again, Makayleigh may be exaggerating. She's very studious and often doesn't accept marks that others would.

"Same here," I agree solemnly. "I only got sixty percent on my midterm."

Makayleigh stares at me in shock as we pass a cluster of talking Nymphs. We recognize them from our Field Practice class.

"What?" she breathes. "There's no way what you did was worth sixty percent. That's total BS."

I smile at Makayleigh's urge to protect her loved ones. She's a lot like Nora in that way.

"It's fine," I try to dismiss – though I know it isn't. "I'll just have to work harder."

I'm about to take a breath to try and get my bearings before History class when my eyes dart straight ahead. There's Cole, walking down the hallway with Taylor. She looks *regal* with her flowing red hair and crimson trenchcoat.

My heart skips a nervous beat when Cole looks at me and gives me one of those 'boy waves' with his index and middle fingers pressed together.

At least it's an improvement from last time.

I'm too stunned to respond right away. Eventually, I give him a small wave.

"I didn't think you two could stand to be in the same realm together," Makayleigh murmurs to me as the two Shifters pass us.

A sting of regret hits me like an angry hornet. I hate lying, and I hate secret-keeping, too.

But I know I can't say anything to her – or to anyone.

If I push too hard...

"He's become marginally more tolerable," I try to explain, causing Makayleigh to snicker.

"If you say so," she responds, pulling her phone out of her black jacket. "Oh, Alan wants to know if the gang can come to his place tonight. Pizza and video games," she pretends to scoff – but I know she loves both.

"That sounds fun. I'm in," I reply.

I'm not good at video games, but I like watching other people play. Plus, spending time with people who don't know about the ghost might help me feel less unnerved.

But that does nothing to extinguish my guilt.

I'm keeping so many secrets – the ghost, my relationship with Cole...

It's too much.

Fifteen

COLE AND THE CURIO

I go through Friday in a daze. I know I have to come clean to Diego about what I saw on Wednesday night. I just don't know how.

I'm still pissed at Ryker – and I'm not too thrilled with Lucy, either. They're both scum. This is why I hate girl stuff and relationships.

This is also why you should never trust any race other than your own.

Diego knowingly frowns at me when I meet up with him after Field Practice class.

Damn. He knows something's bugging me.

"What's up with you today, Hudson?" he asks.

He's not wrong to be suspicious.

Diego must be picking up on my discomfort about the Curio.

A Curio will give off this *vibe* that other Shifters can feel, too. If they're not wearing or touching it, they'll still be able to Shift – but if they get too close, they'll be weirded out.

I didn't want to tell anyone about this – not even Arya. Not being able to Shift – my true nature – is a prison sentence. But I need to be honest with Diego – at least about this.

I finally yank down my black hoodie to reveal the gold necklace. Diego's jaw drops.

"That's a fucking *Curio*!" he breathes, reaching out a hand to grab it.

Most Shifters wouldn't touch a Curio or something thought to be one. But Diego's different.

The Curio must do something to Diego: he winces and lets go of it as fast as he can.

"Holy shit! That thing is fucked up! Why are you wearing it?" he asks as we begin to make our way back to the dorms.

If I start talking now, there's no going back.

"I almost killed Johnson a couple of days ago," I admit as we pass some Shifter girls on their phones.

This afternoon was supposed to be chill. We were going to get some shut-eye before pizza night. The only thing is, after I spill the beans to Diego, he won't want to nap.

Diego laughs once. "Why? You know he could probably send you straight to Hell. It's probably where you're going anyway, but why get an early boarding pass?" he adds, causing me to glower up at him.

This is it.

"He kissed her – Lucy. Outside of Feara," I confess after a long and weird silence.

I kept trying to talk myself out of being honest – but that wouldn't be right. Diego's my best friend. I suck at being honest with people – and I know that's not a good thing. I owe Diego the truth.

Diego stares at me, his hazel eyes looking – well, *not* what I expected. I figured Diego would already be on his way to ripping Ryker apart. Instead, he looks weirdly calm. Must be the shock.

"Did she kiss him back?" he asks.

I frown. I didn't expect that. "I don't know. Maybe," is all I answer.

I doubt that will make things better. Maybe I shouldn't have said anything in the first place.

Who cares if Lucy kissed him back? Something had to have happened for Ryker to make a move like that. Neither of them are innocent.

"Qadir found me after I Shifted that night. He calmed me down."

There's no reason to tell Diego that our Shifter professor scared the shit out of me as the Cuda.

"The Curio was what I got instead of expulsion," I finish.

Diego frowns at me. "So, you can't Shift," he seems to think out loud, "which means if the ghost comes back for you, you're a goner."

He's still not saying anything about Lucy. Or Ryker. Then again, this ghost shit is way bigger than that. Poor bastard has to pick and choose his battles.

"Already thought of that," I state sourly. "And Frow spelled it so only she or Qadir can take it off."

"Damn," is all Diego says. He looks deep in thought – and not in a good way.

"Well, looks like you'll need me around, for protection," Diego smirks.

I bet he's using jokes and shit to ignore the fact that Ryker kissed his girl.

"Shut up, Jasper," I order as we close in on Feara.

"Maybe we can get walkie-talkies. You can radio me if you're scared," he continues, biting back a cackle.

"I've never felt safer in my life," I grumble, making Diego laugh his annoying, I-got-you laugh.

"But seriously – what will you do if the ghost zeroes in on you again?" Diego inquires.

We're at Feara now. The snow is getting thicker. I should be used to Winter, being from Houssan, but I still think it's a drag. Diego loves it, though. Even though he's staring at me intently, you can tell he's not in a hurry to get inside.

I shrug. "I dunno," is all I say, but for the first time, I wonder if Qadir's decision to 'Curio' me was on purpose. Not just so I can't Shift in general, but so I can't get involved with the ghost any more than I already have.

Fuck. I feel even more helpless than before. Worse than that, I'm letting everyone down – even shithead Ryker. I won't be of any use to anyone if there's an attack. And if *I* get attacked, someone has to help *me*. I'm not used to needing help.

Things will only get worse from here.

Things are pretty shitty, already. The Curio has made my life more fucked up than usual. I have this weird *pins and needles* feeling all the time. I feel it even when I'm sleeping.

This stupid POS may cost me my life – and my friends', too.

Friday night is cold and boring – so far, anyway. Diego goes to hang out with Lucy – probably to chew her out, but I don't ask for details.

I look down at the golden necklace around my neck that I've been covering up with hoodies and t-shirts. It might as well be a fucking ball and chain (what's the word for that – 'ironic?').

I'm a prisoner. This thing is depriving me of what makes me, well, *me*.

Even if I can't change this, I'd still like to think that I could be of *some* help to our ghost-hunting group. I'll just have to figure out *how* to make myself useful.

The Tedla can't help me now. It's a first.

And it sucks balls.

I can't just sit here in my dorm, feeling sorry for myself. I need a distraction.

Plus, it's Friday night. Since when do I just sit at home, by myself, when the weekend is here?

Since Diego got a girlfriend.

Since I'm still too weirded out about being seen with mine – if that's what she even is.

Part of me wishes I didn't feel this way about her – that I wasn't so wrapped up in the 'what other people will think' kind of thing. But even if I feel crappy, I know I'm doing the right thing. I've grown tired of people staring at me and trying to figure out my business. It started with the Tedla and Germain thing – and then ended with stupid classmates and loser Enchanters. Lukas is a good example.

I just want to be left alone – for people to know nothing about me.

I don't think Arya understands that, which worries me. Sure, I could explain it better – but I also think my 'let's keep this quiet' thing makes her feel shitty, too. Then you factor in bitches like Désirée and Arya must feel even worse. I don't want to hurt her the same way, but...

The Dining Hall thing distracts me. The entire school was buzzing about the half-Nymph's pasta being set on fire by Désirée Chapin.

What would I have done if I'd been there?

Part of me knows I wouldn't have done anything to stop it. I'm mostly relieved I hadn't been there, so I didn't have to make that call.

I pull my phone out of my jeans pocket, deciding to call or at least message her. Calling would be better, but I do not sit around on the phone for hours at a time.

It's probably a lame thing to text. Expressing myself isn't my thing.

It's embarrassing, but I keep checking to see if she's read it. So far, no dice. Maybe she *is* pissed at me. She didn't seem that way in-person, though.

I don't know what to think. I don't know Arya as well as I could by now. I wish I could've made more of an effort.

If I don't do something more to show her I'm into her, she may close up for good. The problem is, I suck at girl stuff. Diego has always loved teasing me about that.

Here goes nothing.

Walking into Meera's lobby is humiliating–not just for the usual reasons. I feel like I'm *grovelling*, or whatever it's called.

I'm standing in front of Room 407. As I'm about to knock, I realize there are no sounds of life from the inside. No talking, shuffling around. The Curio may stop me from Shifting, but it doesn't stop me from having heightened senses.

Don't panic.

So the girls aren't home. Maybe they're out. That would explain why Arya didn't answer me.

No need to freak out.

But the ghost is getting reckless – maybe even careless.

Crashing parties.

Getting close to the dorms.

Letting its little zombie henchmen interact with students.

Who knows how many other zombie-attacks have happened since Halloween? Maybe their victims didn't live to talk about it.

For a split second, I think about breaking the door down. If they've been taken, there could be clues inside. Or, if they're in there and not breathing–

Don't think like that.

If the ghost showed up, the girls would scream and attack it. Call attention to themselves.

Don't panic!

Too fucking bad! I'm busting through this door. Nora was already targeted once. Who's to say the ghost didn't return for both of them?

"Cole?"

I turn with the call. Nora and Anja are staring at me like I've grown a second head.

Nora frowns at me, suspicious. "What are you doing here?"

Fuck. Now I gotta explain myself. I guess I hadn't really thought of Nora seeing me, which was pretty dumb, since she lives with Arya. At least Nora's not zombie-slash-ghost bait. But where's Arya?

I try to look casual. "Looking for Arya."

Nora looks concerned, or mad. Anja looks stumped.

*Did Arya tell Nora about us? What is **us**, anyway?*

That's kind of why I need to talk to Arya.

Maybe I'm overreacting. Everyone knows Arya and I hate each other. No one knows the truth. Maybe Nora's worried because Arya's 'bully' is looking for her.

"For Mentor stuff," I try to add.

Nora looks even more suspicious. "At nine PM?" she asks, folding her arms.

I shrug. "Qadir's on my ass," is all I explain.

"How poetic," Anja responds flatly.

Obviously, Nora has filled her in on who I am because Anja doesn't seem thrilled that I'm looking for her friend.

I'm used to having a reputation that precedes me, as Diego says. Germains usually have one – but not in the same way that *I* do.

"Is she here?" I inquire, even though I already know the answer.

"No," Nora responds. "She's hanging out with sane people."

Well, at least I know Arya's not in trouble. But I'm disappointed I won't be seeing her tonight.

Damn! I don't like this! All these *feelings* I have for someone I used to hate! For a *Nymph*!

They're impossible to ignore. They're making me do crazy shit. I feel *drawn* to her. She's like the Curio – trapping me against my fucking will.

"Hilarious," I counter. "Fine. Catch you later."

As I walk past them, Nora grabs my arm.

She has an Earth Affinity. Nymphs and Enchanters with those powers are usually super happy-go-lucky. But right now, Nora looks pissed, and her grip is pretty intense. She eyes me defensively.

We may be working together, but she doesn't trust me.

"Leave Arya alone," she warns.

I roll my eyes at her threat. "Have I done anything super-shitty to anyone lately?" I counter, interested in hearing her response.

"Just because we haven't seen it, doesn't mean it hasn't happened," Nora is quick to fire back.

I'm surprised. Here I was, thinking I'd stumped her. Nora must be pretty dead set on keeping me away from Arya. Maybe she *does* know more than she's letting on...

"Think what you want. I really don't care," I tell them, even though I'm not sure if that's exactly true.

Nora lets go of me. "I've been experimenting with poison ivy lately," she tells me in a creepy voice.

Huh. Poison ivy. It's not really how I want to spend my weekend.

"Later," I tell them, continuing on my way faster than usual.

Nora and Anja snicker behind me. I tell myself I don't care. But maybe I do – a little.

Sometimes, being alone is, well, *lonely*.

I unlock the door and enter my dorm, close to nine-thirty at night. I had to smoke beforehand. I'm surprised Professor Qadir or the Headmistress didn't jump out of the shadows at me while I was lighting up.

I know what I'm walking into. Diego is home, blasting rock music – specifically, *The Drug In Me Is You*, by Falling In Reverse. My Shifter hearing can pick out the tune even if Diego's wearing headphones.

Anyway, this isn't a good sign.

Diego lowers his headphones when he sees me.

"Hey," I greet him, turning halfway to close and lock the door.

"Hey. Where'd you go?" he asks. "I keep thinking we need to have some sort of chip on each other now that we're all getting targeted."

I give him a *look* as I approach my bed. "Out for a smoke," I lie.

It's not a *complete* lie, but it's not the whole truth.

If anyone could help me with my Arya situation, it'd be Diego. But I don't want to go there. Plus, Diego's got his shit to deal with.

Diego nods in my peripheral vision. I sink onto my bed, rubbing my flaring temples. For a Nymph with an Earth Affinity, Nora packs a fucking wallop.

"If we try to stick together, the ghost won't be able to pick us off, one by one," I think out loud.

"Awwww, look who's all *go team*," Diego throws at me, his hazel eyes sparkling with fucking glee as he makes fun of me.

He's all jokes so I won't ask about Lucy.

"Shut the hell up," I snap, pulling out my phone from my jeans pocket. I'm surprised to see a message from Arya.

> Just got back from hanging out with Makayleigh and Alan. You?

Well, that explains why she was radio-silent.

Nora was telling the truth. I guess I'm not very trusting of people, either. She and I have *that* in common.

Diego cackles, adjusting his headphones and resuming his rock meltdown. His hazel eyes look tortured when I glance at him. He looks busted up beyond repair. But he says nothing about it.

Being free of Lucy is the best thing for him, even if he looks and feels like shit.

"So... Things are good?" I finally ask.

Diego looks surprised by my question. Due to his Phoenix senses, he doesn't adjust his music or lower his headphones. He does glance at me briefly before asserting,

"I'm still alive and not zombie bait. I guess I'm good."

That's *not good.*

"Jasper," I finally order, after an awkward silence.

"Ryker and Lucy have a thing for each other," he confesses without looking at me.

I can't say this surprises me. It's not like you can kiss someone you hate. I know this better than anyone.

"It happened while Ryker was helping her control her powers."

"Did you kill him?" I ask.

Diego turns his head from side to side, considering. "I wanted to. But there's no point. Setting him on fire wouldn't solve anything."

I disagree, but I know it's not the time to be a dick.

"Lucy said she wanted time to figure out what she wants." Diego fiddles with his phone, maybe changing songs.

She wants time to figure out **who** *she wants.*

"Thanks for having my back," Diego adds but still doesn't make eye contact.

"I wish it never happened in the first place," I admit.

Diego doesn't know what I mean. If he had never fallen for someone outside of our race, his living Hell never would have happened.

This could have been avoided.

And I'm making the same mistake.

Sixteen

ARYA'S SATURDAY MORNING

I'm just getting out of the bathroom after showering and dressing. Nora and Anja are going for a Winter nature walk in the Nymph's Field, so they are complying with the Academy's strict rules.

They invited me, too, but I didn't want to be a third wheel. Not only that, Headmistress Frow wants me to 'stop by her office this morning.'

I don't know what to expect. Her email was brief. That's definitely not like Leona Frow, who likes schedules, timing, and details.

Maybe she was too busy to explain herself. Whatever the reason for the rendez-vous, I'm terrified she's discovered our ghost-hunting meetings.

I walk to my unmade bed, towel-drying my hair. I pull my pink duvet over my tangled sheets and pick up my phone. Mom texted me just a few minutes ago.

> Good morning, honey. Do you want to video chat sometime today?

As I begin to answer, my phone vibrates. I never get notifications all at once like this.

I'm even more surprised to see that Cole is the sender.

Want to get breakfast?

I'm stunned. Cole doesn't seem to be the 'let's get breakfast' type of guy. Then again, I don't know him well.

I'm also excited that he wants to hang out. Maybe I was wrong about him being embarrassed of me. Maybe Cole's just a private person. I should probably ask him about this when we're together, though. I was too nervous to bring it up. Now, I really want to know.

Yeah. That sounds fun.

I hope that doesn't sound too silly. I'm still trying to figure out how to talk to Cole in a way that's *not* insulting, defensive, or aggressive.

Cool. Is nine okay?

I look at the time on my phone. It's eight-thirty. If I hurry up to fix my hair and choose a better outfit, nine o'clock should be okay. Better still, I'm almost positive it's Pancake Day.

I'm looking forward to this more and more with each passing second.

Sure. I just have to stop by the Headmistress' office on the way.

I keep thinking about the reason for the meeting.

Could Professor Xhao have told Headmistress Frow about my 'ineptitude' in Field Practice class?

Before I can run with that theory, Cole messages me again.

> What'd you do this time?

I roll my eyes at his teasing, but a smile plays on my lips. I stop smiling as soon as I realize that.

*My God. I **do** like him.*

Wasn't the kissing and Halloween party enough to tell me that?

*How does he feel about **me**, though?*

My thoughts swarm around inside me like vultures circling a dead animal. I'm so confused. But this is why I'm going to meet with him.

Even though Cole acts cool and collected (when he's not raging mad, anyway), I'm sure he has questions for me, too.

> Nothing!

I send him another message so he knows I'm not mad at him.

> I don't know why she wants to see me.

> Weird. TTYL.

Wow. If *Cole* thinks the situation is weird, something is *definitely* wrong. Maybe it *is* about our meetings. But if that's the case wouldn't everyone else be called in, too?

I'm rushing to get ready. I don't bother drying my hair. I hastily apply some mascara and lip gloss. Tugging on my boots and racing out the door, I barely remember to message Mom.

The walk to Gomada Academy is quick, but my anxiety prolongs the trip.

When I finally get to the Administration side of the school, I look for Headmistress Frow's study. I know I should have its location memorized by now – but here I am, heart pounding, looking for the golden letters plated on the wooden door that could spell out my demise.

If Professor Xhao told Headmistress Frow about my poor performance in her class, I worry the Headmistress won't entertain my version of the story.

Nora was right. I should have said something sooner. When I tell Nora about her *rightness*, she'll be tickled pink.

Headmistress Frow's office door is closed. She leaves it open, even ajar, a lot of the time – making herself available to her students.

This is suspicious.

Is she trying to ward off the ghost? But why do that when spirits can move through walls and doors?

I knock lightly on the door. A strange silence ensues.

I should be thinking about what to say if Headmistress Frow asks me about Professor Xhao. All I can think about right now is the ghost.

There's still so much about the spirit that remains a mystery to us. Has one of us ever *seen it* walk through a wall? Could it be more human than ghost?

I snap to attention when I realize that more than a few seconds have passed since I knocked on the Headmistress' door.

"Headmistress Frow?" I call, knocking again.

Could she be doing errands, or speaking to a colleague elsewhere? These are all likely possibilities, but I'm still worried. Am I being paranoid, or did something happen?

It's getting hard to tell. Everything in Gomada seems to be *piling up* – the ghost, my bullies, bad teacher experiences, and a new relationship. It's hard to keep track of it all.

When the quiet continues, I decide to let my anxiety get the better of me. I turn the doorknob in an experimental, I-may-get-into-trouble-for-this kind of way.

It's unlocked. If Headmistress Frow isn't in her office, there's no way she'd leave it unlocked!

I open the door slowly. "Headmistress Frow, it's Arya Will–"

Everything seems neat and tidy, like always. Nothing seems out of place – except for the fact that it's pitch-black in here and Leona Frow is nowhere to be found. Her laptop is open as if the Headmistress was in the middle of something before stepping out for a quick minute.

Maybe I'm just getting worked up over nothing...

I'm backing out of her office when I discover two beady eyes staring at me. I almost throw up from fear.

That's her Familiar, I realize.

He's poking his head out from around her desk. Why is he on the floor?

Big birds freak me out, so I jump a mile when the hawk leaps and flies up to me. His actions are quick but not malicious. He seems insistent.

How could a bird be insistent or anxious? Then again, Familiars are very intuitive. After spending more time with Ryker and Lucy, I've seen the intelligence of Familiars first-hand – even freaky ones, like Zola, the black panther.

Leopold doesn't get too close: he hovers at eye level and cries out to me. I can actually see *fear* in his eyes.

"Where's the Headmistress, Leopold?" I ask, certain he'll know what I'm saying.

Leopold flips backward and flies back to where he was before. I rush behind him, a sudden lump in my throat making it hard to swallow.

When I see what's in front of me, I cover my mouth and scream.

"Hey," Cole says into the phone.

I'm shaking so badly that it's hard to tell if his voice is trembling, or if it's all me.

"Where are you?" he asks. "Did you get in shit with Frow?"

"You need to come!" I explode before he's finished talking.

"What happened?" he asks, calmly but firmly. He's not kidding around anymore.

"In her office. Please come," I weep.

That didn't make sense. But I can't be logical right now.

He just has to get here.

I need him.

"Calm down. I'm coming. I'll be there in two minutes. Lock the door. Don't let in anyone else but me."

I don't know why Cole suggests that. It's not like the ghost – who's probably behind this – can be stumped by locks. I'm numb and disoriented. I blindly do what he says.

It's hard to move once the door is locked. I don't want to go back. But I know I need to.

I find the light switch and turn toward the desk. Unnerving shadows evaporate, illuminating the Headmistress' body. Her dead body.

Leopold is sitting next to her, his head bent low and red wings folded against his sides. His eyes are sorrowful. Mine are filled with tears.

A brief but loud knock on the other side of the wooden door makes me jump.

Have two minutes already passed?

Have I been frozen here for that long?

I turn around just as Cole says, "Arya, it's me."

I unlock and open the door. Cole opens his mouth to say something, but I grab his arm and yank him inside.

"Okay, what the fuck is – holy shit," he breathes, kicking the door closed as soon as his green eyes dart behind me.

Cole does something surprising. He rushes to the Headmistress, crouches next to her, and places his fingers on her neck. Leopold stays motionless as he works.

He's checking for a pulse.

Why didn't I do that?

Cole looks up at me, interrupting my thoughts. "She's dead," he announces, letting go of the limp person who was very much alive yesterday.

Leopold lets out a guttural, mournful cry. He begins to flap his wings, hopping from the carpet to the Headmistress' desk. Cole ignores all of this and gets back to staring at the Headmistress.

"You found her like this?" he asks. He's no-nonsense and calm right now, but he looks pale.

"Yeah," I tremble. "I – I got worried when she didn't answer the door."

Cole approaches the Headmistress' desk. He leans around the still-pushed-in chair and grabs for the drawer to her desk that we'd broken into just a few weeks earlier. I'm shocked when he pulls the drawer open in a lop-sided kind of way.

Cole begins to dig through the desk. "Huh," he says – maybe more to himself than to me.

"What?" I inquire, not sure why Cole's looking through drawers when we need to do something about the Headmistress.

"All that shit about Izaak Johnson is missing," Cole reports, continuing to shuffle through the desk.

"You think she was murdered, and that stuff was taken?" I gasp.

Cole frowns at me as if I'm missing something. "Pretty much," he responds. "If she's dead and stuff's taken from her desk, that's pretty damn suspicious."

I frown back at him. "So, you think Izaak took the photos and the newspaper clipping? Or someone who knows him?" I can't help but counter. "Why would all that be worth killing someone?"

Cole shrugs. "I'm not a detective. But this is shady as shit." He closes the drawer and looks over at me.

"What do we do? We need to report this," I begin to fret, on pins and needles.

Leopold is still erratic atop the desk. I now wonder if he led us there on purpose.

Cole has done a masterful job of ignoring the Familiar, but it looks like he's getting annoyed.

"There are cameras out in the hall," he says as if I should know this by now.

It shouldn't surprise me that Cole knows where the security cameras are within the school's walls.

"We need to report this to Greyson. Security. Somebody," he finishes solemnly.

There's a small pause between us that's filled with Leopold's yowls of sadness. Cole turns and shoots the bird a *look*. I'm surprised when Leopold glares right back at Cole and makes one final exclamation aimed at Cole's face. Cole rolls his eyes to the ceiling and then looks at me.

"Don't mention the stuff that's taken," Cole advises me. "But I think we need to have a bigger conversation with Ryker about his long-lost uncle."

I don't know much about Ryker or this 'long-lost uncle' of his. Ever since I got turned down by Ryker, I haven't wanted to spend a lot of time with him. But this is important.

If the Headmistress is dead, I'm assuming that her death is

somehow connected to the ghost and the abductions that are taking place on school grounds. It seems like Izaak Johnson has something to do with all of that – especially if his photos and newspaper clippings were taken from the Headmistress' desk. Who knows what more could have been taken from the school without us noticing?

If Ryker can shed some light on his uncle, we may be one step closer to figuring out the mystery that's been plaguing us since the beginning of the year.

And it may reveal the identity of Leona Frow's killer.

Henry Greyson is walking away from us just after telling us 'to stay close by or in our dorms, in case we need to answer more questions.' I'm nervous, but it's probably a routine thing to say during a murder investigation.

A murder investigation.

Is that what things are coming to? Murder?

Granted, we assumed the abducted students were murdered, too – but they were very much alive the last time we saw them.

Then again, we don't know if all of the taken students have been *returned*. And we don't know what the ghost is using them for – or when it will decide they are disposable. We also don't understand why any of this is happening, and it's only getting worse.

Cole and I are standing in the hallway. To our left is Leona Frow's office. Gomadian security guards are everywhere – in the Headmistress' office, in the hallways. We hear their voices carrying from one end of the hall to the other. It's scary, even though I know they're here to help. One of them mentioned that the

Headmistress' murder may cause the King and Queen of Vyquean to send over more military personnel.

Since the Vyquean monarchy rules over Chimara and Gomada, I guess it makes sense that the King and Queen would be involved in something as big as the murder investigation of a school official.

It's still weird to say that a 'King and Queen' will take action in a crisis like this, not a President. Further proof that I'm in a really different realm – one that's nowhere close to being as comforting or as familiar as the Overworld.

Cole jerks his head to the left, capturing my attention. "Come on," he tells me.

I frown at him in confusion. "But–" I begin to protest.

"Greyson knows where to find us," Cole interrupts, turning to look down at me. "Let's get something to eat." His green eyes look different than they did just a minute earlier.

I swallow a lump in my throat. I'm starving, though I didn't realize it until now.

I guess Cole is right. There's nothing more we can do – right now, anyway.

The Dining Hall is filled with celebratory voices of students enjoying their weekend. I wish I could shut them out. I'm so disoriented that the noise is making me light-headed and nauseous. It just doesn't feel right that people are having fun after Leona Frow's tragic end.

I look up at Cole, wondering what he's thinking. He still looks pale, but otherwise, it's like nothing happened.

I'm not sure if he'll be okay with this, but I feel like I need to be closer to him – closer than I am right now.

I still can't believe that the Headmistress is gone. She seemed like a kind person – and now, she's no longer living.

It's not fair.

I'm reminded of Grandpa's sudden death. Grief tugs at my throat, making it difficult to function.

Any one of us could be next. It's too much for me to handle. If Mom and Dad had suggested I come back to San Francisco today and not a few weeks ago, I might have gone home and never looked back.

I reach out and take Cole's left hand. I know he doesn't want people to find out about us, but surely this has to be different. Someone *died*. Cole and I discovered the murder scene. I can't go through another second of this without some kind of human contact.

It looks like Cole is letting this hand-holding happen. He doesn't let go of my hand as we go down the aisle of a half-full room of eating students. It's hard to read him and even harder to keep my composure. Despite my internal battle, Cole's close proximity and touch are comforting. His hands are the opposite of what I expected. Instead of being rough and yellowed from cigarettes, they're smooth and warm.

I could get used to this.

I hope it continues – especially when I feel scared, helpless, and confused, which is pretty much all the time. Those feelings should have been discussed as prerequisites in September's welcome email from Gomada Academy.

We get into line, Cole angling himself so we're still standing together. The soft, comforting *safeguard* between us shatters like cheap glass when someone calls Cole by his last name. He drops my hand and turns. I turn, too, though I already know who called him.

Diego is filing into line with Taylor. It looks like they were in the middle of a conversation that got interrupted when Diego spotted his close friend.

"Man, you're hard to track down!" Diego goes on, smacking Cole on the arm as if in reprimand.

Cole narrows his eyes at his friend. "What am I, your wife?" he snaps back.

Taylor scoffs at Cole's retort. "I told you to look here first, Diego," she tells Diego, as if *she's* reprimanding *him* now. "You know what Cole's like on Pancake Day."

Diego grumbles something in agreement. I'm too busy trying not to cry in front of three Shifters and a room full of dining students and faculty to get what he's saying.

Taylor suddenly looks down at me, causing me to swallow back the enormous lump in my throat. "Hey, Arya," she greets me.

I'm surprised she remembers my name from the first day of school. I remember asking her if she knew Cole because I was trying to track down my Mentor before doing anything else.

I nod and give her a small smile, knowing that if I talk, it'll sound weak and pathetic. No need to tell the entire room what I already know.

Even with ghost abductions and murders, Cole still sees being with me as some kind of dirty, embarrassing secret. Him dropping my hand like I'm radioactive waste and not his date or girlfriend is the only clue I need to know the truth.

All I'll ever be to him is a secret.

And I'm not okay with that right now.

"Want to have breakfast with us?" Taylor asks me. "The way these two eat, one of us may have to perform CPR on them."

I clear my throat. "No, thanks. I'm not hungry."

Cole's green eyes dart to me in my peripheral vision.

"This *is* the food line, you know," Diego teases me. His hazel eyes look playful, not mean.

I give him a tiny smile. "Just came for coffee," I tell him, glancing at Taylor. "Next time, okay?" I check, so she doesn't think I'm being rude.

I'm stunned that I can make this much conversation under the circumstances.

Taylor waves her hand dismissively, her red ponytail moving as she goes. "Sure!" she smiles. "Catch you later."

Before anything else can happen, I turn on my heel and rush into the kitchen. I know from Dining Hall rules that if you're just getting a drink, the beverage bar inside doesn't require waiting in line. Hopefully Taylor and Diego just think I'm forgetful and not purposeful in my actions.

I guess I just figured that Désirée, Samuel, and Professor Xhao would paint target signs on my back. I thought Cole was finished with all that. But now, I find myself longing for a good fire battle with Samuel, or a catfight with Désirée. Even a demeaning one-sided argument with Professor Xhao would be preferable.

Cole hurting me like this – maybe without meaning to, which doesn't make it any less painful – is much worse than any threats or demeaning comments my enemies could ever dish out.

It's hard to unlock the door to my dorm. My hands are shaking so badly that I try four times before I succeed. All I can think about now that I'm alone (sort of – there are Nymphs around but I'm invisible to them) is the dead body I saw earlier this morning.

The dead body.

Is that what happens when someone dies? Their identity and dignity are stripped away, and they're demoted to being called 'the body?'

Grandpa's funeral swings into view. I wish I had his pocket watch with me right now.

A chill spins down my spine when I realize that my *time* may come faster than it should (pun unintended).

Leona Frow's sudden demise was no accident. I don't have a lot of money, but I'd bet my bottom dollar that the ghost had something to do with the murder. And if it did, that means we could all die.

These thoughts make me shove open the door even faster, somehow without spilling my coffee.

I stop dead in my tracks.

The Headmistress is on the carpet before me.

I blink hard, thankfully seeing an empty room when I open my eyes. But when I close them again, the Headmistress haunts my mind. I don't think that mental image will go away anytime soon.

I lock up, hating my solitude. Nora and Anja probably won't be back for a while. Or, they may just be arriving now and will have something to eat before going back to their dorms. Either way, I'm by myself – and it's awful.

I know I could take advantage of this free time to video chat with Mom, but I don't think I'd be able to do it without begging her and Dad to pull me out of school.

As desperate as I am to go home, part of me thinks it would be the wrong decision to make.

I need to stay and protect Nora, Anja, Makayleigh, and Alan as best I can. Besides, if those *strategy meetings* ever happen in real life, I know those *on the inside* (as Diego likes to say) will need to be available to help.

If one person drops out, the rest could all die or get captured. I don't want to be the one to make it worse, even deadly, for everyone else.

I force myself to sit on my bed. My body doesn't want to bend. I place my barely-touched coffee on my bedside table. I pull my phone out of my jacket pocket (I'm still wearing my coat?) and look at the screen, just for something to do. I'd rather not be on my phone right now, but I need a distraction – any distraction.

I'm sorry, Arya.

I'm surprised Cole sensed my hurt feelings from before. On the other hand, it's not so unbelievable. Cole picks up on a lot of little details that others easily miss. But that doesn't make everything suddenly okay.

I'm not the kind of person to ignore or push people away, but I know I can't talk to Cole right now. I may say or do the wrong thing, and I don't want that to happen.

In addition to being hurt, I'm slowly becoming angry. Angry that Cole doesn't care about my feelings enough to move past his discrimination against Nymphs. Maybe if I knew he'd act differently, an apology would be worth more. But I'm honestly not sure if he'll change his ways.

What if I'm not enough?

I have no other texts – just the regular shopping emails from stores with upcoming Christmas sales. I close up my phone and place it on the bed, knowing I'm nowhere near ready to be thinking about Christmas.

Tears pour down my face, tainting my soft and dry pink duvet. I didn't know Leona Frow well at all – to me, she was in charge, the head of the school, someone to be feared and respected – but she didn't deserve to die. No matter what kind of a person she was – and I'm assuming she was kind, if she was so focused on things like comingling of the races and education for children – she didn't deserve to be murdered in cold blood.

Speaking of which, *how* was she murdered? I never saw any blood or gashes. It was almost like she just *dropped*.

Could it be that she had a heart attack or died of natural causes? But if that's the case, why was her office broken into at the same time?

No. This has to be murder. And we have to figure it out quickly before more people die. Maybe even one of us.

I'm so intent on my thoughts that I practically jump a mile when I hear the door unlock from the outside.

The door opens, revealing Nora. Her long black hair is pulled up into an effortless bun. Her black hiking boots have mud, slush, and caked dirt around the edges. She must have enjoyed her morning date with Nora. I'm happy Nora can still find some joy amidst the terror of living within the walls of Gomada Academy.

Nora takes one look at me and gapes. "What happened?" she gasps.

More tears fall down my cheeks. I've officially lost it.

Nora is by my side in an instant – coat and all. She sits on my left and places her arm around me. "Who do I have to kill?" she asks, though her tone is tender.

I might have laughed at that had the situation not been so horrific.

"Headmistress Frow is dead," I finally murmur, hearing the words coming out of my mouth in a foreign way. They don't belong to me. They don't belong to this world. They shouldn't be spoken out loud.

I can feel the tension in Nora's shoulders when she stiffens beside me. "What?" she breathes. "She's dead? There's no way! She's one of the most powerful Enchantresses in all of Gomada. It's probably just some dumb rumour."

"I saw her," I confess quietly. "Security from Vyquean and Gomada are everywhere."

Nora's jaw drops. "Oh, my God. Arya, I'm so sorry that happened to you."

I hesitate. As much as I want to unburden myself, I don't want to give Nora any more details. They're too awful to be sharing with other people. What happened to the Headmistress isn't some funny anecdote that should be recounted.

"The King and Queen of Vyquean may show up," Nora muses, causing me to look at her. I keep thinking she'll elaborate – Nora knows more about Gomadian politics than I do – but she never does.

"The ghost did it?" Nora inquires, though it's not really a question she's asking.

"That's what I think," I concur weakly.

The room is spinning all over again.

Nora looks at me, her blue eyes determined. "Well, if the ghost is starting to murder people, we need to do way more than backdoor gatherings. We need to actually do something."

Our phones vibrate loudly.

Frow was murdered. We're going after the ghost, ASAP.

Cole.

"How does *he* know about it?" Nora breathes. It looks like she's reading and re-reading the group chat message in surprise.

"He saw her, too," I finally admit, unsure if I should be saying anything about Cole. At the same time, I'm too drained to be worrying about things like secrets and lies.

Nora frowns at me. "So, I'm assuming he's your boyfriend now," she shocks me to my core by asserting. "You kiss him and never say a word about it again, but he creeps up in every story you tell or shows up when you least expect him, like some kind of viral infection."

I don't know what to say. I've never been good at keeping the truth from people.

On the other hand, I still don't know what Cole and I are to one another. That makes me feel a little better when I say what's truly on my mind.

"I don't know," I finally confess. "I – I think so."

Nora sighs. "I know he's your first, but just watch yourself, Arya. Guys like Cole aren't as fun as they seem. Especially him." She arches an eyebrow at me. "Once we're done talking about murders and spirits, I want to know all about this weird relationship of yours – and to tell you how bad of an idea it is."

Seventeen

COLE'S IN HOT WATER

Even though breakfast with my friends is just like old times – no Enchantress girlfriends, no 'ghost hybrid' stuff – I still feel like shit. And it's not just the Curio.

Arya's reaction to me letting go of her hand as soon as my friends showed up...

It was bad.

I guess I understand why she wanted to be close like that. Somebody just got murdered. I tried hard to give her what she wanted, but I choked in the end.

"You know her replacement will be twice as strict, Hudson."

Diego and I are in our dorm. He's playing a handheld video game. I'm listening to music, but nothing's really working in getting my mind off how badly I treated Arya.

Nothing's loud enough to drown that out.

I shrug. I can hear what he's saying over my music. "Whatever. If we all die, what does it matter?"

Diego is sprawled out on his bed. He turns around and glares across the room at me. "How d'you *really* feel?" he challenges me, putting down his console.

I roll my eyes. I'm in too much pain to smile, even though I did this crap to myself.

More or less on topic, is Diego feeling better, or is he just using more tactics to push his own shit to the back burner?

"Just saying what everyone else is thinking. If we all go after the ghost, some of us might not make it back," I continue fervently.

"Speaking of going after the ghost," Diego begins, moving his long hair away from his shoulder, "you're gonna have to tell them about the Curio."

I don't like the sound of that. But I know Diego is right.

I've only had the Curio for a little while. I guess I thought I had time to figure a way out. But now that Frow is dead, we'll have to move faster. That means I need to come clean about the Curio and that I may not be able to help if we go into battle against the ghost.

It's not like Qadir's gonna have a magical change of heart and just remove the damned thing from my neck if I ask nicely. I feel like a trained dog and not a person. And there's nothing I can do about it.

Or is there?

I may not be able to get the Curio off on my own, but thinking about this *change of heart* stuff snaps me out of my pity party.

I can feel Diego's eyes on me as I get up.

"Where're you going?" Diego demands. "What about the meeting?"

"It's only at five," I remind him. Like I'd forget about the meeting I just planned. "I'll be back long before then."

"Smoke break?" Diego asks, making me turn to look at him. His hazel eyes pierce into mine. "Dude, didn't you just smoke after breakfast?"

He sounds like Mom. Dad doesn't care enough to talk to me about things like smoking.

I shrug. "Your point?"

Diego rolls his eyes. "Nothing. Forget I mentioned it. You'll be huffing and puffing going up the stairs in about five years."

"Whatever," I scoff, putting on my boots and walking out.

The truth is, I'm not going outside to smoke. Diego doesn't have to know the real reason – even if it would've gotten him off my back. Sometimes, when I smoke too much, he rides my ass.

As soon as I close the door behind me, I pull my phone out of my jeans pocket. This won't be very comfortable, but I know I have to do it while I still have the chance.

Before the meeting.

Before more things go to shit.

> Can we meet?

I send the message before I change my mind.

I'm surprised to get an answer as I'm walking down the hall, passing some Shifters who are making out. They better live it up before the ghost comes back and kills all of us.

> I have to video chat with my mom.

> No worries. Just want to talk.

I suck at texting. Hopefully, she knows what I'm getting at. Between dead bodies, ghost attacks, and abducted students coming to get us, I have no clue what's happening anymore.

> I might be free later.

I almost fall down the last three stairs to the main floor of Feara.

I should have expected this. I did a stupid thing, and now I'm paying for it. The thing is, I'd probably do it again. I just can't help it. I'm a judgemental asshole, and so are a lot of the people at this school. Hell, even Nora gave me shit about looking for Arya the other night. I just don't know how to make things better.

I almost slam into some big-ass red-headed guy who's just opening the door to go up and not down. I don't know him, that's for sure. He passes me and gives me this *look*, like he wants to slam my head through a wall.

Get in line, pal.

I don't show him any kind of reaction which seems to piss him off even more. But he leaves me alone. Maybe he's too brainless or chicken to fight me. Or maybe he senses that a Curio is nearby, and doesn't want to mess with me.

Whatever. I don't want to get a life sentence with this fucking necklace because I kicked this guy's ass. I don't have time for losers, anyway.

What do I say to her? She didn't say 'no,' but she sure as hell didn't say 'yes,' either.

If I say nothing, I could lose her for good. But I genuinely don't know what to do.

Maybe if I'd give in to her now and again, instead of running the show, she may feel better about things between us.

I need to regroup. I can't do anything about Arya right now. I need to figure out how to come clean about the Curio. If I'm lucky – which never happens – maybe I'll figure out an answer to my problems with Arya, too.

I go for a smoke (sorry, Diego) near the Shifter's Field, using the wind as a cover.

It's not easy getting back here. Vyquean security guards are everywhere. It's starting to snow and snow hard, making them look freaky. I'm not a huge fan of law enforcement or authority, and it looks like other kids around here feel the same way. Students of all races are staring warily at the guards.

News of the Headmistress' death is spreading. Of course, the King and Queen send in the big guns when a Headmistress gets killed – but not when students are taken.

At least the Shifter's Field isn't as busy. Only a few Shifters are sparring up ahead. I'm far enough away that they can't see what I'm up to, and the wind is carrying my cigarette smoke in the opposite direction. Leaning against a tree, I try to take a few deep breaths, but nothing calms me down.

I'm so fucking stressed!

People are getting *murdered.*

The ghost is using kids as zombie bait.

I can't Shift because I was a dumbass.

The girl I like hates my guts because I was a moron.

One shitstorm at a time, I try to tell myself.

The Curio. I need to tell everyone about the Curio.

This has to be dealt with first, despite how badly I feel about what I did to Arya.

I hate talking about personal shit, but this will affect everyone. I couldn't have picked the worst possible time to be stuck with a Curio.

Maybe if I just come clean at the meeting (sort of, because Ryker and Lucy will be there and I don't want them to know I saw the kiss they shared), it'll be okay.

But how is *any* of this okay? People could fucking die because I lost my temper!

Stomping my cig under my boot, rage pokes at the backs of my eyes. I try to stop it, but its warmth spreads through my body like a small fire gaining momentum inside a dry forest.

I can't give into it this time.

I take a breath, letting the north wind seep into my lungs. It counteracts my self-hate and I begin to feel better.

I'll tell them at the meeting. No going back.

Just don't screw it up.

I gotta stop digging myself into these *holes* all the time.

I think about Frow, how her body looked, how rough it was to realize that she was dead.

I feel sorry for her. She was a pain in the ass (and I'm sure she felt the same way about me), but she didn't deserve to die.

If I get my way, the ghost won't be able to kill anyone else.

The Shifter's Field begins to lose its touch because I can't come up with any more solutions to my never-ending list of problems.

It's mid-afternoon. I go home to an empty dorm room. I text Diego to see if he wants to hang but he tells me he's with Lucy for the rest of the day. This piques my curiosity.

Maybe she's made her *choice*. I just hope it's a choice in Diego's favour – not just because he's my best friend but because rejection will cloud his senses and we need all hands on deck right now.

Enchanters and Enchantresses – they think they're so much better than everyone else.

Slumping against my bed, I pull out my phone and wonder what to say to Arya – for the trillionth time. Leaving her hanging isn't something I'm proud of, but I'm afraid to make things worse if I give her some half-assed response.

I guess if she dumps my ass, I won't have to worry about the judgement and ridicule from everyone. She wouldn't have to worry about it, either. It's not like Arya's Nymph friends will be accepting of her dating a Shifter. And even if they would be, they'd change their tune if they found out that Shifter was *me*.

Maybe it would be best for everyone if I just let her go.

But if that's the right thing to do, why do I feel like shit?

Being with Arya is something I want.

She's different from me. She's not super-negative. She's nice –

not an uptight bitch like the other girls around here. She's not full of herself. She's got a cute laugh. She's hot. And she doesn't make me feel like a freak. She's seen what I am and doesn't ask questions.

Maybe she doesn't know about the link between the Tedla and the Germains because she's a Nymph. That shouldn't surprise me. What surprises me, though, is how *good* it feels that she either knows and doesn't care or doesn't want to find out at all. Both make me feel more like myself when I'm with her.

What the hell does all this mean? If she makes me feel all these things, does that mean that I...

I must have fallen asleep (I can't seem to do that at night – shocker) because a loud knock at the door makes me sit up. I'm groggy. My temples ache. I ease myself off the bed, my phone almost falling off my chest when I do.

Fuck. I guess I never texted Arya back.

More shit to add to the never-ending pile.

I toss my phone onto my bed, staggering to an upright position. I avoid my tired and angry muscles and approach the door.

Ghosts can't knock, so I guess I won't be dying today.

When I open the door and see Arya with a pissed-off look on her face, I rethink that theory.

"Uh, hey," I mumble, rubbing my hair that's probably sticking out all over the place. I must have pulled off my beanie before falling asleep.

Arya doesn't look fazed by my shitty appearance or grogginess. "What's your problem?" she demands instead.

Well, that makes sense.

"Come in," I respond, opening the door wider.

She rushes inside. I close the door, ready to apologize for not texting her back and then for being a judgemental dickhead.

"I can't believe you could be so narrow-minded and cruel!" she rants, turning to face me as I lean against the door.

My heart is pounding in my ears, even if I look like I can't be bothered right now.

"The Headmistress was *murdered*, and you can't even hold my hand in the Dining Hall? Are you that embarrassed of me?" she snaps.

"I'm sorry," I respond, folding my arms.

"'Sorry' isn't going to magically make things better, Cole!" she counters.

Her brown eyes are full of tears, but she looks angry as hell. This is the angriest I've seen her – or *made* her – and I've seen her pissed quite a few times by now.

"I get it." I lean off the door. "I wasn't trying to–"

"Be a jerk? Hurt me? Are you kidding?" she interrupts. "The entire school hates me because I'm half-blooded, and you're making me feel even worse!"

Tears pour down her face. I open my mouth to try talking again, even if I know there's probably nothing I can do or say to make this up to her.

This is all my fault.

"I thought I could sneak around if it meant being with you, but it's not enough!" she cuts me off by asserting. "When I needed you, you couldn't give enough of a shit to even try!"

She must be really mad if she's swearing. I can see her shaking. I don't think she likes confrontation. I can't say I blame her for saying all these things – but that doesn't mean they don't hurt like a son of a bitch.

I kind of figured this would be a double-whammy for Arya – but now I know for a fact that it is.

What was I thinking? I was a total dick to her this entire time. Even though I really like her, it's pretty damn obvious I can't get past this whole 'she's a Nymph' thing.

I gotta be honest with her.

"I know I'm an asshole, okay?" I tell her firmly.

She doesn't budge an inch at my assertion.

"D'you think you're telling me something I don't know?" I add.

Maybe now isn't the time to pick a fight with her. It'll probably get me in deeper shit than I was before. But fighting with Arya is like lighting a match. It's weird, but this feels *normal* to us. Maybe because we spent most of our time together arguing.

I also can't help but think she looks sexy when she's mad at me. Her deep brown eyes narrowed at me, her arms crossed in defiance, her agility in matching me, a comeback for a comeback. It's fun watching her stomp away from me, too. Since she doesn't do this with other people, it feels kind of… unique that she does it with me.

Man, I'm fucked up.

"Oh, I think you're aware of it," she answers without missing a beat. "You only care about yourself. You don't think for one second about how your actions hurt other people."

"You don't know what you're talking about," I respond, causing her eyes to widen.

"Oh, really?" she shouts back. "Who are you actually *nice to*, Cole? Maybe just Taylor, for obvious reasons!"

I frown. "What the fuck does Taylor have to do with anything?" I demand, dumbfounded.

"A hot Shifter you don't mind being seen with in the halls? You tell me," she retorts.

I can't help it – I laugh once. "Are you actually *jealous* of Taylor?" I scoff.

A blush colours her cheeks. "Shut up!" she orders.

"You're right," I smirk, approaching her now.

Arya looks caught off guard by everything I'm doing. I'm loving it.

"She *is* hot. She is a Shifter," I go on, leaning my head close to hers. She doesn't move, but her eyes search mine angrily.

"But she's not you," I finish quietly, causing Arya's face to get redder. "I care about you," I admit softly.

"No!" she exclaims, shoving me away from her. "If you did, you'd accept that I'm a Nymph – which is the equivalent of the nicotine patch to you."

I can't help but scoff at that. "Good God," I groan.

"What, am I wrong?" she challenges me, her pink sweater with a melting dusting of snow on it not matching her tone or her eyes. "What do you possibly have to say that could make things better?"

I didn't know how to label how I was feeling until now. Standing here in front of the girl who has put up with all of my shit longer than most people ever have is proving something to me. Maybe the nap helped. Maybe she needed to verbally kick my ass like this for me to admit it to myself.

Once I say it, there's no going back.

Is what I'm going to say strong enough to change her mind? Strong enough to change *mine*? What about everyone else in this damned school?

"I love you."

Arya stares at me, a blank look on her face.

Maybe she doesn't believe me. Maybe she thinks I'm out of my mind. And maybe I am. Ghost abductions, near-death experiences, and this fucking Curio have me spinning out of control.

But what gets me into even more of a spiral?

Her.

She does.

And I can't deny it anymore.

I take one step closer to her when silence fills the room. "Arya," I prompt.

Say something. Hit me. Scream at me. Just do something.

The anger is drained from her face. I can't tell what she's thinking. Her body language doesn't give me any clues, either.

Maybe she's processing. She probably thinks I'm incapable of loving or being loved. Me being anti-Nymph probably doesn't help.

I don't expect her to tell me how she really feels. I'm probably the worst boyfriend (if I even am one) in the entire realm. I don't deserve her. But she has to know where I stand, especially if this is the last time we'll ever spend together by ourselves.

She frowns up at me. "Since when?" she demands.

I'm surprised she wants to find out more about my confession.

Swallowing a big-ass lump in my throat doesn't make this new 'revelation' any easier to admit. "The campfire."

It's true. The campfire is when it all started to click. Sneaking out to tail the Headmistress changed things, too, but it wasn't until the Shifter campfire that I noticed her.

It's all been downhill – a crazy rollercoaster ride – since then.

Arya is stunned that I've come up with this kind of an answer, an explanation. It looks like she believes me more than before. Could things be starting to click for her, too?

We are fire and gasoline, which is the only explanation for what comes next.

Our mouths crash together without warning but with fucking intensity.

She tastes amazing.

It's already hard to breathe.

I grab a fistful of her hair, pulling her ponytail out of place. Her arms are around my neck. My other hand is on her back, pushing her closer than ever.

Her vanilla scent and candy-flavoured lips ignite something inside of me. I'm so turned on right now. It's impossible to hide. I just hope I don't freak her out. It's not like we ever talked about this.

My heart feels like it's gonna explode as our kiss deepens. It's hard to think straight with my tongue brushing against her teeth and her hands clutching my neck, cutting off my oxygen even more than before.

My tongue is weaving its way inside her. Her hands are tangled up in my hair that's gross, but she doesn't notice or care.

I pivot myself so I can bend down and scoop her into my arms. She's like putty, folding around me like she was meant to do it. My hands cup her perfect bubble ass so I can wrap her legs around my sides.

She's fucking flexible – maybe because she can fly with her Air Affinity, who knows? – and it makes me even harder to think about how that elasticity could be used later.

Arya has both hands plastered to me as she digs her teeth into my throat. My eyes practically roll to the back of my head. I've never been kissed like this before. I've never been *wanted* like this before.

I hesitate as Arya and I continue to make out. Does she want to go further than this? Weren't we just in this huge stalemate? What if she's not ready?

I place her on the floor so she can back away if she wants to – but instead she grabs my hoodie and yanks it over my head. My staticky hair flies out but I ignore it. I grab her neck and snake an arm around her lower waist, begging her to do more.

Good God, she's taking off my t-shirt now.

I run my hand along her stomach, hearing her breath coming out in short, quick gasps. WIth both hands firmly on her waist, I begin to kiss her throat, her pulse on fire.

I'm startled when a strangled moan escapes her. Running my hands under the seams of her pink sweater, I look at her pointedly.

"Just do it," she breathes – or begs – which honestly makes the room spin.

Pulling her sweater over her head reveals a white lacy top. I can see a hint of a pink lace bra underneath.

Pressing my fingers into her collarbone, I trail my other hand across her chest. She stares up at me, lips parted and brown eyes wide with arousal and surprise – maybe she's surprised *by* her arousal.

I can pick up another scent in the room she probably doesn't want me to know about. It tells me she's just as turned on as I am. I don't say anything about it, but I'm on the brink of losing control.

If we're all gonna die, Arya and I might as well go out with a bang.

Eighteen

ARYA'S NEW ASSIGNMENT

The smell of coffee and the buzz of students enjoying what's left of their weekend increases my sensory overload as I walk into the café.

Gomada Academy has a few services on campus that students run. The coffee shop is one of them. It's almost always busy, earning its well-deserved title as the 'hub of campus.' Lines are always long. Baristas rush about, filling orders and decorating lattés.

I usually can't stand coffee. My lack of sleep and inability to comprehend what just happened to me means one thing and one thing only:

Coffee to process and decompress. I'll need the caffeine if I want to have a prayer of functioning.

That's why I'm here at all. The café is usually avoided by me unless it's absolutely necessary (or if I have a craving for hot chocolate).

After waiting in the queue and finally receiving my order, I sit down at a vacant table near the wall. Shutting my eyes and gripping my to-go cup, I try to concentrate.

I went to Feara to confront Cole. He was being a total jackass! Instead of crying, I needed to do something.

However, I didn't expect that I'd do *him*.

What just happened between us?

It was animal-like, erratic, out of character. And I told him to 'just do it.'

Oh, my God!

Was it the passion, or stress of the moment?

We always have heated arguments. When we argued while hating each other, the fire kept burning.

This time, we extinguished it.

Making things more complicated, that was my first time. My first time ever.

My first time was with Cole Hudson – a Shifter, a judge-mental and discriminating jerk.

But I can't help but remember his good qualities – even if they sometimes seem to be in short supply. He's observant, protective, loyal, and thoughtful – when he wants to be.

And then there's the way he makes me feel physically...

I never thought sex with someone – which always seemed to be scary and unrealistic – could be so *primal*. That it could feel so good. The space between my legs is still trembling, throbbing, soaking wet. It's hard to sit still – or sit at all. I can still remember my head spinning during *it* – how it was hard to think, move, even speak.

What does it all mean? Was having sex with Cole a responsible thing to do?

If I have to ask myself that question, I'm pretty sure the answer is 'no.'

What's more, Cole told me something awful before I left. It explains why he's been acting so withdrawn lately. It doesn't excuse his behaviour – but it certainly *explains* it.

My phone vibrates madly, scattering my thoughts. It's not the same kind of vibration I'd get when a phone call would be coming in. I don't recognize the pattern at all.

This is weird.

I pull my phone out of my leggings' pocket.

I'm surprised to see a red 'ALERT' on the screen. It's from Gomada Academy. Usually, I only get those if there's a severe weather event in San Francisco or if a child has been abducted.

One quick glance around the café reveals other students pulling devices out of pockets, backpacks and purses. Startled gasps meet my ears.

I turn my attention back to my phone, my heart in my throat.

ATTENTION STUDENTS,

What you are about to read will be difficult to process. Please bear that in mind as you go through this email.

Headmistress Leona Frow was found dead in her office this morning. Vyquean Security is suspecting foul play. Due to the already-troubling circumstances surrounding the academy as of late, the King and Queen of Vyquean are issuing a state of emergency in Upper Gomada.

You are not to leave campus under any circumstances. You are to stay in your dorms unless it is time for classes or meals. All academy sports, clubs, and extracurriculars will be postponed indefinitely.

When leaving your dorm, you must do so with another student. Freshmen and Sophomores: use your partner from the Mentorship Program. Juniors, Seniors, and Masters: you will be assigned a partner who lives in close proximity.

All of this is subject to change without notice. More updates will ensue as we receive them. A new interim Headmaster/Headmistress will be appointed while we investigate the death of Leona Frow.

If you have any questions or concerns, you may bring them

to the attention of the Interim Headmaster/Headmistress once appointed.

Julian Gillies, M.D. SH.
    Head of Security, Vyquean Division

That makes it official.

I assumed Gomada Academy would eventually address this, react accordingly to Headmistress Frow's murder – yet it's strange that they leave out the missing students and the ghost.

Are the King and Queen really declaring a state of emergency in all of Upper Gomada? That's pretty extreme. Yes, the school is *in* Upper Gomada, but if the monarchy gets involved...

Things are going to get worse.

Glancing around the room now, I suddenly feel like I've stepped into an alternate dimension. Students are leaning close to one another at nearby tables, whispering concernedly. Adult men and women are circling the outer perimeter of the café and the hallways branching off to different sections of the school.

There's even more security now than there was before.

I close the alert on my phone, take a breath, and go to the group chat. My phone has been vibrating since I stopped reading my email, but I was too dazed to do anything about it until now.

> This state of emergency bullshit isn't going to stop us.

Thank God I'm alone when I read this message from Cole.

He's not just the leader of our ghost-hunting group. He's not just my Mentor or the guy that I kissed.

He's the guy that I slept with.

And now, the school wants us to be in even closer proximity than before.

No time to sort out my feelings.

We gotta talk here instead of meeting up. Be ready by five o'clock

Aye Aye, Captain.

I can almost *hear* Nora's sarcasm through the screen. I'm even less inclined to share about my loss of virginity with her.

As usual, Ryker and Diego react with a laughing smiley to Nora's message. They love it when she does this kind of thing to Cole.

Speaking of Ryker, I haven't spoken to or even seen him for several days. I sometimes see him with Lucy. I'm assuming he's helping her control her duelling Affinities.

How can we decide anything of importance over text? Can we at least communicate verbally?

I'm not surprised that Lucy is resisting this change. I imagine it's happening due to the school's stricter rules and increased security.

Too risky. Vyquean security is everywhere. They'll patrol the dorms. You don't wanna mess with them or have them hear the wrong thing.

I'm shocked by Cole's detailed response. Despite the confusion between us, he's taking his leadership role seriously.

It's a smart move. They may know some kids are poking around. Qadir and Frow were already suspicious before.

Diego is right. It's better to avoid any extra scrutiny if we can help it.

I'm also terrified of getting caught. After Cole and I had to report what we saw to Greyson, it's not a huge leap to think that we're all going to be under closer surveillance – especially if faculty or staff see the rest of the 'group' associating with Cole and I.

If that means we have to talk over text, so be it.

I suck in a tortured breath and write,

> Do you think they have our names?

Who knows what these Vyquean guards have been told about us?

My heart skids to a painful halt when Cole answers me.

> Probably not. But it doesn't hurt to lay low.

> Guards are in Gleera's common rooms.
> Asking us to go back to our dorms.

> Just saw a guard argue with an Enchanter
> who was minding his own business.

Ryker's messages prove that it is safer not to take chances this time around. No more sneaking out to Feara using different routes. No more clandestine meetings.

Maybe after what happened between Cole and I, text meetings are the way to go.

"Hey, you. What are you doing?"

I jump a mile at the verbal interruption. A pair of suspicious blue eyes are leering at me.

A Vyquean security guard is hovering close to my table, looking at me like I am a juvenile delinquent. In some ways, maybe I am.

My pulse races in response. What do I do?

I think he's a Shifter with a powerful alter ego based on the damp feeling I get. It's scary, but nothing compared to what I feel when I see the ghost.

I pick up my to-go cup of coffee to show him. "Just having coffee," I respond quietly.

The guard narrows his eyes as I put my phone away.

"Well, you can take your coffee and go back to your dorm," the Vyquean guard counters gruffly.

I have no other choice. I get up from my chair and leave, coffee in hand. I feel the guard's eyes on me as I exit the coffee shop and rush for the front doors to the Academy.

What if he thinks I'm doing something rebellious? What if he follows me back to Meera? Despite what Cole said, I'm sure every single guard has our names after we discovered Leona Frow's body.

The adults are looking in all the wrong places. What's more, they only seem to be doing something now that a grown-up has died. Though I'm stricken over Leona's death, I'm also frantic over the students who have gone missing right under the noses of the Academy.

Plus, why hasn't the school mentioned anything about the missing students attacking their contemporaries?

It's impossible for the school to hide all this.

We know who – or what – is responsible for these horrendous acts. The only problem is, we can't leave campus to fight the ghost or even save those missing students who are being manipulated by an evil entity.

But after tonight, I'm hoping all that will change.

As scared as I am to break the rules, I am willing to do it to save those students who don't deserve their fate.

Nora and I are quiet in our dorm. We're mentally preparing for our *meeting*, which will start any second now.

All Nora and I can really hear is the distant, quiet chatter of people in the hallway. After what I saw coming back to Meera, those murmurings don't belong to Nymphs or other students.

Vyquean security guards are everywhere.

Even though the alert on my phone kind of prepared me for that, their presence still unnerves me. They're creeping around campus like spiders crawling under a rock.

My phone vibrates, scattering my thoughts from Vyquean guards to ghosts. I hear Nora's phone vibrate too. When she scoffs in an annoyed way, I'm quick to open up the notification on my phone.

> We need to come up with a new plan.

> No, really?

I'm not surprised that Nora is annoyed by Cole's 'stating the obvious' – but she doesn't know what I do.

Cole is tortured by the fact that he can't Shift. Due to Headmistress Frow's demise, only Professor Qadir can remove the Curio he showed me earlier. Now that the stakes are higher, Cole must feel guiltier and more helpless than ever.

Punishment or not, the Curio has put us in danger. Cole was very clear about that today.

> It's a long story, but I can't Shift. Not for a while.

Cole's announcement in the chat is shocking to me. The way he told me this afternoon... He looked ashamed.

Everyone reads his message. Some are already writing responses as Cole is trying to write one of his own.

> Diego and I can't sweep the ghost like we wanted to. This leaves Diego and the rest of you at a disadvantage. I'm sorry for that.

When I first met Cole in September, I never thought he'd be the kind of person to apologize for anything. He has been doing a lot of that lately – the question is whether or not he is sincere. It certainly seems this way now – even *before*.

I glance at Nora. She's staring at me with a quizzical expression.

"Did you know about that?" she asks as our phones go off again.

What do I say to her? I think fervently. *I don't want to betray Cole's confidence or cause him further embarrassment. I'm sure it took a lot for him to admit that to everyone in the chat.*

At the same time, I know I can't lie to Nora. I'm getting tired of keeping secrets, lying, and sneaking around.

Even after having it out with Cole, it's not like we resolved anything. In fact, we probably just made things worse by sleeping together. Still, I don't feel good about lying. It's been hard enough to keep the ghost and 'zombie students' from Mom and Dad – I don't want to keep a boyfriend from them, too.

The least I can do is tell the truth and make sure Cole's dignity remains intact.

"Yeah," I tell Nora. "He just told me today."

Nora makes a 'hmph' sound, moving her long black braid off her shoulder. "Well, at least he tells the truth *sometimes*," she grumbles, getting back to her phone.

You can't Shift? Since when?

This is a disaster. If one of us can't defend ourselves, we'll be the first one the ghost attacks.

Lucy speaks the truth once again, leaving Ryker's question unanswered.

That's what I'm counting on.

I gape in shock at Cole's message. Even Nora follows suit with a gasp, even though she's not his biggest fan.

You're going to be bait, buddy?

I thought Diego and Cole were together. Maybe Diego is voicing his question so everyone in the chat can see it, too.

Yeah. The ghost has already come for me before. Probably still has it out for me because of last time we tangled.

There's an uncomfortable silence in the room as Nora and I think back on Cole Shifting and attacking the ghost to protect Nora.

If I can lure it out, the rest of you can finish it off.

And what if we can't do it without you? Not to be all doom and gloom, or anything, but this isn't good.

Ryker's counter to Cole's strategy pretty much voices what

Nora and I are thinking. The whole point of this plan was that we would be stronger as a unit. If one of us can't perform...

We're switching the plan around. We know more about the thing now. It's probably not a ghost at all. Just a monster. A monster means we can kill it.

A monster?!

A monster we've never heard of before with frightening mind-control powers sounds just as bad as a ghost haunting campus and offing people – but that's just me.

Cole sent another message, so I quickly get back to reality (what a crushing, supernatural reality it is) and catch up as fast as possible.

Ryker and Lucy are stronger now. They can combine their Affinities to immobilize it. Nora's my back-up. Diego and Arya can sweep it in the end.

Sweep it?!

Nora grumbles about being Cole's 'back-up' as I type a hasty,

What does that mean?

It means you're taking my place and finishing it off with Diego. It'll work. Trust me.

I stare at Nora, horrified. "That's *not* going to work," I protest.

She frowns at me. "Are *you* going to tell him that?" she asks me. "It's not like any of us are getting out of this scot-free. There's gotta be a reason why Cole put you with Diego."

"Yeah, but what kind of rational reason could there be?" I can't help but panic.

My voice is shaking. So is the rest of me. As much as I want to help, I don't know if I want the responsibility of *finishing off* the ghost.

My phone's screen timed out shortly after I started speaking to Nora. It vibrates in my hands. I'm too afraid to check it, though.

"I mean, I've gotten better since September, but–" I begin.

Nora fixes her blue eyes on me. "You've come a long way since September. Don't let Professor Xhao mess with your head. As much as agreeing with Cole makes me want to vomit, I think he's right in putting you at the end."

I wish I could believe her. Nora's improved so much since September – and even then, she was a strong partner. I have no doubt she'll be able to use her new poisonous, thorny vines to trap and hurt the ghost – and protect Cole if needed. If anyone is capable of finishing off the ghost, it's Nora.

I hate thinking this way, but it's easier for someone like Nora to tell me I've improved. She's a full-blooded Nymph with more power. Getting to her level would take much longer for someone like me. But I give her a small smile in thanks, because she's trying to be kind.

This is the plan. I need to accept it. I'll have to train harder to get past those creepy Vyquean security guards.

As fear stricken as I am, I know I need to try and help.

It's not just about the six of us.

It's about the school.

It's about the realm of Gomada.

It's about our Headmistress, who didn't deserve to die.

It's about those captured students being manipulated.

I know I can't ignore the rest of the meeting. More messages are coming in. I begin to read.

Willow and I can handle it.

Is Diego serious?

I can barely remember Diego's last name, yet he's confident we'll work well together. I don't think we've even had one conversation so far. I'm sure he's nice, but I've never had a reason or the courage to approach him about anything.

Also, what kind of creature does he Shift into? Judging by how big and strong he looks, it must be powerful. How am I supposed to complement or assist with *that*?

> Lucy and I can pin the ghost down long
> enough for Diego and Arya to finish it off.

Lucy doesn't agree or disagree with Ryker, but I see she's read the message. Maybe she's as nervous as I am. It's not like she and Ryker have an easy job. If she has feelings like doubt and anxiety, I've clearly misjudged her, too.

> My poison component is coming in well. I'll
> make sure it doesn't move – or that when it
> does, it'll hurt like a bitch.

That's Nora's first contribution to the meeting, but it has a profound impact on the conversation.

> Damn, girl! I'd hate to get on YOUR bad side!

I can't help but smile at Diego's joke. It's probably the first time I've smiled all day.

> Board up the door.

> Shut up, Cole. You're next.

Ryker and Diego both put a laughing reaction on Nora's message.

> Fuck. Take it easy, Leith. I can't even
> Shift now.

My phone vibrates once more. It's a text from an unknown number.

> Hey, it's Diego. Not sure how much you know
> about Shifters, but this is what I turn into.
> We'll pair up nicely together.

An incoming MMS message appears. As it loads, I begin to type a message back to Diego.

My eyes widen with alarm when I see an image of an enormous bird against a black sky. It's full of fire. It looks like someone took it with their cell phone. My guess is Cole. Since they are so close, maybe they know each other's alter egos.

Something tells me that Diego's just as secretive about his alter ego as Cole. They're never with other Shifters.

Wait.

I know why Cole paired me up with Diego.

He wants us to attack the ghost from the air – maybe cash in on the element of surprise.

> Hey. I don't know much, but I'm sure we'll be
> able to figure something out.

> Glad you're cool with it. We'll have the
> element of surprise on our hands. That's what
> Cole's counting on.

It surprises me that Diego and I are on the same page. Maybe we will work better together than I thought. More to the point, *surprise* might be the only thing we have going for us against an anthropomorphic ghost.

A new message in the group chat distracts me from the

notion that Diego and I will have to meet up to work on our combined attack. Even if we're both going to be flying, I'm assuming it still involves some strategy. I know my flying has improved, but I'll need to hone my skills if I'll be working under duress.

> And when, pray tell, are we embarking on this revamped mission?

I'm sure Cole is annoyed by Lucy's tone, but he answers her in a diplomatic way – more civil than I would have thought.

> Good question. I'm thinking as soon as possible, before things get worse. Maybe tonight or tomorrow.

Tonight or tomorrow?
Nora flinches from my right.

> No way! That gives us zero time to prepare.

> You've had days to know what to do, Leith. Arya and Diego are the only ones scrambling. And me, too, since I can't even defend myself.

> Cole's right. We need to get a handle on this before the school tightens up on security or more people get taken. It's not like we know about every single abduction that's happened. More kids could be going missing. There's no time to waste.

Ryker's long message is one of many. It's hard to keep track of who's saying what. If we were in the same room, we'd be talking all at once. It's chaos.

> If we do it tonight, there's a good chance we'll get hurt, or worse. This is crazy!

I can't help but agree with Nora.

> Ryker and I haven't had nearly enough time to train. I don't know why you're so gung-ho about fighting tonight.

> If we don't do anything now, and the King and Queen swing in with more guards, we won't be able to sneeze, let alone fight a ghost hybrid.

> Not to mention the fact that more people could die!

Diego and Cole are going head-to-head against Lucy. This is bad – and surprising, since Diego and Lucy are dating.

Fighting amongst ourselves will just make things easier for the ghost and the zombified students to get to us.

> This is bedlam. We're all going to die if we don't plan this further.

I'm happy that someone as tough as Lucy is speaking the truth even though she's getting outnumbered.

> Arya?

I'm stunned by Cole's inquiry. Maybe he's asking because I'm the only one who hasn't said anything yet. I've been so busy trying to keep up with the chat that I didn't even think about adding my voice to the fray.

Part of me wonders if Cole would have been quick to ask me for my opinion if things hadn't changed between us. But now's not the time to think about that.

> I don't like going in without more practice, but I also think it's dangerous to keep waiting.

Alright. We can vote on it, then. If you want out, tell me now or suck it up. We'll be tougher to beat in a group of six. But I'm not gonna force anyone.

There's silence in the chat as everyone reads Cole's message.

I think this will end badly, but I won't leave my roommate hanging. I'm in.

I turn to the right and give Nora an emotional look. I don't want her to feel like she *has* to do something to keep me safe – but the fact that she's willing to do this for me is very touching.

"Are you sure?" I ask her.

Nora sighs. "We have to think about the other students and the school," she elaborates. "It's not just about us. And I don't want you, Anja, or anyone else suffering if I could have done something to stop it."

More messages come in that stop us from our one-on-one conversation.

I'm in. We gotta do this now.

Same here. We can't waste any more time chatting.

Ryker and Diego are ready.

I disagree, but I won't let you Neanderthals do this alone. I'll be there.

I'm quick to write underneath Lucy's pompous response.

I'm in, too.

Alright. We can talk more about when and how we'll sneak out. Just give me some time.

Cole's final message brings the meeting to a close.

I look at my watch. My open books and pile of homework have done nothing to distract me.

It's close to nine o'clock. I'm on-edge about the time and have been obsessively checking clocks everywhere. Even at dinner, it was all I could do to stop thinking about the plan.

Nora seems to be the same. She was very quiet at dinner. Anja even asked her if anything was wrong, to which Nora responded with an, 'I'm tired' excuse. I know Nora felt bad about lying to her girlfriend – but we both know it's best to keep what's happening a secret.

If we involve Anja or anyone else in this mess–

"Okay. I'm ready."

Nora is standing up from her desk, pulling on the black hoodie draped on her bed. She enjoys earthier colours, but I know why she chose this shade for tonight's heist.

"Okay. I'll see you in a while," I tell her as I get to my feet.

"See you then," Nora agrees solemnly.

Nora and I share a quick but meaningful glance as Nora gets ready to leave. We're being delusional by saying we'll 'see each other later.' That may not happen. There may not be any kind of *later* after tonight.

Nora lingers at the door, giving me one last look before unlocking it. She's gone in a flash.

Sneaking out after curfew isn't Nora. She's been dreading this – breaking school rules, facing the enemy, all of it – ever since the new plan was set in motion.

The thing is, this problem is bigger than all of us. The ghost (or whatever it is) trumps everything else. We all know it, even though we don't necessarily say it.

I glance at my phone when its dull vibration alerts me to a chat message. I take a shallow breath when I activate my lockscreen and see the news from Nora.

I'm out. Thanks, Lucy.

Cole, Ryker, and Lucy have been strategizing since today's meeting. It turns out that Ryker and Lucy can manipulate what other people see by tapping into both Light and Dark energies at once. I don't know how they do it, but it clearly works because Nora's off campus and away from prying eyes.

Lucy Chapin having these kinds of powers frightens me. I still don't know if I can trust her. Ever since she and Désirée targeted Nora and I at the beginning of the school year, I haven't felt comfortable.

Bullies like that don't just *change*. Well, maybe they do – but usually, it's for the worse.

Hot waves of hypocrisy and guilt hit me hard when I consider my feelings for Cole. It's not like we've had time to talk about our relationship, but I've definitely given him chances to redeem himself – more than I've ever given Lucy.

So, maybe bullies *can* change for the better. Maybe my experiences at my former high school and with the Chapin cousins have tainted how I view adolescent tyrants. But now isn't the time to think about that.

Great. Two down, four to go.

Right. Cole was the first to sneak out since he's posing as the *bait*. He needed the extra time to get himself into position: the very spot where Lukas Crabtree was abducted weeks earlier.

I can't bear to think about Cole purposefully putting himself in danger like that – explaining why I tried to distract myself with homework all evening, with varying success. Despite our tumultuous relationship, I don't want anything to happen to him.

But I can do nothing about Cole's new part in this plan. The ghost has been targeting him for a while. His inability to Shift makes him most capable of luring the spirit out into the open.

We still think the spirit has been watching us from a distance – meaning it knows about Cole's Curio and is counting on him being vulnerable. Still, we hope it doesn't know *everything*: like the fact that Nora is hiding in the wings.

I'm putting my phone down when it vibrates suddenly. Cole has sent me a text message.

> You okay?

> I know sneaking out isn't your thing.

My insides twist at his messages. Cole is being thoughtful, even though we're smack-dab in the middle of breaking out of Gomada Academy to fight off a ghost with psychic powers.

Even after everything that's happened between us.

Even after the awful things I said to him.

I was wrong about the ghost trumping everything in our lives. As much as I wish Cole wouldn't be so intent on keeping our relationship a secret, it means a lot to me that he's making a private effort like this.

> I'm okay. Just nervous.

I'm too shy to say anything else to the guy who made me moan in ecstasy just a handful of hours ago. Thank God he can't see my face right now.

It'll all work out. Just stick to the plan.

Are you okay?

Yeah. Things are fine.

Part of me wonders how honest Cole is being right now. I'm sure he's putting on a brave front, but it *must* be bothering him that he can't Shift. It's his worst nightmare to be unable to protect himself against a supernatural threat. I get that he's trying to use it to his advantage, but–

I jump out of my chair when I hear a strange tapping on my window.

That's the signal. Ten minutes must have passed since Nora left. We're going one by one to err on the side of caution.

I cross over to the window, looking down to see billows of black smoke contorting higher and higher into the frosty air. I know from our debriefing that it's Ryker.

Things are still kind of weird between him and I – but less so since the moment I kissed Cole. I just don't think I realized it until now.

I fixate on the black smoke. It flickers in response. I close my eyes, feeling a strange numbness coursing through my body.

I'm startled when I look down and see the same black tendrils seeping around me. I knew this would happen, but it's still frightening.

I'm currently invisible so long as Ryker channels both Affinities. This magical barrier even helps us to open doors without getting detected.

I know I can't stay still as a statue in my dorm room while Lucy, Ryker, Nora, and Cole are out there. Ryker and Lucy told us their power has limits, too, so I shouldn't dawdle.

I approach the door, pulling out my fully-charged phone on the way.

Just leaving now.

Lucy and Ryker see the message first.

Go quickly, Arya. As soon as I can drop the barrier with you, it'll be easier to get Diego out.

Crap! How much time has passed since Ryker's power absorbed into my body?

I move faster due to my guilt. If Ryker gets tired or his concentration breaks due to overexertion–

I unlock and open the door to a brightly-lit hallway and three Vyquean guards.

A chill spins down my spine as soon as one guard makes eye contact with me.

Oh, my God. She's looking **through** *me. She can't see or hear me.*

The spell may have worked, but I'm not sticking around and risking things. The sooner I get out of here, the sooner Ryker can cloak Diego.

I close the door as quietly as I can. I shuffle past the conversing guards who lean casually against the walls.

My heart thumps erratically in my chest as I sprint headlong through the crunching snow. Little green specks of dying grass stick out of the white clay-like snow, trying to cling to life.

There's enough snow to leave footprints, which worries me. I can't remember if that is still possible with the cloaking spell – and I have no time to look.

I reach the boarded-up gates, armed by two large Vyquean officials. One of them looks like he could be a Shifter.

I can't waste time. I just hope I'll be able to do this under pressure.

Running for the fence that houses Gomada Academy, yet imprisons us, I concentrate as best I can. I focus on my wings – what they look like, what I see when I fly, how I feel when I'm airborne, the tug of the wind against my body...

As I near the dark fence, I worry that nothing has happened. What if I can't summon my Air Affinity enough to activate my wings? I'll be stuck here!

I grit my teeth, trying hard to fight back angry tears that push at the backs of my eyes.

Professor Xhao was right.

No! I want to prove her wrong! I want to prove them all wrong!

Being half-human is who I am. I've never felt ashamed of it before, and I won't let Professor Xhao or anyone else berate me for it now!

I'm shocked when two bright lights jut out from either side of me. My wings!

The guards don't notice the bright white wings or the sparkles they give off against the rough wind as I sail over the fence with relief.

Once over the gate, I try to focus on the dark ground below and on the specifics of our strategy.

Cole wants us to meet up in our assigned pairs. Lucy will meet up with Ryker once all of us have gotten out. Nora is staying close to Cole in case the ghost comes before the rest of us can surround it. I need to find Diego.

Taking a deep breath, I find a small hill past the entrance to the Gomada Thicket. I land, retrieving my phone from my jacket pocket. Maybe I'm too full of adrenaline to deactivate my wings. They're pinned at my sides. This will save time for what comes next.

> I'm out. Thank you, Ryker.

> Awesome. Diego, I got you. Head out in a
> minute or so.

Ryker is probably circling back to Feara. It must be hard for him and Lucy to conceal not only themselves but another person, too. Their training over the past few weeks must have really paid off because we wouldn't have been able to break out of school without them.

> Hurry the fuck up.

My heart stops beating when I read Cole's message in the group chat. I answer quickly.

> What happened?

I can't sense anything, but I'm not too far away from Cole's position. Wasn't Lukas attacked just a few yards away?
Nora responds next.

> I sense something dark and creepy. Similar to
> how I felt last time.

Oh, my God! The ghost is already in the Gomada Thicket!
Cole can't defend himself!
If Nora's the only one there to help, they could both die – or worse!
She was only supposed to be the surprise back-up if Ryker and Lucy can't trap the ghost first!

> We can't help without a location.

Maybe Lucy is the only other person answering because Ryker is preoccupied with getting Diego off school property. That leaves me and Lucy to assist.

Despite the bluntness of her message, I know she's right.

There's fog! Hurry!

I can tell Nora's scared because of the typos and extra periods in her message.

Sweat pools at the back of my neck as I remember Nora's near-abduction. Now, Nora *and* Cole could be next. *They* could be the zombie minions controlled by the ghost, attacking students without a mind of their own.

I know what I have to do.

I dig my bootheels into the snow as much as I can, getting ready to take off. I spread my wings, which feel stiff after a while of inactivity.

I jump a mile and spin around when someone clears their throat from behind me. I'm pretty sure it's not the ghost (what kind of monster clears phlegm to get your attention?). Still, I don't like being snuck up on anymore.

Lucy frowns at me. She's wearing a black trench coat with a gold scarf. It looks like she's heading out for a movie date night, not sneaking out of school to track down a ghost hybrid.

"Hey. Have you seen Ryker – or Diego?" she asks, an odd expression drowning her blue eyes.

I'm confused by this, but I don't comment on it. "No," I respond. "I'm guessing they're still trying to get out."

"Well, we can't pair up the way we were supposed to if the ghost is already present," Lucy muses, which was what I was thinking, too.

"Cole wants us to stick to the plan if possible," I remind her, though I know that stalling and waiting aren't wise.

Lucy arches a perfectly-tweezed eyebrow. "That ship has sailed. And since when do you care what Mr. Hudson has to say about anything?" she challenges me.

Eerie silence fills the thicket at her statement.

"Last I checked, he and my cousin were taking turns on who could humiliate you most," Lucy continues.

I scowl at her to cover up my feelings for Cole. "If this is your way of asking me to team up with you tonight, you're off to a great start."

Lucy rolls her eyes but a small smile betrays her would-be sarcastic response. "We don't have to braid each other's hair or go shopping," she asserts. "We just need to work together *now* to ensure our classmates don't get themselves killed."

Maybe she's given up on trying to befriend Nora and I. Part of me feels bad about that, because I don't like believing the worst in people.

What was I just thinking before, about mean girls and bullies having the potential to change?

"That's good, because braiding hair isn't my forté," I affirm.

Lucy gives me a grin in return.

We both tense up when a sudden gust of wind blows through our hair and clothes. Lucy shudders, but something tells me it's due to more than the wintry weather.

"How are we going to find them?" I ask her. "My plan was just to fly overhead and look," I add for context.

Lucy gives a small gesture with her right hand, facing into the Gomada Thicket. "You can follow me by foot or from the air," she surprises me by asserting. "I didn't truly feel it until I got closer to the Thicket, but..."

We both look toward the deep, dark woods. Before I know it, we're sprinting headlong into the unknown. I'm not a huge fan of the dark, or creepy thickets, but my desire to save Nora and Cole trumps my fears. I just hope we're not too late.

"But what?" I press as I follow her.

Usually, Lucy is all too excited to lecture us about something she knows. Now, she's quiet.

"There's a surge of dark energy that's almost impossible to ignore!" she exclaims from up ahead. "It was a small pull when I got off campus, but now... !"

"You think it's the ghost?" I call as I try to keep up with her, but it's not a question.

"It's odd, though!" she pants, her voice carrying over the howling wind. I'm using up all of my energy to keep up with her. "If it was a ghost, I don't think it would give off this kind of energy!"

I frown as I follow Lucy through the dark and uneven terrain. I don't understand. If this ghost is evil, *wouldn't it* give off dark or evil energy? But what were Ryker, Diego, and Cole saying about the ghost having human-like tendencies? I myself have considered that from time to time. It's not like a ghost can be injured by a bite from a Shifter... Right?

We really don't know what we're up against.

What is the identity of this monster that's threatening to undo Gomada Academy?

Nineteen

COLE'S WEAKNESS

I'm sweating bullets as the creepy as fuck fog snakes around my feet, trying to keep me pinned to the ground. I just don't feel paralyzed – yet.

The ghost is trying to freak me out, trap me inside my own head. And it may actually work because I can't Shift to save myself!

I have no idea of the ghost's position. All I know for sure is that it's *here*.

Nora must sense it, too. She's around here somewhere as my back-up in case the ghost jumps my ass – though right now, I don't think there's any *in case* about it.

It's fucking *happening*.

I look down at my Curio. I'm so frustrated that this stupid necklace that I *should* be able to snap into a million pieces is stopping me from Shifting. It's stopping me from protecting my friends. Protecting myself. Protecting Arya.

Basically, it's stopping survival.

I never asked to be the group leader. I never wanted the

238

responsibility. But I still feel like the failure that will get everyone killed.

*Remember that you hurt the ghost before. If you can do that, it can't be **all** ghost.*

Maybe there's still a chance, after all – Curio or not.

My feet are ripped from the hard snow. I'm airborne. Before I can take a breath, I'm hurtled backward against the wind.

I fly what feels like dozens of feet backward. I hear a dull *whoomp*. I'm numb as my face hits the packing snow with a small *thud*.

Am I choking? Am I dying? Is my back broken? How the hell did I get flung backward like that?

I realize I'm clutching my chest after a second or two. I got the wind knocked out of me.

Holy shit, that hurt!

If only that would have broken the Curio. But my luck isn't that good. I still feel it around my neck, its magical energy stopping me from Shifting into the Tedla.

Speaking of the Tedla, I can feel it rattling around inside of me. I can't tell if it's angry, frustrated, or scared.

Scared.

That's a bad sign.

My vision is clearing –maybe things got foggy when I got slammed into what I'm guessing was a tree.

Black mist surrounds me. It looks different than the black fog fingers. It almost looks like dark energy – similar to when I saw Ryker pick the lock using his Darkness Affinity the night we tried to save Lukas.

Is another Enchanter out here? It's not like Ryker or Lucy chucked me across the Gomada Thicket just now. Maybe it's not the ghost at all. But how does that explain the creepy fog fingers?

And where the hell is Nora?

Nora may hate my guts, but she's too nice to leave people hanging – even me. Her absence is a big-ass red flag.

Did the ghost or whatever-it-is get to her first?

Even though I know it'll blow our cover, I turn my head around (which hurts like a bitch) and yell, "Nora!"

Silence.

"Your little Nymph friend can't come out to play, Shifter."

I want to flinch. The voice is menacing, but it's not the ghost's. Instead, I look up, facing my enemy head-on. Whether I can Shift or not, I won't back down from an opponent.

My vision is tainted from the blackness of the night and the pestering snowflakes. But the voice sounded close by.

What did this creep do to Nora?

Where is everyone?

How badly am I hurt?

Am I going to die out here?

Before I can even open my mouth to say, 'show yourself,' the mysterious threat appears.

Like I thought, it's not the ghost. No hole-like eyes. No fog. That weird, damp feeling isn't there, either.

It's a human. A man. He's dressed in all black, with a hood pulled up over his head. I can sort of tell that his skin is dark.

The only thing I know for sure is that he's an Enchanter. He has that Enchanter vibe that Ryker, Lucy, Lukas and Désirée have: I'm better than you.

Is this guy working for the ghost? He knows too much and he's clearly out to get us.

*Or is **he** the ghost?*

Didn't Ryker mention that Enchanters and Enchantresses can't 'manipulate their body chemistry,' or whatever? So what's going on?

"Who the fuck are you?" I demand, though I'm not in a position to *demand* anything.

I'm injured, I have no idea where my teammates are or what he's already done to them, and I'm alone out here in the dead of Winter with no escape.

I'm screwed.

He laughs a small laugh. "Still pompous and entitled, even on death's door," he purrs, which freaks me out more than the 'death's door' comment. "I should have expected nothing less from a Germain."

*How the **fuck** does he know I'm a Germain?*

I grit my teeth, angry and frustrated. I'd ask him, but it's not like questions are getting me anywhere.

I guess people could potentially know about me. If they know about my grandpa and who his kids are, they could track me down. But it's still weird.

"Where is she?" I ask instead, wondering if he'll slip up and tell me about Nora's whereabouts.

I hate to admit it because she's an annoying bitch, but I'm actually worried about Nora. The world must be ending.

"Which 'she?'" the man prompts instead, causing me to see red. "I'm sensing there's more than one girl involved in this suicide mission of yours."

My vision is dimmed again, this time by searing hot pain. It's like my insides are on fire. I choke back my own vomit.

I knew yanking on my Curio would do fuck-all, but I guess I had hope, which was even stupider. I gnash my teeth, warm puke smashing against them as I pull harder. No use. It's not coming off.

Damnit!

There's nothing I can do! I'm so mad I want to scream. When I pull harder and my vision goes black, I *do* scream.

"It's a pity you aren't able to Shift," the douchebag chuckles. "It would have made for an interesting battle. You shouldn't have been so rebellious, Cole."

He's grabbing me by the collar of my hoodie, yanking me upright. I still can't see. My hands are clutching my damned Curio.

"I see much of myself in you. Take it from me – you won't like being the odd man out."

What is he talking about? How the fuck does he know all this about me?

I'm too weak to retaliate. Trying to take off the Curio has completely fucked me up. Maybe the Enchanter knew that would happen when he brought up Arya being here, too. He wanted to weaken me.

Whatever. I guess this is how I die. At least I only had seventeen years of family shit to deal with. The Tedla can choose someone else – someone smarter, a rule-follower, a dedicated Shifter. Not some lazy-ass guy like me who'd rather avoid the tough stuff or play pranks on people.

A *crash* from behind me fills the clearing, causing me to let go of the Curio. My vision wavers and the guy loosens his grip on me.

A big-ass tree branch falls into the Gomada Thicket. Maybe this is why the guy is now stepping back from me. I collapse to the ground as soon as he does, holding my throat. The sound of the fallen branch reverberates in my ears. I'm disoriented but relieved as hell that the branch didn't crush me.

Then again, I'll most certainly die out here. If it's not gonna be the branch, it'll be something else.

I feel so fucking helpless! I'm not used to feeling this way! I hate it!

Even if I'm going to die, I know this might be my only shot. Now that the weird guy is stepping away from me – why? – I struggle to my feet. I'm halfway there when a *swooping* sound almost breaks my eardrums for the second time tonight.

I swing back onto my knees. I know what's happening (finally). I duck my head and sure enough, sweltering heat plasters the air above me.

I look up just in time to see the end of Diego's flaming red tail as he blasts a wave of fire at the guy who is now backing up, but laughing. Asshole.

"Well!" he cries, holding both hands in front of him. Dark magic pulses through them and meets the fire blast head-on. "So this is the Phoenix. A little lacklustre, wouldn't you–"

Just when I think Diego's fire may not be enough to get rid of this shithead, spirals of white and black travel through the flames in some kind of trippy way.

It almost looks like I'm seeing things. The man who must be an Enchanter cries out when the Light and Dark Affinities clash with the fire and ultimately overpower his dark energy blast. His hood falls back, revealing brown eyes, dark skin, and a pissed-off glare at Diego and Ryker.

Ryker is sitting on Diego's back, gripping the vibrant feathers at his neck. He's combining his Affinities with the Phoenix's power. I'm surprised they're working so well together–but it's not like they have a choice. We can always rip Ryker a new one later. We just gotta be alive to do it.

Something weird happens when the Enchanter lays eyes on Diego and Ryker. All I can hear is the flapping of Diego's wings as he blasts another wave of fire at the man.

I keep thinking our adversary will use another Affinity against Diego and Ryker, but it doesn't look like he's going to. He's just scowling and blasting more dark energy out of his palms.

"Wait!" Ryker yells.

I'm shocked out of my mind that Ryker is actually telling Diego to *wait*.

Is he nuts? Is this some kind of Enchanter loyalty crap? There's no way we can wait!

I've made up my mind about this guy. He's not some foot

soldier for the ghost. This jackass *is* the ghost. I don't know how he did it, but it has to be him.

He's a mind controller and a murderer. There's no telling what he'll do next. It's not like there's a *cap* on the bad stuff he does. There's no way we're fucking waiting!

Ryker's no longer fighting. Diego is doing all the work. I yank at the Curio again, but I know if I pass out, I won't be any good to anyone – if being *less useful* than I am now is even possible.

What the hell are we going to do?

"Ryker!" I snap, but I know it's pointless.

I can tell from all the way down here that Ryker has stopped using any kind of magic.

He's done.

I'm going to kick Ryker's ass from here to Valis, where most Enchanters come from – but we gotta survive this first. It may not happen.

Diego's struggling under the pressure of the dark magic coming from the hoodie-wearing guy.

Diego is powerful and capable. But even someone like me can see that this opponent is dealing from a different deck than the rest of us. He's older – maybe Qadir's age – meaning he's had more time in the field. And the magic he's using...

It's bad. And it looks like it's really hurting Diego.

I tug on the Curio again, fighting back the nausea and the haziness. Black splotches splash across my eyes.

I stumble when Diego shrieks in pain – the darkness overtook his fire. He's sailing backward, smashing into a tree a few yards behind me. I don't know where Ryker was in all of that, and part of me doesn't care anymore.

I'm trying to tear off the Curio when the guy approaches me again. He didn't even break a sweat with all that fighting. Bastard!

He grabs me by the collar with one hand, a creepy sneer on his face. "I know your father," he tells me – which might be one of the reasons why he wants to kill me. "I do hope you reserve a space in Hell for him."

I'm too nauseous and disoriented from the Curio suppressing my Shifting abilities that I'm barely able to muster out an eye-roll and a 'fuck off' to the unnamed guy about to kill me.

I wish I'd done more with my life than just being a dick – but there's no use worrying about that now. I just hope this messed up Enchanter doesn't go after my parents next. If only I could have warned them–

The evil dude holds out his free hand, which distracts me. I see a swirl of blackness growing from it.

This has to be it.

Our enemy screams suddenly, letting go of me. I drop to my knees like a sack of bricks, jagged pain running down my body. Then, it's gone. Weird.

I look up just in time to see the hooded guy keeling over and howling in pain as intense white electricity courses through his entire body.

Holy shit, he's getting electrocuted!

That has to mean–

"I should have known how helpless you would be without female assistance."

I'm too fucked up from the Curio to glare behind me or fire back a comment of my own at Lucy. But I can smell her – and Arya, too.

I'm just relieved that the girls are here and not dead.

As soon as the Enchantress steps beside me, she places one hand onto my wet-with-sweat forehead. At first, I think it's weird. When I start to feel better, I realize Lucy is using her Light Affinity to heal me.

"Took you long enough," I grumble instead of thanking her – which I know will come later, even if Lucy and Ryker have been pissing me off lately.

Lucy scoffs at my reaction and lets go of me. "You're welcome," she spits in return.

It looks like Arya took the evil guy by surprise because she has him where she wants him.

Thunder churns from overhead. I smell burning flesh.

I can't see Arya, but she must be behind the enemy. She and Lucy must have approached the clearing from different angles.

The Enchanter finally drops to the ground, electricity sizzling his clothes and causing him to scream and laugh at the same time.

Lucy holds out both hands. A massive amount of light energy hurtles toward him, lighting up the entire black clearing.

That's a good idea! Use Light against Dark, I can't help but think, though I'd never say that to Lucy.

When the laughing but still sort-of-injured Enchanter collapses into the snow, I'm finally able to see Arya. Electricity is crackling from her palms, crashing into the man. Those damned black splotches are still coming at me, but I can see from here that she's shaking and her nose is bleeding.

Lucy is beside me; her brow furrowed in concentration as her light energy injures her opponent. She's tired but not out.

I underestimated Lucy's power and calibre as an Enchantress – but she still has Diego and Ryker wrapped around her little finger.

Still, she showed up for us tonight. I can't deny that.

Just when we think we got the guy on the ropes, he swings up and turns around in a crouched position, letting Lucy come at him without defending himself.

"You are *weak*!" he throws at Arya, thrusting a huge-ass blast of darkness at her.

I see a flicker of pure fear on Arya's face. It's not like I know her well, but I can tell what she's thinking now.

Arya knows he's figured out she's a half-Nymph and is using it against her.

The blast shoots through the electricity in a second. Both blasts take her out.

"Arya!" I scream.

"Fuck!" Lucy exclaims.

I've never heard her swear before.

Arya is lying on the ground – unconscious or worse.

I'm stumbling for her in a blind rage. I want to kill this guy and then kill him again. I've never felt so angry before. Even Ryker kissing Lucy didn't get me this bad – and I had to stop myself from killing him that night.

The Tedla is going nuts inside me. It wants to kill, too. Our minds are linked, but our bodies aren't in sync. I can't Shift, and it's pissed about it. There's nothing I can do but stay human.

It's hard to run even though I've let go of the Curio. Maybe I tried to get it off for too long and now I'm damaged beyond repair.

"Don't!" Lucy calls to me, yanking on my arm. "You'll get caught in the blast! I can't guarantee your safety!"

My safety? What am I – a five-year-old?

Lucy is now shooting a blast of light magic from one hand and dark magic from the other at the evil-ass Enchanter.

He stumbles, but he's not down. He's still facing Arya. It's like he's taking some kind of messed up pleasure in her being hurt before he attacks her again.

Come on! I yell to the Tedla. *Just ignore the fucking Curio and get out! I can't let her die!*

But it's not like either of us has a choice.

The Curio *will* stop us.

It'll stop me from saving her. I might as well have stayed home tonight for all the good I'm doing now.

"Lucy!" I all but wheeze to her. I'm hunched over, trying to fight against the Curio again.

Lucy looks down at me as I try to yank at the spelled necklace.

"Get this motherfucker off me!" I cough.

Lucy actually gives me a sad look as she continues to aim her duo-magic at the Enchanter who's ignoring her. He's just taking the damage as he watches Arya. He's so fucked, it's outrageous.

"I can't," Lucy tells me. "Only the person who spelled it or placed it on you can take it off."

She did her homework learning about Shifter history. But that's not the point. I was hoping Lucy could somehow take this cursed thing off of me. At least Frow made Qadir able to take it off because now that the Headmistress is dead, I might have been stuck with this thing forever.

But if Arya dies, I don't think anything else matters.

Dark energy comes spiralling toward Arya's limp body. I don't know if she's dead or out cold – and honestly, either one is fucking terrible.

"Take me instead!" I yell, not giving a fuck who hears it.

Lucy stares at me like I've just stripped naked and ran through campus.

As I'm yelling, a bright light sweeps through my vision. Large red eyes and a flaming face are now in front of Arya.

Diego.

He's back, and protecting her.

He blasts fire at the dark energy, flapping his wings. Smoke and flames flicker off him and fill the blackness of the Gomada Thicket. Snow and ice sizzle as he counterattacks.

Thank God!

With Diego and Lucy attacking him from either side, the ghost-Enchanter asshole looks more nervous than before. I think he underestimated Diego – especially now that he's pissed off. When Diego is mad or attacked as a Phoenix, his power increases and he goes nuts. His red eyes are larger, filled with anger. He'd be able to burn down an entire continent if he wanted.

I don't know what to do. It's Lucy and Diego against a

strong-ass Enchanter with a huge chip on his shoulder. It was supposed to be six-on-one. This isn't good. Everyone is going to die. And I could have stopped it if I just could've Shifted!

The Enchanter turns and glares at me. He's literally *on fire* but is limping toward Lucy and I. I don't know how he's doing it. I'd be impressed if I didn't want to see him dead.

"Fine, then!" he laughs at me, probably answering my *plea* from before.

That's what it was. I'm not ashamed to admit it. I'd rather him take me than do anything to Arya. I never thought I'd jeopardize my life or fucking lay it down for a Nymph, but here I am.

And I'd do it again.

The Enchanter is getting closer. He's almost engulfed in flames. Diego is hovering above his head, blasting fire onto him.

I don't know how this asshole is still alive.

Beside me, Lucy's eyes are twitching and her nose is starting to bleed.

We're fucked.

A large, gray cloud suddenly hovers over Lucy and I. Lucy frowns at me as she's trying with all her might to control her powers and to keep 'em coming.

"It isn't me!" I protest.

"Of course it isn't!" she snaps, panting now. "You've been utterly useless this entire time!"

Lightning strikes the forest floor and surrounds Lucy and I, making the unnamed guy laugh as he gets closer to us.

"Half-powers won't stop me!" he taunts, throwing his arm behind him. Arya sails through the air and smashes into a nearby tree in the clearing.

She screams as she flies. Her cry gets cut off when she hits the trunk. As soon as I hear the crash, I shut my eyes. I can feel the electricity disappear even though I can't see it.

"Arya!" Lucy cries.

"I'm gonna fucking *kill you*!" I scream, opening my eyes.

I'm using all my strength to pull on the Curio, fighting against the nausea and pain coursing through my body.

"You?" the Enchanter chuckles as Lucy drops to her knees and throws up.

Both nostrils are bleeding. She's puking blood.

I kneel slightly, reaching out a hand to clasp Lucy's arm in support. She may be a bitch and an Enchantress, but she doesn't deserve this. She's crying and shaking as sizzling flames surround us.

Now, it's one-on-one.

I don't want to leave Diego alone in this fight. He doesn't deserve that, either. But with Lucy, Arya and I taken out, Nora nowhere to be found, and Ryker wussing out, it seems to be the only way.

"I'll take all three of you!" he eggs us on menacingly. "The half-Nymph isn't worth my time!"

"How pathetic, picking on children."

The voice cuts through the flames from Diego. It even freaks out the Enchanter. He whips his head to his left. I follow his glance, seeing Professor Xhao standing at the edge of the clearing. She's wearing a purple cloak with the hood pulled over her head – but I'd recognize her nails-on-a-chalkboard voice anywhere.

"What else would you expect from Izaak Johnson?" comes a voice I know all too well.

Holy shit, that's Qadir!

Lucy and I can barely turn our heads to look behind us. Professor Qadir is walking into the clearing, wearing his typical suit-and-tie combo.

The profs must have seen and heard the flames, the commotion, and the random electricity. I guess we didn't think much about that part of the plan.

Teachers being here can only help – and *that's* something I never thought I'd say or think.

Wait.

Izaak Johnson?

That's Ryker's uncle.

Maybe that explains why Ryker suddenly tapped out – but it doesn't explain why he'd be okay betraying us and leaving us here to die.

Izaak bares his teeth at both professors, looking pissed as hell that he was ambushed.

Does he know them? I guess they're all more or less the same age. If Izaak knows my dad, he likely knows the profs.

A huge-ass thundercloud hovers above Izaak's head. Professor Xhao's eyes go white. She's tapping into her electrical component. I guess I should've guessed that she possessed an Air Affinity. It explains why she picks on Arya so much.

"If you continue to hurt my students, I *will* kill you," Professor Xhao tells Izaak calmly – as if murder and shit are just *things* that she does during the day, like her taxes.

"And she'll have help."

Qadir's head snaps to the side, and his entire body spasms. Ripping sounds and brown flecks of clothing go everywhere.

The Cuda replaces Professor Qadir in seconds. At over seven feet in height, it more than eclipses the man that stood in the same spot.

From above Izaak, Diego squawks, his red eyes alarmed. He's only seen Qadir's alter ego once, during Field Practice. Even though I've seen it recently, I'm still scared as fuck the third time around.

Izaak laughs and holds his hands out. "Go ahead and try!" he jeers. "I'm still leaving with exactly what I want."

Thick purple lightning bolts shower Izaak with a slight wave of Professor Xhao's hand. As he's being electrocuted, a tornado whips through the Gomada Thicket. Diego cries out as he's knocked off course above Lucy and me.

We're smack dab in the eye of the tornado.

That was purposeful. Xhao is protecting us.

Okay, so *we* may be safe, but what about Arya?

We can't see shit. My nerves are on overdrive.

"The boy was never my target!" I hear Izaak laugh.

Fuck!

I hear a crazed scrambling over the howling of the wind, and I know it's Qadir. A creepy-ass howl of laughter cuts through the air. Peeling of flesh and ear-splitting screams pierce my eardrums.

That's Qadir, laughing his hyena laugh and ripping Izaak to shreds.

I gotta say, this right here could make Qadir my mentor. Someone I actually respect – not another adult to avoid.

"*That's* your Shifter Professor?" Lucy yells at me over the tornado and the hysterical laughter.

"What's wrong with that?" I shrug weakly.

The tornado wanes and is flung into the air. As it carries the nighttime clouds with it, it slowly dies down until it's nothing but a strong breeze.

The clearing is a fucking warzone. Trees have come down. Flames are eating snow. Blood is everywhere.

Qadir is pacing in front of us, snarling and grunting. Blood is dripping from his muzzle.

Professor Xhao is nowhere to be seen. But I don't give a shit about that.

Where's Arya?

Where's Izaak?

Acknowledgments

I can't fathom that the second book in the Gomada Academy Series has been published. It has been a long and winding road to get to this point. A lot of fatigue, pain, self-doubt, and intimidation almost halted me from putting out another book. Being an indie author is difficult. You constantly compare yourself to others around you, even if you don't want to. You wear as many hats as you possibly can: you're a writer, an editor, a publicist, a reader, a skeptic. You try to juggle all of those responsibilities alongside your other commitments. At times, you just want to quit. *What makes my book special?* You might ask yourself.

What I've learned is that it's not about the stats, numbers, notoriety, or reviews. It's about creating a body of work you are proud to call your own. It's about connecting with people who value your work and enjoy it – be they a select few or many. It's about the people along the way that cheer you on, push you forward, urging you to follow your deepest passions.

To my husband Nathan, who is always encouraging me to better myself and to follow my heart's desire: **you** are my heart's desire and I couldn't have done any of this without your unwavering support. To my son, William: you might have pulled me away from Cursed Campus work countless times, but each and every moment spent with you is priceless. I am honoured and blessed to be your mother.

To my mother, Marie: thank you for sharing your love of writing with me. It's because of you that I am here. To my brother, Frank: thank you for singing my praises, taking care of me, and for your steadfast friendship. To my father, Jim: thank you for reading my fanfiction and for being the light and legacy I want to emulate. I miss you.

To my in-laws and my husband's extended family: thank you for your encouragement and love. Your investment in my author career has been humbling. I love you all.

I of course owe a debt of gratitude to my editor, who has a near-magical way of moulding my clumsy manuscripts into material more than suitable for publication purposes. I so appreciate you!

My Midnight Tide Publishing family has been there for me through thick and thin. I appreciate each and every one of you. You inspire me at every turn.

And lastly, to the person reading this. There may not be a 'ghost hybrid' haunting you, but there might be something in your life that is holding you back, keeping you locked in fear. You are more than enough. Seize the day and conquer whatever it is that is making you feel inadequate. You can do it.

Happy reading!

Cynthia Brubaker

The Official Playlist

1. Beggin' – Måneskin
2. The Drug In Me Is You – Falling In Reverse
3. Wrecking Ball – Miley Cyrus
4. Birds – Imagine Dragons
5. My Dilemma – Selena Gomez
6. Loaded Gun – COMET
7. Kiss Kiss Kiss – Danica The Morning Star
8. Jerkface Loser Boyfriend – Emily Osment
9. Electricity – Ashley Jana
10. Work Bitch – Britney Spears
11. Warriors – Imagine Dragons
12. Bad Romance – Lady Gaga
13. Demons Awake – Sierra Pilot
14. Crush – Jennifer Paige
15. Lips Are Movin' – Meghan Trainor
16. Fireworks – First Aid Kit
17. Dark Paradise – Lana Del Rey
18. If You Want It To Be Good Girl (Get Yourself A Bad Boy) – Backstreet Boys
19. The Weakest Shade Of Blue – Pernice Brothers
20. Too Close – Alex Clare

About Cynthia

Cynthia Brubaker lives in two worlds. One is populated with loved ones, her cat, and coffee. The other is a realm made authentic by the words she uses to create vivid characters and unique adventures.

Cynthia has been writing since childhood but became serious about her craft in the Spring of 2020. Since then, fantasy (urban, dark), romantic suspense, and contemporary romance works have been her passion. Her début romance novel, Masquerade, was published in June of 2022. Her true sanctuary is writing fantasy and supernatural-themed novels.

In a word, Cynthia can be described as "quirky." She can usually be found sipping coffee, cuddling her cat, hugging her husband, and/or attempting to navigate the wondrous waters of being a first-time mom.

More from Cynthia

Masquerade

Gomada Academy

Gomada Academy

Cursed Campus

More Books You'll Love

If you enjoyed this story, please consider leaving a review!

Then check out more books from Midnight Tide Publishing!

Call of Death by R.J. Garcia

A story of first love that catapults into a rollercoaster ride of suspense.

Hannah Priestly is an obsessive-compulsive California girl attending an English boarding school with the usual teen problems. She doesn't fit in at school and is falling in love with her best friend. But when she wakes up knowing the name of a notorious serial killer at large, Norman Biggs, her life goes from complicated to scary, and her visions only grow darker.

Rory Veer is Hannah's easy-going, romantically challenged friend and school crush. When Norman Biggs unexpectedly appears in Rory's reality, terror is set in motion. It is Rory who must acknowledge a past he has denied if the mystery is to be unraveled.

Thrust into a terrifying future, they must find a way to change fate before it catches up with them.

Available Now

Bound Island by G.D. Roman

Brye, Lenna, and Tara have lived their entire lives on an island surrounded by mists and protected by magical bonds. Nothing could be more perfect. Until one night, when magic begins to fray at the seams, and their lives change forever.

The Healer–Brye's healing abilities are her pride, making her the best match of the season. If only someone were interesting enough for her. Until she catches the eye of Prince Gareth, the least interesting one of all.

The Mist Maiden – Lenna has lived her life in the shadow of her sisters. Until Beltane, when her magic explodes. Now, she has been chosen to be a Mist Maiden, protector of Avalon. A role she was never destined to play.

The Warrior–Tara knows that she is meant to be more than being someone's mate. A warrior through and through, Tara strives for the extraordinary. No matter the cost. Even if that means she might have to sacrifice her growing feelings for Aiden.

As Avalon slowly becomes an island lost in the mists, will the sisters strengthen their bonds and save their home, or will they break apart forever?

Available Now